ACCLAIM FOR CURVEBALL
AT THE CROSSROADS

"Baseball and the blues, two American originals, come together in this striking -- no pun intended -- tale of faith and perseverance. Like baseball and the blues, CURVEBALL AT THE CROSSROADS is enticing and seductive, a story that will stay with you long after the last pitch."

- **Jay Busbee, author, "Earnhardt Nation", writer, *Yahoo! Sports***

"The deal-with-the-devil is a favorite story motif. This book puts it in a baseball context. This is a fun read with vivid scenarios which could easily be adapted to video. Loved it."

- **Patro Mabili, radio host, WMNF 88.5 FM (Tampa, FL)**

"Curveball at the Crossroads" is a wonderful first novel that is a multi-layered story that moves along at a brisk pace to its final pages with writing and a story that is guaranteed to please."

- **Gary Roen, senior book reviewer, Midwest Book Review**

"Baseball and the Blues. Are there any greater American creations? Nay, I say, and first-time author Michael Lortz has merged these two cultural pillars with his excellent new novel, "Curveball at the Crossroads."

"People who know me know I love the Blues — it's my favorite musical genre, especially Delta Blues — making Michael's book a must-read for me and anyone else whose passions include the Blues and baseball."

- **Ryan Whirty, writer/historian, The Negro Leagues Up Close and Society of American Baseball Research**

"Lortz brings his key characters to life, the humble, conflicted Reliford, the conniving and crafty devil and a slew of others that provide meaning and substance. His chapters are short (66 of them), which works perfectly for those of us with ADHD. They end vividly in well-crafted cliffhangers that make Crossroads difficult to put down because you want to see what happens next, which should be the point of any well-written book."

- **Chris Humphreys, SportsChump.net**

"This book was awesome. I enjoyed the way the author wove history, culture, and more into the story line. I found myself hooked and was not able to put the book down. Hoping there's a sequel because I fell in love with the main character's journey! Definitely recommend to anyone who is a sports lover!"

- **TJ Pittinger, manager: Big3Rollup podcast, host: Peek2Pitt podcast, Double Fries No Slaw podcast, and Bourbon on a Budget podcast**

"Enjoyable book about a young baseball pitcher who makes a Faustian deal with the devil. Author Lortz does a good job creating several memorable side characters and shows promise for future work."

- **John Porter, co-host, Time for the Blues radio show, 89.1 WCVN, 90.1 WMVE, 93.1 and 107.3 VPM-Music (Richmond, VA)**

"I am normally not a big fiction guy, but I really did enjoy reading your story. It took a surprising turn late I was not expecting!"

- **Jason Collette, columnist for Rotowire, podcaster at Fangraphs.com**

"A fun and entertaining blend of baseball and fiction. It is a quick and engrossing read that blends sports and fable to create a unique take on making a deal with the Devil. It is very relatable if you're familiar with flash-in-the-pan sports stars who disappear almost as quickly as the burst onto the scene. Except this tale includes a supernatural twist that may make you wonder why those real life stars vanished."

- **Steven P. Ericson, PhD, Geographer of beer, culture, sports, and urban environments**

"I liked it. It was good."

- **The Author's Dad**

Dedicated to

My mother who inspired my love for books and my father who taught me about baseball and the blues.

Say the name "JaMark Reliford" to baseball fans and they'll shake their head and lament lost talent.

Say the name "JaMark Reliford" to people of the Mississippi Delta and you'll hear a much different story.

CHAPTER 1

Welcome back to Eagles baseball, fans. Wherever you are in the Delta, I want to thank you for listening. I hope you are cooler than we are here at the ballpark. It's a hot one, as usual.

We are in the top of the sixth inning here in Rosedale, with your Eagles leading the Natchez Bulldogs six to nothing. Been quite the game for JaMark Reliford, as he is pitching a gem. They might as well be rubies or emeralds he is throwing up there because those boys from Natchez haven't made contact yet. This could be our first-ever regional championship if he keeps this up.

Here comes the Natchez number seven hitter and second baseman, Johnny Smith. Like all the other Bulldogs, Smith struck out his first at-bat.

Reliford winds up. A fastball on the corner and Smith was way behind. Strike one.

Smith didn't look like he had a lot of confidence there. Must be tough for a freshman to face JaMark.

Reliford winds up again. Another fastball. Smith swings and misses. Strike two.

As hot as it is out there, JaMark has been cool as lettuce. He doesn't even look like he is breaking a sweat.

Reliford toes the rubber and looks in at his catcher. Although I think we all know what's coming. He winds up, and there is a beautiful slow curveball. Smith doesn't even take the bat off his shoulders, and that's strike out number sixteen for JaMark.

Now coming up to bat is the Natchez number eight hitter, left fielder Hillabee Williams, Jr. Although a junior by name, Williams is a senior by class and has started all four years for the Bulldogs. He has some speed, so if he can make contact he might be able to steal a base on JaMark.

Reliford winds up. There is another fastball right down the middle. Williams gives it the ol' college try but is a bit behind. Needless to say, that's *strike one on the high schooler.*

Gotta wonder if any of these Bulldogs are going to hit JaMark tonight. He has pitched amazing for us all year, and word is there is even a big league scout in the stands tonight. This might be the best game of JaMark's Eagle career.

Here is the windup. Another fastball, this one on the inside corner. Williams thought it was a little inside, but not tonight. JaMark's control has been just about perfect. I don't think that umpire has called a ball on any pitch he has thrown all night.

JaMark steps back on the mound and looks in to his catcher. The count is zero and two, in the top of the sixth, with the Eagles leading six to nothing.

JaMark winds up and …
Oh, my God."

CHAPTER 2

The baseball rolled slowly through the short-cut grass. It tumbled twice stitch-over-stitch before coming to a stop near the dirt of the third baseline, ten feet from the batter's box.

Although the ball was in fair territory, no fielder made a move. No runners ran, and no one called timeout. No one was watching the ball. Not the players on the field, nor the batter, nor the players in the dugout, nor the fans in the bleachers of the Rosedale High School baseball field.

On that humid, muggy evening, deep in the Mississippi Delta, no one saw the ball come to a stop.

Every eye in the stadium was instead watching the player laying at the end of the pitching mound. The player rolling on the ground where the dirt met the grass. The player clutching his arm, screaming in pain.

Prior to his final start in the final game of the Rosedale High School baseball season, JaMark Reliford was the Rosedale Eagles' ace pitcher. He was a seventeen-year old phenomenon, already one of the most accomplished athletes in the history of the largely agricultural region of Northwest Mississippi.

With Rosedale High tucked deep in the rural farmland, most baseball people were leery of the drive to see JaMark pitch. At the behest of his high school baseball coach, however, one Major League scout made the drive that night.

During the regional high school championship against the Bulldogs from Natchez High School, JaMark had been better than perfect. Through the first five innings, none of the seventeen batters from Natchez High School made contact with the ball. JaMark struck out every batter he faced, and had yet to throw a pitch out of the strike zone. Everyone in attendance knew the Natchez nine had no chance.

As word spread throughout the crowd that a scout from the Major Leagues was in attendance, the masses grew more excited, cheering every pitch and roaring with every eventual strikeout. During its history, Rosedale had seen its share of musicians attain big city riches, but never an athlete. The fans of Rosedale baseball were on the cusp of history. One of their own was about to make it.

In the sixth inning, with his team leading six to nothing, disaster struck. On his sixth pitch of the frame, a loud pop emanated from JaMark's left shoulder, shattering the shoulder at the joint and leaving the star pitcher writhing in pain. As coaches, players, and the crowd looked on in horror, JaMark's last high school pitch rolled meekly across the field, stopping near the third baseline.

Some called the incident a tragedy. Others called it a shame. Some said it was hubris and humility catching up with a person growing "too big for his britches." In an article for the local newspaper, the baseball scout who saw JaMark's arm dissolve into a limp mass of muscle called it "possibly the biggest instantaneous loss of baseball talent ever."

CHAPTER 3

Before his injury, JaMark Reliford was counting on his arm to get him out of Rosedale, where his family lived well below the poverty line.

When he was a child, JaMark was skinny and somewhat fragile. He was so skinny, people took to calling him "rail-thin". He was definitely as thin as a rail, but rails are made of steel and so, unlike JaMark, they are not fragile. Along with his narrow stature, JaMark suffered from an undiagnosed case of Marfan's Syndrome possibly carried on his father's side, causing his fingers to grow abnormally long. The Marfan's and his lack of strength made his early years difficult, as he struggled with simple tasks such as using scissors, peeling onions, or throwing a football.

Sensing JaMark could be hurt playing football or any other contact sport, his Uncle Rufus suggested he take up baseball.

"A man can't play if he can't play," Rufus said to JaMark as he presented the six-year-old his birthday present of his first bat, ball, and baseball glove. "But in baseball, brains beats brawn every time. It's a thinking man's game. Like chess."

Although JaMark's physical home was never broken, and the walls and roof stood sturdy, the structure of his nuclear family split when he was a child. A year after receiving his baseball gifts, JaMark's father, Jerome Reliford, was arrested for stealing desserts from Rosedale's only all-you-can-eat buffet during JaMark's seventh birthday party. What would have been a minor misdemeanor turned into a longer sentence when Jerome's lawyer misled the court by claiming Jerome could not have stolen desserts as he was allergic to food. Unfortunately, the defense's case failed to hold water when Jerome failed to hold down his lunch. Going along with his lawyer's lie, Jerome threw up a ham and cheese sandwich while sitting down on the stand. The judge threw the book at the defendant, his lawyer threw up his hands, and Jerome was thrown in jail for making a mis-masticated mockery of the court. Following his release years later, Jerome took to the life of a rolling stone, getting satisfaction by gathering moss until the bright lights of a big city beckoned and he was never heard from again.

JaMark's mother, Marie, further splintered the family tree three years later. Marie was never happy in Rosedale, as she moved to the town because of her father, Claudius, a famous gnu racer who pitched razors in Scandinavia. Claudius was a downhearted man who lost his fortune and his mind when his wife eloped with the famous German skeeballer Augustus McFuger. Marie tolerated her new town and nation and grew up as any normal, blonde-haired, blue-eyed Norwegian girl would in the predominantly black-haired, brown-eyed Mississippi Delta. But after her husband Jerome was put in the state pen, Marie ran away with a freelance writer who wrote run-on sentences about marathons.

After his parents left, JaMark moved in with his father's mother. LaRosa Reliford was a kind-hearted, religious woman who held the dual honors of being the best cook in Rosedale and the town gossip. A long-time generational descendant of the area, she could talk turkey and townsfolk, rap on roasts and rumors, and wax poetic on pies and politics. For most of his teen years, however, JaMark wanted nothing to do with his grandmother's social status. While keeping his possessions at his grandmother's house, he laid his head in the bed of many affectionate female friends.

Since he was introduced to baseball by his Uncle Rufus, a longtime family friend, who was neither related to his mother nor his father, JaMark met success at every level, from the Rosedale Little League to the Rosedale Teen League. He even received an unheard of spoken invitation to join the Rosedale High School team before he entered high school.

As he developed, JaMark built his arm strength throwing piles of spoiled strawberries off Rufus's strawberry fields. Rufus was the most successful strawberry farmer in the cotton-heavy Mississippi Delta, and JaMark assisted where he could, hurling expired produce over the farm's eastern fence. Little did JaMark know that by following his uncle's instruction, he was tossing the spoiled fruit on the field of his uncle's closest local competitor, Monsignor Hiram Laggums.

By the time Uncle Rufus was arrested and sentenced to five years in the state penitentiary for aggravated agricultural sabotage, JaMark was an ace pitcher for Rosedale High. His powerful arm, honed from hours of strawberry hurling, gave him the fastest fastball in the Delta, and his abnormally long fingers put an unnatural spin on his curveball, making it nearly unhittable to legions of local leaguers. When they talked about JaMark, many throughout the Delta called his curveball "Legba", the fieldhand name for the spirit who led souls to Hell. For most, Hell was facing JaMark and taking the slow walk from the batter's box back to the dugout.

Off the pitcher's mound, JaMark also developed a reputation. His talent on the field made him a local celebrity, and he acted as he thought a celebrity should. He posed for cameras, belittled opponents, was late for games, and rarely, if ever, attended practice. His careless lifestyle also permeated his social life, as he delved into youthful vices and bacchanal behavior.

Prior to his senior year of high school, JaMark had twice been picked up for underage drinking. He was never arrested, however, as he was well-known among local authorities, many of whom found his charm and baseball skills an impressive combination. Despite his lack of discipline, everyone, from coaches to parents to the local press, thought JaMark was a good kid who was just a bit misguided.

As his fame and notoriety grew, the on-the-field reputation of JaMark Reliford became less local and increasingly national. People wanted to know about the kid from Mississippi who one local scribe dubbed the "Delta Darling with the Mississippi Missile." Others used less alliterative terms but wrote just as glowingly.

The night before his final high school game, after hearing

a Major League scout would finally see him, JaMark limited his extracurricular activities to only a rendezvous with his high school fling of the moment, passing on his usual late-night liaison with a liter of liquor. That night, with the scout in attendance, and without alcohol slowing him down, JaMark rose to the occasion.

Until, with the score six to nothing, his sixth pitch of the sixth inning brought his dreams crashing down.

CHAPTER 4

In the years following his debilitating shoulder injury, JaMark swirled in a mire of depression. He worked an even number of odd jobs, drank heavily, and shunned all responsibility. His arm, meanwhile, stayed in either constant pain or occasional numbness, a steady reminder of his shattered dream.

Six months after his injury and four months after he and his classmates concluded their graduation commencements, JaMark was sentenced to twenty days of community service for disrupting the peace. According to the court docket, after a day of heavy drinking, JaMark passed out behind the car of Rosedale's only pizza delivery service, severely altering the driver's ability to deliver pies. As part of his punishment, JaMark was required to don the uniform of the delivery service and apologize to the households whose enjoyment of their pieces of pizza was disrupted that night.

The next year, JaMark was again in trouble with the law. While employed for a graphics company responsible for spray painting company names on the sides of select Rosedale businesses, JaMark was accused of leaving his secondhand scraps, his worn waste, and his used refuse at each customer site. While he first denied the charge, video surveillance at one establishment proved JaMark was, in fact, littering while lettering. JaMark dropped his defense, pleaded guilty, and was sentenced to twenty-five days of community service.

JaMark's downfall culminated in a small juke joint in a town not far from Rosedale. On the night of May eighth, on his twenty-first birthday, JaMark, in a fit of drunken rage, assaulted the establishment's barkeep and knocked him unconscious. According to witnesses, the bartender, an old teammate of JaMark's, thought it would be funny to serve the former star a vessel of beer with a cracked handle. When he presented the drink to JaMark, witnesses claimed the barkeep jokingly said, "Happy Birthday, buddy. Here is a broken pitcher for a broken pitcher." Witnesses then claimed a somber but far from sober JaMark accepted the drink, and, holding the handle, swung the pitcher of beer with his good arm at the bartender, shattering both the glass and the bartender's face.

Still somewhat of a local celebrity, the court was lenient on JaMark, ignoring his prior misdemeanors and ordering him to do ninety days of community service for this new crime. While serving his community, however, JaMark was required to stay under house arrest, where the judge figured JaMark would be forced to face the wrath of the family and friends who had stuck with the embattled former ballplayer.

Although all of JaMark's aunts, uncles, and other distant family had cut ties, cared little for his actions, and refused to talk to him, after his third arrest, JaMark's grandmother emerged as a voice of reason. She again allowed him to stay in her home throughout his communal payback on the condition he clean up his life. Although supportive and sympathetic, she often chastised him and bemoaned his wayless ways.

"You were bad before," she told JaMark as they left the courthouse, "but at least you made people happy. Now you just actin' like you got the devil in you."

10

CHAPTER 5

After three months of his grandmother's lecturing, and after the conclusion of his community service and associated house arrest, JaMark decided to leave Rosedale in an attempt to clear his mind, find himself, and start anew.

On a clear Thursday night, two days after the end of his house arrest, and six months after his bar room incident, JaMark left his grandmother's home with only a backpack of clothes, a pack of cigarettes, an old baseball glove, and a bottle of Mississippi moonshine. Being that Rosedale was not a very big town, JaMark left rather quickly. But leaving town was only one of his goals. He still wanted to wander, clear his mind, find himself, and start anew if at all possible.

On the second night of his travels, JaMark stopped at a large oak tree on the Rosedale side of an intersection between two weather-worn dirt highways. Instead of taking any of the three roads away from where he came, JaMark decided to rest at the base of the large oak tree. He had walked continuously since he left, stopping only to swig his bottle of moonshine or relieve himself. He ate on the go, he smoked on the go, and he thought on the go. At the crossroads, he did not feel like going anymore.

As he sat at the base of the tree, he pulled out the bottle of Mississippi moonshine. He put the bottle to his mouth, but the once familiar taste became incredibly sour and made him nauseous. Without a second thought, JaMark hurled the bottle towards the highway junction. It shattered on impact, splattering the road with its remaining contents.

Confused, but still seeking a temporary buzz, JaMark lit his last remaining cigarette. The smoke coursed its way through his lungs, but he again felt nauseous. Almost instinctively, he flicked the lit cigarette from his hand.

JaMark watched the cigarette fly through the air, flipping end over end, shedding its ashes, and landing near the broken moonshine bottle. Unimpressed with his throw, JaMark closed his eyes and tried to sleep at the base of the old oak tree. Exhausted, he was asleep in moments and failed to notice the nascent blaze growing from his volatile mix of alcohol and fire.

While he slept, the fire burned in the crossroads, first feeding on the alcohol and then on the dirt, as if the earth itself was soaked in moonshine. Within moments, the spark turned into a full blaze. Unlike a usual fire, however, the blaze was contained in the middle of the old intersection.

Before long, a hole grew in the middle of the fire that burned at the crossroads. From the blazing flame and the depths of the earth emerged a figure – a tall, slender, well-dressed man in a black suit, tie, and matching top hat. Once fully emerged from the earth, the man spread his arms and extinguished the blaze. After dusting the ashes and soot off his suit, the man walked towards JaMark.

JaMark felt a tap on his left shoulder, both the surprise and pain waking him from his short slumber. He struggled to open his eyes as his body still wanted to sleep despite his brain alerting him of a presence.

Stunned and disoriented, JaMark saw the tall, well-dressed man with the black suit, tie, and matching top hat standing over him. The man stuck out an old, weathered hand.

"Come with me, and I will turn your life around," the man in the black suit said.

JaMark stumbled on his words. "Do I know you?"

"I'll make your life better than you can imagine or even dream of," the man in the black suit said. "Your arm, your life. It will all be better."

Although still half asleep, the mention of his arm and the idea of being able to throw again sparked JaMark's curiosity.

"What do you want from me?" JaMark asked. JaMark learned from his grandmother that nothing was ever for free, especially in the market of life help, guidance, and assistance.

"I want a guarantee," the tall man in the suit said slowly in a deep tone that belied his tall, wistful frame. "A guarantee you will always put me first. If you put me first, your arm will never hurt again. However, if you put anyone else first, everything I give you will disappear."

The man paused and stared at JaMark.

"And I will take your soul."

Without giving the notion of his soul a second thought, JaMark shook the outstretched hand of the man in the black suit, agreeing to offer him first dibs on a soul he thought little of in its present state. The man smiled and walked towards the intersection of the dirt highway. JaMark watched the man disappear through the still smoldering hole in the middle of the crossroads. In moments, the crossroads were quiet once again, and JaMark was again asleep at the base of the old oak tree.

CHAPTER 6

When JaMark awoke the next morning, he felt more refreshed and alert than he had in years. The pain in his left arm, once a somber reminder of days past, was gone. He swung his arm several times, and to his amazement, he felt as if he was sixteen again, physically strong and spry.

Was it a dream, or was there really a man who gave him hope?

JaMark decided to test his renewed strength and spryness. He walked gingerly to the center of the crossroads and grabbed the largest jagged shard of glass from the bottle he discarded the night prior. He threw the piece of broken moonshine bottle as far as he could down the eastbound highway. The shard flew in the air with such velocity and power it lodged almost completely into a tree several hundred yards away.

JaMark stood in amazement of his rediscovered strength. Within the hour, he picked up as many of the pieces of the broken moonshine bottle as he could and deposited them all into nearby signs and trees. Most surprisingly of all, he felt no pain.

His mind clearer, JaMark looked down the road from which he came and decided he would return to Rosedale. He knew he would still be looked at as the failed phenom, but he thought without the burden of an injured arm, perhaps he could make something of himself again.

After two more days of walking, JaMark crossed back into Rosedale city limits. He laid low, returning to his grandmother's house and subjecting himself to her lectures. Although he threw dozens of pieces of glass a few mornings before, and the steady pain was gone, JaMark was still unsure of himself.

To his grandmother's approval, JaMark stopped drinking and smoking. He tried a cigarette a few days after his return, only to find it still caused the same acrid taste it had under the old oak at the crossroads. JaMark considered the foul taste a reminder of changes he needed to make.

Within months, and with growing confidence, JaMark began to put his life back together and became a productive member of society. He patched up most of his relationships with his aunts and uncles, found employment at a local auto repair shop, and, most important to his sense of well-being and belonging, he returned to the baseball field.

Although he began as a seldom-used outfielder for the local semi-pro team, JaMark quickly found his way back to the pitcher's mound. After the team's ace hurler, a middle-aged pizzeria owner, had to be hospitalized with a case of gingivitis, the manager of the team, a lounge singer who moonlighted as the pizzeria's delivery person, asked if anyone had any experience pitching. JaMark didn't raise his hand, but a teammate who played against JaMark in the Rosedale Little League couldn't help but inform the coach of JaMark's dominant past.

Before the game, as several players took batting practice, the manager approached JaMark about pitching.

"I hear you used to pitch," the manager said. "You interested?"

"I did," JaMark said. "But I injured my arm a few years ago, and I'm not sure what I got left."

"Son," the manager said, "the other night, I saw you throw a laser beam and hang a man out to dry at home plate from in front of the Al's Dry Cleaning sign in right field. If that ain't irony, I don't know what is. But don't you go telling me you can't throw a baseball."

JaMark smiled. "Alright, I will give it a shot," he said.

That night, on the small semi-pro field, on a humid and muggy Mississippi evening, JaMark took the mound for the first time since his senior year tragedy. After a few successful warm-up pitches, he wound up and threw his first pitch six feet behind the batter and into the crowd. JaMark cringed as he saw the ball almost strike a man wearing a black top hat.

The sight of the black top hat scared JaMark, but also calmed his nerves, as he remembered what the man at the crossroads said months before.

'I'll make your life better than you can imagine or even dream of …"

As a child, JaMark had imagined flying cars and monsters under his bed. He also imagined that one day he would help his grandfather find revenge on the skeeballer who stole his wife. But on the field that night, he imagined he was again the best pitcher the Delta had ever seen.

JaMark took a deep breath and returned to the pitcher's mound. He glared deep into the eyes of his catcher and nodded his head after receiving the hand signal for a fastball. With the same wind-up he used throughout his youth, JaMark threw the next pitch directly into the glove of his catcher. The umpire called it a strike.

After the batter swung and missed at the next pitch – another fastball – JaMark's catcher signaled for a curveball. JaMark again nodded his head up and down in approval. With the grip feeling natural in his abnormally long fingers, JaMark wound and threw a breaking ball that baffled and befuddled the batsman. A veteran of the Delta semi-pro league, the batter had never seen a ball do what JaMark had made it do. The umpire called "strike three," but the man didn't need to hear it, as he already turned and walked towards the dugout.

Although he pitched the entire seven-inning game and threw well over 100 pitches, JaMark felt no pain the next day. Throughout his shift at the local auto repair shop, all he could think about was baseball. He wanted to get back on the field again, to feel the rush he felt on the mound. He was excited for the first time in years.

CHAPTER 7

By his third game on the mound and his third victorious pitching performance, JaMark knew his curveball was as good as it had ever been, and his fastball was faster than before. Batters he faced in high school, now facing him again years later, told their teammates JaMark was harder to hit as a semi-pro than he was as a high schooler.

As his confidence on the mound grew, so too did a sense of humbleness and grace. JaMark carried himself differently than he had years earlier. He was even able to be on time.

While his life on the field was improving, JaMark's social life also took a turn for the better when Uncle Rufus, recently released from prison, introduced him to a woman from the local church. The woman, Miss Betsy Belvedere, was Rufus's caseworker and helped Rufus settle into his new career as Rosedale's first wholesale tofu distributor.

"Son," Rufus told JaMark, "I found health and a good heart in prison. I see you getting healthy, but you need a woman to help your heart."

At first, things went well with Betsy and JaMark. New in town and not knowing his history, she went to his games and gave him her support. He, in turn, took her out for pizza.

On their third date, their growing relationship faced its first roadblock. As planned, JaMark picked Betsy up at her house and drove her to the local movie theater. As they walked towards the building, JaMark saw a man in a black suit, tie, and matching top hat.

The man walked side-by-side with JaMark, who walked alongside Betsy. As they approached the door to the theater, the words of the man from the crossroads rang in JaMark's mind.

"Always put me first …"

JaMark took a step ahead of Betsy, opened the door to the theater, and held it open for the man in the black suit, tie, and matching top hat. The man tipped his hat as he passed the threshold. Betsy paused for a moment before she passed JaMark, and gave him a confused look.

After the movie, JaMark and Betsy held hands and walked in synchronized steps on their way to JaMark's car. JaMark forgot about the run-in with the well-dressed man and was glad Betsy enjoyed the movie, *Zombie Tomatoes 4: Catch Up With Murder.* He never thought a woman who went to church religiously could be such a fan of people rising from the dead.

CHAPTER 8

Before long, word spread that JaMark was back on the ballfield. People again started writing words about JaMark, and the words were published in local newspapers, and the words were heard on local sports radio. Word even travelled to JaMark's former high school coach, who came to a game the following week and watched JaMark strike out sixteen batters in six innings and make grown men look foolish. His former high school coach then said words to the Major League scout who saw JaMark years before. Although the scout was leery, based on the importance of the words, he again agreed to drive from Memphis to the rural Mississippi Delta to see JaMark pitch, but only after JaMark's former high school coach agreed to buy the travelling scout dinner and the first post-game pitcher of beer.

As his old coach and the professional scout watched, JaMark nearly single-handedly won the game for his local semi-pro team. Without a tragedy of injury, JaMark was able to pitch all nine innings. He not only didn't allow the other team to score, he also struck out every batter, as he had during his final high school appearance. Although JaMark felt it, after the game, the scout stated that his radar gun gave undeniable, irrefutable, and indisputable proof that JaMark was indeed throwing faster than he did during his high school years.

"Thank you for coming, sir," JaMark told the scout after the game. "I hope to hear from you someday."

Someday arrived faster than JaMark thought. Immediately after leaving the small semi-pro ball field, the scout called his supervisors from the Saint Petersburg Saints. Like the scout, they were hesitant to discuss a player from the sandlots of rural Mississippi. They preferred amateur players with professional grooming and upbringing and preferred they play on fields with working scoreboards. After weeks of negotiations, and several additional reports of JaMark's semi-pro dominance, the scout finally convinced the Saints to offer JaMark a contract.

On May 8th, on his twenty-third birthday, two years after he met the man at the crossroads, JaMark signed his first contract to play professional baseball. Unlike more traditional signees, who make millions before swinging a professional bat or throwing a professional ball, JaMark agreed on a bonus of only $700 and a new set of run-flat tires for his used 1992 Camaro. The bonus was a godsend for JaMark, who was still only making minimum wage at the auto repair shop and was still rolling on the same tires he had on his car in high school. Where he was going, however, he wouldn't need the old Camaro. Five years after his high school injury, JaMark was finally leaving Rosedale to play baseball.

One week after he signed his contract, JaMark left for Cheyenne, Wyoming to meet his new team. The trip was JaMark's first outside of Mississippi, and as he walked throughout the airport, he didn't see anyone who looked like him. While they all had similar facial features, none shared his complexion. One man at the terminal slightly resembled his Uncle Rufus, but that was only when he smiled. And despite his wisdom, Uncle Rufus rarely smiled.

As JaMark arrived at the stadium, before he had the opportunity to meet his teammates, he was greeted by his manager, Joe Shetler. Shetler was a career minor league manager and a simple man with a Napoleonic complex who lived an easy life but was hard on his players.

"I heard about you years ago," Shetler said as he stuck a pointed finger at JaMark's chest. "Rumor had it you were one of the best young arms in the South. Fast to the plate but even faster with the bottle. You do that here, and you'll find yourself back in Podunkville."

JaMark was taken aback by the man's forwardness. He wanted to tell his new manager he was a changed man, but Shetler left before JaMark could say a word.

22

JaMark followed Shetler from the parking lot, through two corridors, and to the home team locker room. There he found a uniform and a set of new equipment, including shoes, socks, and a new glove. JaMark smiled as he had been using his old glove since his days in high school and was thankful for a fresh and less odorous piece of equipment.

As he did on the Rosedale semi-pro squad, JaMark started on the bench for the Wyoming team, this time buried in the distant plains of a minor league bullpen. Based on Shetler's initial reception, JaMark knew he would have to start at the bottom and earn his new manager's trust.

After three weeks, JaMark still hadn't pitched in any games. Game after game, he was passed over for younger talent with more ludicrous signing bonuses. Despite not seeing any game action, JaMark participated in as many pitching practice sessions as possible with his coaches. Eventually, the clamor to use the Mississippi hurler was too loud for Shetler to ignore. The manager could no longer resist his coaches, his players, or his will to win.

JaMark made his first professional appearance in organized baseball on a balmy Wednesday night in the beginning of summer, with clear skies and the full moon rising high over the Wyoming wilderness. Once the game began, the serene environment was jarred by the steady noise of the crack of the bat and the collective groan of the hometown attendance. The score was four to nothing in the top of the first inning, and the bases were loaded with no one out when Shetler finally called for JaMark to relieve the starting pitcher. The Cheyenne starter had started the game successfully, but his pitching did not share the same success.

As the batter who led off the game took his place for a second time in the batter's box, JaMark walked atop the pitcher's mound, toed the rubber for the first time, and stared in at his catcher. He saw the familiar signal for a fastball – a single digit placed downward in the catcher's groin area.

"This is no different than Mississippi," he told himself before immediately realizing it was a lie. It was dryer and much cooler in Wyoming than in Mississippi, and there weren't swarms of mosquitoes to contend with on the field in Wyoming. He also had a new glove, new shoes, a new hat, and he received a salary for taking the field.

"All these things are true," he replied to himself, "but you won't make another dollar if you don't pitch the ball and get this batter out."

In his mind, this was a logical conclusion.

JaMark wound up and threw his first fastball towards the catcher. Although a bit higher than the strike zone, the batter swung and missed. JaMark followed that fastball with another, which was called a ball, as it was inches outside the batter's strike zone. A third fastball, and another ball, this time too high. JaMark stared in at his catcher for the fourth time. Another fastball. He wound up, fired, and the batter fouled the pitch into the stands, even though the pitch was also a few inches outside.

With two strikes on the batter, JaMark knew what he wanted to throw. The catcher put down the sign for a fastball, and JaMark shook his head, wanting to throw the only other pitch he knew, a pitch he knew the batter would be unable to hit. The catcher didn't put down the signal for a curveball, but only pounded his glove with his ungloved hand to show JaMark he was ready.

JaMark stood still on the pitcher's mound, his long fingers embracing the ball in a curveball grip he knew by instinct. He wound up and let the ball fly, snapping his wrist at the perfect moment to get the perfect spin on a perfect curveball. As gracefully as the ball flew, the batter's swing was equally ungraceful. His stance broke from the violence of his missed attempt, and he fell to one knee before standing and walking to the dugout.

Shetler was impressed, and while he wasn't the type to compliment, he yelled the tried and true baseball axiom to JaMark, "Atta boy, now get the next one!"

JaMark got the next one, and the one after that to end the inning. He went to the mound for four more innings, struck out ten batters, walked one, and gave up two hits. Meanwhile, his team was able to score five runs to take the lead, and with his bullpen mates pitching the final four innings, JaMark would get his first professional win on that clear, Wyoming summer night.

Convinced by JaMark's effort on that Wednesday in Wyoming, Shetler decided to make JaMark a regular member of the team's starting rotation. While he pitched well in the first two starts, winning both, his third starting appearance made him a household name among the homes of the small mountain town.

Three and a half weeks after his first appearance, and six weeks after he joined the team, on a Sunday in early July, JaMark took the mound against the team from Boise, Idaho. JaMark had never been to Idaho, but his grandmother did buy Idaho potatoes, and JaMark enjoyed them. So he held nothing against the team from Boise on a personal level, but as he took the mound and began pitching, people wondered if the Boise team had slighted JaMark in some way. Which was impossible, as they had never met.

In the first inning, JaMark struck out the first three batters, throwing only the necessary nine pitches. In the second inning, he threw three more strikeouts, needing only nine more pitches. In the third, three strikeouts, nine pitches. By the fourth inning, most of the crowd started whispering the pattern to each other, careful not to disrupt the action on the field.

JaMark continued his masterful performance through the middle innings, never tiring, and never losing control. Every pitch was a strike, either swung at and missed, or called so by the umpire, who seemed to be enjoying the ease of his nightly duty. Although there were the occasional foul balls, they were never on the second strike, and hence never extended the at-bats. No batter put the ball in play, and each batter made the resulting, depressing walk back to the dugout after his at-bat.

While the Boise pitcher did not pitch a bad game, he was outperformed by JaMark. The one run the Boise hurler allowed in the sixth inning was enough for JaMark's teammates, as they needed to score only once to support JaMark on that magical night. There was even a whisper in the dugout as they batted in the eighth inning that none of the team would take the field except for JaMark and his catcher, but Shetler put an end to that idea.

"This ain't no sideshow," Shetler announced. "You want to join the circus and be a clown, be my guest. But remember this, clowns don't get post-show tail, unless you want to snuggle up to the bearded lady."

Convinced doing nothing in the field would be better than sleeping with a woman with facial hair, the team took the field in the ninth inning.

CHAPTER 9

elcome back to Cheyenne baseball. Glad you could join us on this beautiful Wyoming night. For those of you just tuning in, beautiful does not begin to describe the game JaMark Reliford has pitched for us tonight. My goodness is he on the cusp of history.

It's the top of the ninth and JaMark Reliford not only has a shutout, he not only has a no-hitter, he hasn't even thrown a pitch called a ball all game. According to our stats guy Jason, JaMark has thrown seventy-two straight strikes. In case you ever wondered how many pitches it would take to strike out every batter on three pitches through eight innings, JaMark has done it.

Here is the first batter of the inning, the Boise second baseman, the number seven hitter, number four Derek Taylor. Taylor has been struggling of late, with only one hit in his last fifteen at-bats.

The first pitch from JaMark is a fastball, and a swing and miss by Taylor means its strike one. Taylor was way behind on that one. JaMark doesn't appear to have lost any velocity on his fastball all game.

The next pitch, another fastball, and Reliford is now up 0 and two on Taylor. Our trusty stats guy Jason just informed me JaMark threw a pitch ninety-seven miles per hour in the first inning and that first fastball to Taylor was ninety-eight miles per hour. So he is actually throwing faster. Not too many pitchers can do that.

You gotta feel for the Cheyenne fielders tonight. They've been on the field all game, and not one ball has been hit to any of them. You know they are rooting for JaMark, but still, they gotta be bored.

Here is the 0 and two pitch to Taylor. It's another fastball, and Taylor didn't even take the bat off his shoulders. He just stood there. The umpire hadn't even called strike three before Taylor was already walking back to the dugout.

Batting second in the top of the ninth for Boise is third baseman Marco Mestoban. Mestoban, like the rest of his teammates, is 0 for the day.

Like the rest of the lineup, he has struck out in each at-bat.

JaMark starts Mestoban with a fastball at the knees for strike one. I don't know if I have said enough about the movement of JaMark's fastball tonight. He is throwing so hard, that fastball looks like it is rising in the strike zone.

The second pitch to Mestoban is another fastball. This one on the inside corner and Mestoban tried to get his hands out in front, but failed. Strike two. Mestoban looks completely overmatched.

Reliford winds and delivers. High fastball that Mestoban swings at but misses. Strike three and now there are two away. We are down to one batter left for history.

JaMark steps off the mound and rubs the baseball. Is he even thinking at this point, or is the game just coming naturally to him?

Now down to their last out, it seems the Boise manager is going to his bench. Oh, this should be interesting ..."

CHAPTER 10

In an attempt to shake JaMark (mentally, of course, as shaking the pitcher at any point in the game would be a violation of baseball rules), the opposing team manager decided to pinch-hit for the third batter of the inning. The substitute batter actually did arrive in a pinch, as he had just been assigned to the club on a rehabilitation assignment from the Major Leagues. When Dustin Pershing, a veteran with five years in the Majors, entered the ballpark and heard what JaMark was doing, his professional ego and curiosity grabbed hold of him in a spiritual sense and he grabbed a uniform and a bat and decided to face the young Mississippi left-hander.

JaMark peered in at his catcher to see the familiar one-finger fastball sign as Pershing took his place in the right-hand side of the batter's box. JaMark wound up and threw. The big leaguer swung and connected. The horsehide sphere soared deep into the night air down the left field line, curving foul just before the left field foul pole. JaMark gulped, his confidence rattled for the first time that night.

As JaMark took his place on the pitching mound, Pershing resumed his place in the batter's box. JaMark again looked in at his catcher, again saw the fastball finger, again wound up, and again hurled a fastball towards the catcher's target. Again the bat hit the ball, and again the ball flew far into the clear night, again missing the left field foul pole and fair territory by inches.

Again JaMark gulped. One more pitch, he thought to himself.

Taking a deep breath, JaMark took the mound for what he hoped was the last pitch of the game. Pershing took his familiar position in the box outlined for batters just as JaMark took his position on the mound designated for pitchers. JaMark looked in to his catcher. Two fingers flashed in his catcher's crotch, the familiar sign for a curveball. Like the people of the Delta, the people of Wyoming created a name for JaMark's nearly unhittable breaking pitch. They called it "Ninninbe", the Shoshone tribe name for an ancient race of people who shot arrows from the mountains at people they did not like.

JaMark glanced at the mountains beyond the outfield wall as he began his pitching motion, hoping the Ninninbe would be with him and would strike down the final batter who stood between him and the end of the game. He knew they were there. He could feel their eyes on him.

The ball spun from JaMark's elongated fingers and flew through the air towards the catcher. The air around the ball started to flow, and because of the spin JaMark put on the pitch, the ball started to move towards the direction of less resistance, causing it to veer off its original projected path.

JaMark and his catcher knew the new projection of the ball, and his catcher began to move to where he predicted the ball would go. Seeing the seams of the ball when JaMark released it, the batter also tried to predict the movement of the pitch and began his swing towards what he thought would be a predicted point of impact.

After a mighty swing and a failed estimate, the Major League veteran heard a loud roar from the seats behind him. Although thousands across the vast expanse of Wyoming would say they were at JaMark's perfect pitching performance, in reality, only 732 people were witness to history. But those 732 voices bounced off the mountains, echoed, and reached the decibel magnitude of thousands.

By the end of the game, almost all of those in attendance knew what they saw. If they didn't initially, then someone in the crowd told them. Except for a man who wandered out into the far right field bleachers in the fourth inning and fell asleep in the stands. Even though he wore a black suit, tie, and matching top hat, those who saw him meander towards the bleachers assumed he partook in one too many alcoholic beverages. The ballpark attendees who saw him decided to let him sleep and planned to wake him after the game, as they were too busy watching JaMark pitch. Following the game, ballpark personnel went to the bleachers to wake the sleeping man only to find he had disappeared.

After the game, the local media – one aspiring twenty-two-year-old recent college graduate who spent evenings at the ballpark writing filler for the town newspaper – sought to capture the slice of baseball history that had just come to pass in the small Wyoming stadium. As Jennifer McDavidson ran from the press box towards the home clubhouse in a race against no one but herself, JaMark celebrated in the home clubhouse amidst his teammates' hugs and congratulations. Even Joe Shetler had soft words and a firm handshake for JaMark.

Moments later, the eager reporter frantically entered into the clubhouse.

"JaMark, can I talk to you?" asked an out of breath McDavidson.

"Sure," JaMark answered, speaking slowly so the young writer could catch her breath.

"JaMark, you just did what no one else has ever done in the history of baseball," McDavidson said. "You threw a truly perfect game! You struck out twenty-seven batters on only eighty-one pitches! That is history!"

"Well, I don't like to make a big deal of things," JaMark answered. "I was pitching well. My fastball was moving, and I was getting a good break on my curve. And the defense did a great job out there."

In the background, a few of JaMark's teammates chuckled at their mention.

"JaMark, come on, man," pleaded McDavidson. "You just pitched a historical game. You did something no one else has done. Ever. Eighty-one pitches! Twenty-seven strikeouts! Please don't give me the stereotypical post-game pitcher platitudes."

"Well, I was able to establish the fastball early in the count to most of them," JaMark answered. "I knew I had the shade to my advantage in the early innings. And I ate a bologna sandwich before the game. Maybe that helped."

Again, JaMark's teammates chuckled at JaMark's answers and McDavidson's increasing frustration.

"Ok," the young reporter said, giving up. "Look. I need something. Can you at least give me a quote? Maybe who you'd like to give thanks to for such a great game? I can run with that."

JaMark looked at the short, spectacled reporter as he thought of his answer.

"That's a good question," JaMark said. "I'd like to thank my teammates. My manager, for putting me on the mound. My grandmother, for putting me on track. My Uncle Rufus, for getting me into baseball. And my girl, who decided to stay in touch even though she still knows little about baseball. Oh, and the fans. I'd like to thank them for coming out."

With JaMark's quotes in hand, McDavidson walked out of the clubhouse to file her report. JaMark's teammates took the place of the reporter, surrounding JaMark again and offering their congratulations on his historic game. After many of them left to paint the town red in his honor, JaMark straightened the items in his locker, headed out of the clubhouse, and departed for the team hotel. Although his arm felt fine, he was tired and was ready to call it a night. He was asleep by midnight, sleeping through the racket his teammates made when they returned several hours later.

By the next morning, JaMark was a sports world phenomenon. Led by McDavidson's write-up and a few dozen posts on social media, news of JaMark's perfect game was the talk of the sports world and even had a brief mention in the non-sports world. When JaMark realized the extent of his achievement, he smiled, as his ability finally got him positive acclaim, even though he still had to borrow money the next day to order extra toppings on a post-game pizza.

Such is the life of a minor leaguer, he told himself.

CHAPTER 11

After one more week in Wyoming, including a follow-up eight-inning, one-run pitching performance that was only sub-par when compared to his previous perfection, JaMark was informed he was called up to the next level of the Minor Leagues. With a blessing and firm handshake by Joe Shetler, JaMark left his Wyoming team to report to his new ballclub in Mobile, Alabama.

Due to a pilot error and a missed connection, JaMark failed to link up with his new team in Mobile as they already departed for a contest in Chattanooga, Tennessee. After calling his new manager, JaMark was told to stay the night in Mobile at the best hotel his minor league salary could afford.

That night, after scuttling away the roaches and sweeping the cigarette butts off his motel bed, JaMark attempted to relax by watching the only English-speaking show he could find on the black and white hotel television. He hadn't seen a coat hanger used as a TV antenna since he was a child, so he was proud of himself when he was able to pick up a local televised bingo match. From what JaMark could ascertain, the challenger, a spritely young lass from the Ancient River Retirement Home, was about to upset forty-three-time champion, ninety-seven-year old Gertie Dupree. While the challenger only needed an I-18, Gertie was staring at an empty card.

JaMark's attention was taken from the bingo match by a knock on the door. JaMark opened the door and saw the same man with the black suit, tie, and matching top hat from the Rosedale movie theater and, more importantly, the crossroads. JaMark hadn't seen the man in nearly a year and almost forgot what he looked like. But now, as the man was standing in the threshold of his motel room, JaMark remembered clearly.

"May I enter?" asked the man, politely.

"Of course," answered JaMark, trembling.

"Do not be afraid," the man said as he entered. "You are famous now. I saw your face in Sports Illustrated. That is very impressive. You made history from what they say."

"Thank you," JaMark answered, still unsure of the reason for the man's visit. As the man entered, JaMark turned off the bingo match.

The man glanced at the television before JaMark hit the off button. "Good match there," he said.

"JaMark, you are going to be a star," the man said as he took his hat off and walked around the small room. He looked at himself in the mirror, adjusted his tie, and turned to JaMark. "As long as you don't screw it up."

A chill rose up JaMark's spine. He was enjoying his talent again and didn't think he did anything to defy the instructions the man gave under the old Mississippi oak tree.

"Umm … I'm sorry," JaMark said. "I don't think I understand."

"I'm sure you do," the man said, taking a seat on JaMark's twin-sized bed. He placed his hat beside a lamp on the wooden night table and stared at JaMark, who stood only a few feet away by the door in the small room.

"Do you remember what you said after your great historical game?" the man asked. "Do you remember who you thanked for that masterful pitching performance?"

JaMark struggled to think back to that night. He remembered pitching, he remembered the results, he remembered his teammates congratulating him, and he did remember talking to the young reporter who wanted him to say something quotable. But after an arduous trip to Mobile, his exact words slipped his mind.

"I'm sorry," JaMark said. "I don't remember."

The man stared at JaMark. "You thanked your manager who had to be convinced to give you a chance, your teammates who did nothing in the field, your grandmother who lectured you, a girl you never see, and an uncle who almost had you

34

arrested for throwing fruit," the man said, his voice growing sterner. "Where was my thanks? Who gave you back this talent? Who made you famous? Who made you who you are today? Me, me, and me."

The man stood up and walked towards JaMark.

"It was all me," the man said. "Who picked you up while you were drunk, whithering away in a small town and made you something again? Me. Who gave you the ability to play again? Me. JaMark, where was my thanks? Where was the 'oh, and thank you to the Devil for making me a baseball player again'?"

JaMark stood stunned. He knew there was something supernatural about the man considering he disappeared into a flaming hole in the middle of an old, dirt highway, but JaMark still wasn't sure if he had dreamt that or not. Although he wasn't sure what kind of magic the man possessed, never did he think he made a deal with the Devil. JaMark tried not to divert his gaze from the man in black as he leaned against the hotel room door.

"Mr. Devil," JaMark said. "Sir, how many athletes have you ever heard actually thank the Devil? It doesn't happen. If there was an athlete interview rulebook, it would be in there. Never thank a deity but God or Jesus. You can't thank Nammu, Ra, or even Zeus."

The Devil peered at JaMark and considered JaMark's point. JaMark peered back, attempting to hide the fear coursing through his body. But he held his composure, almost as tight as he held the door handle behind his back.

"You hurt me, JaMark," the Devil said, his tone softening. "I read what you said, and it hurt. I felt like you didn't appreciate me or anything I have done for you. I just want to know you are thankful for the gift I gave you."

JaMark didn't expect the Devil's demeanor to change as rapidly as it did. He almost felt sorry for the ancient demon. He knew then that he had the upper hand, and he wasn't going to lose his soul or his ability to play baseball that night.

"Mr. Devil," JaMark said. "I am always thankful for what you did. You know I am."

"Then why couldn't you say it?" the Devil said. "Just

once, let someone know what I did for you."

JaMark looked at the Devil, "Even if I did give you all the thanks in the world, people would look at me weird. That reporter might not have even believed me. No one would have believed me. You have to understand that."

"Well, then," the Devil said, regaining his composure and returning to the debonair flair with which he entered the room. "I believe our business here is done. I trust you will have a pleasant evening, and congratulations on your achievements."

The Devil picked his hat off the nightstand and stepped towards the door. JaMark turned the handle and let the Devil out into the muggy Alabama air.

"Thank you for …" JaMark started to say.

"I am sure I will hear of you again, JaMark," the Devil interrupted, putting on his top hat and walking past JaMark into the motel parking lot. "I hope next time we will meet under less stressful circumstances."

JaMark watched the Devil walk down the highway and disappear into the night before closing the door. The Devil's visit scared him, kept him up all night, and, worst of all, made him miss the exciting conclusion of the local televised bingo championship. He kept his mind off the Devil by wondering if Gertie Dupree was able to snatch victory from the dentured jaws of defeat.

CHAPTER 12

The next morning, JaMark checked out of the motel and drove to Chattanooga to meet his new team. Miscalculating the drive and not knowing which hotel his teammates were staying in, JaMark arrived at the stadium four hours before game time. After giving up hope that the opposing team's maintenance crew would let him in early, he sat on a bench by the ticket office. He passed the time by tossing rocks, counting the cracks in the sidewalk, and bantering on occasion with the ticket staff. They also didn't believe him that he was on the opposing team.

Two hours before the game was scheduled to start, the bus carrying JaMark's new teammates finally arrived. JaMark walked quickly across the exterior of the stadium, hoping the grounds staff wouldn't close the fence behind the team bus before he could catch up with them.

Although the fence was still open, JaMark's teammates had already entered the stadium by the time he reached the bus.

JaMark crept into the stadium, careful not to alert the security staff. After walking along the concourse for several minutes, he found a door labeled "Visitor's Clubhouse: Do Not Enter." Defying the sign, he entered and saw a burly man lecturing a group of people partially dressed in baseball uniforms.

The man spun around when he heard the door opening.

"Well, if it isn't the devil himself," the man said in a thick southern accent. "I'll be damned. I thought you weren't ever gonna make it here."

JaMark could feel the eyes of everyone in the room bearing down on him. Being days late and then interrupting a team meeting was hardly the first impression he wanted to give his new team.

"Sorry," JaMark said to his new team, "I missed my flight."

"Hell, that's alright, kid," the man standing in front of the room said. "We coulda used ya last night. Suit up. There's an empty locker over there."

The man pointed to the locker furthest from where he was standing. JaMark found a uniform with his name hanging in the locker along with a hat and a new pair of shoes. While he listened to the end of the man's discussion on teamwork and self-discipline, JaMark quickly dressed, joining his teammates as they took the field, staying with them through the game and after, and finally turning in his rented car after finding the team's hotel accommodations.

Although JaMark failed to achieve the success playing in the Deep South that he had in Wyoming, he had a respectable month with his new team, winning more games than he lost and striking out more than a batter every inning he pitched. Pitching in the Deep South enabled some of JaMark's family to make a trip from Rosedale to see him. Whereas the bridge between JaMark and many people in Rosedale was still burned, his grandmother and Uncle Rufus, escorted of course, by his caseworker, Miss Betsy Belvedere, made the drive through interstates, highways, and byways from Mississippi to Alabama to see JaMark pitch.

Unbeknownst to Uncle Rufus and his grandmother, Betsy made two additional trips to see JaMark, once a week after their first family trip and the other on the last Saturday of the season, which was coincidentally, the last game of the season. With Betsy in attendance, and JaMark coincidentally instructed by his manager to be the starting pitcher on a day he was not normally scheduled to play, JaMark pitched the second masterpiece of his first professional season, a sixteen-strikeout no-hitter. Unfortunately, of the batters who made contact, five of them reached base on errors in the fourth inning, with three of the errant runners making their way across home plate.

JaMark could only take his effort in stride, as his team failed to overcome their fielding faux paus and succumbed to their opponents, losing the game three runs to two.

"You pitched a hell of a game, kid," JaMark's manager said as JaMark sat on the stool by his locker after the game. "Damned if I didn't want them to score a few more for ya."

"Thanks," JaMark said, as he grew accustomed to his manager's proclivity for Luciferic language. Hearing his manager reference the Devil as often as he did didn't scare JaMark as much as it did during his first days with the team. By the end of the season, his manager's colloquialisms only made him aware of the constant conditions surrounding his talent. What JaMark did find strange was that none of the very religious members of the team ever said anything about his manager's chosen verbiage. JaMark once even asked backup catcher Barry Carusowitz, a man known for carrying a Bible in his back pocket during games, if the manager's speech bothered him. To JaMark's surprise, the catcher claimed he never heard the manager say anything of the sort.

After his brief chat with the manager concluded, a teammate yelled from across the clubhouse "Hey, JaMark, there is a woman here to see you!"

JaMark looked at his manager. Unless they were members of the media or team staff, there was a rule against women in the clubhouse. JaMark would need approval to see visitors before his manager dismissed the team or, in case of a road game, they boarded the bus for the hotel. But being that the final game was at the team's home stadium and the players were all headed to their own homes after the game, JaMark hoped his manager would let him see someone from his hometown.

"Hey, skipper," JaMark asked. "Can I take off and see my guest?"

"Hell, you don't need to ask permission," his manager said. "Go ahead."

"Thanks, skip," JaMark grabbed his bags and started to walk towards the clubhouse door.

"Hey JaMark, remember to put me first," JaMark thought he heard his manager say.

JaMark paused for a moment, and turned to face his

manager, who was still facing JaMark's locker.

"Sorry, skip, what was that?"

His manager turned around with one of JaMark's shirts in his hand. "Don't forget your tee shirt," he said, throwing the shirt to JaMark. JaMark caught the shirt, and with a confused look on his face, turned towards the exit.

Betsy stood outside the clubhouse door, leaning on the wall. When JaMark emerged, she ran and embraced him.

"It's great to see you too," JaMark said as she finally let him go.

"You did great tonight even if you lost," she said. "They said you set a record for most strikeouts by a pitcher who lost a no-hitter. I heard a guy in the crowd say that to another guy."

"Eh, it happens, I guess," JaMark replied, slightly disappointed that Betsy immediately started talking about baseball. She was his escape to talk about other things such as politics, pop culture, and why some people chose to eat cake with a spoon instead of a fork. He never understood why people did that, but Betsy finally explained the phenomenon to him in a way that made him not only understand, but also try the spoon method himself.

CHAPTER 13

After leaving the ballpark, Betsy and JaMark went to the finest dining a Minor League baseball player salary could afford, a local diner that specialized in eighty-six-cent burritos. As JaMark frequented the diner after almost every home game, the staff who worked at the diner all knew JaMark and greeted him.

"Wow, you're popular here," Betsy said.

"I go here a lot," JaMark answered.

Before Betsy could say anything in response, a small woman in a small wheelchair came up behind her and asked them to follow her to their seat. Betsy looked closer at the staff and saw they were all in wheelchairs.

As they followed the woman and walked to their seats, Betsy whispered to JaMark, "everyone here is in a wheelchair; that's amazing."

JaMark looked at Betsy and smiled.

"Look around. This restaurant is very wheelchair friendly. It gives people with disabilities a place to work and boost their self-esteem. It was started by the greatest wheelchair basketball player of all-time, Klyde 'The Ride' Emagirios. He retired here and started this restaurant."

"Wow," Betsy said, "that's so heartwarming."

JaMark then pointed her to the main walkway on the floor of the restaurant, which was sloped and slightly unlevel in certain sections to facilitate wheelchair access and egress. JaMark could see Betsy was impressed.

"Wait until you see the menu," JaMark said as they sat down. "Everything here rolls, from the chairs to the tables, and even the food. They serve meatballs, jelly rolls, pigs in a blanket, rolled oats, and for dessert, fruit roll-ups. You should taste the burritos. They are really good."

"You sound like a commercial," Betsy said.

"I guess I do," JaMark replied, suddenly embarrassed by his enthusiasm. "But this place is that good."

"Maybe one day, you can be a commercial pitchman for someone," Betsy said, trying to ensure JaMark that she was not poking fun at his excitement. "You definitely have the skill."

"Yeah, that would be fun. But I have to focus on making the Majors first," JaMark said with a smile.

The awkward pause in their conversation was finally filled when their waitress rolled towards the table.

"Hello, JaMark," she said. "I heard about the game. Is this a new friend?"

"A friend from back home," JaMark answered, looked at Betsy, and smiled. "She has visited before, but it's her first time at the diner."

The waitress smiled at Betsy.

"Well, welcome to the only restaurant on a roll," the waitress said. "As we like to say, we rolled it and sold it, you need it and eat it."

Betsy laughed and ordered meatballs and a jelly roll. JaMark ordered the burritos and a fruit roll-up.

After seventeen minutes and eighteen seconds of catching up and other friendly banter, JaMark became silent. The silence lasted for two minutes and forty-three seconds. Betsy noticed it at one minute and nineteen seconds, as JaMark was normally a good conversationalist, but for the first minute of his silence, she saw he was chewing the last of his burrito.

"You're quiet," Betsy said. "What's wrong?"

JaMark looked at her and sighed.

"I have something I've wanted to talk to you about for a while," JaMark said. "But it's difficult. It might be the hardest thing I've ever had to talk to anyone about ever."

Betsy peered at JaMark with an awkward curiosity. JaMark knew he had to continue talking, or Betsy would ask him to continue, and then he would have to continue talking anyway. He decided to talk before she encouraged him to.

"Were you living in Rosedale the last time the circus came to town?" JaMark asked.

"I don't think I was," Betsy answered.

"Well, there was a monkey who escaped from the circus," JaMark said. "No one knew the monkey was loose in Rosedale until one day it started following Old Man Higgins, the man who tends to the cemetery. It followed him everywhere, and every time he cleaned a gravesite, the monkey threw poop at him. The cemetery never looked better, but Old Man Higgins was always dirty."

Betsy looked at JaMark.

"JaMark, what are you trying to say?" she asked. "I don't understand."

JaMark took a deep breath. "Betsy, I am being followed by the Devil."

JaMark watched as Betsy's eyes grew as she stared at JaMark.

"The Devil?" she shouted. "Oh my God, JaMark!"

In her excitement, Betsy's arm swung across the table and knocked one of her meatballs off her plate and off the table. The meatball rolled off the table onto the sloped floor and towards the door. Before the couple could react, their waitress wheeled towards the door and cut off the wayward ball of meat before it left the restaurant. With a small scooper she hung on the side of her chair, she scooped up the meatball and tossed it into the nearest receptacle. After her swift food rescue, she looked at JaMark and Betsy and smiled.

"Don't worry, dear," she said. "It happens all the time. No need to blaspheme."

Betsy looked at JaMark with a look of embarrassment on her face. JaMark smiled.

"Try to keep this a little quieter," he said in a tone barely above a whisper.

"But JaMark," Betsy said, "the Devil. Is he really following you?"

"Betsy," JaMark said, "I owe the Devil. He helped me get my life together in a way no one else did. All he asks is that I give him a little shout out now and then. In exchange, I get to play baseball. I was so desperate at the time, I thought it was a good idea. It's really no big deal. It's ok, but I wanted to let you know."

Betsy finished her remaining food and looked at JaMark.

"I'm worried for you," she said. "The good book says Satan is not to be played with. Even books that aren't as good warn against dealing with the Devil. As a matter of fact, even bad books say don't mess with Lucifer. Even self-published, un-edited, rambling manuscripts that plump themselves with useless dialogue caution against shaking hands with the Prince of Darkness. It's one thing they all agree on."

JaMark reached across the table for her hand and gave it a light squeeze.

"I'll be ok," he said. "And if I get in trouble, you will be the first person I go to. I promise."

After leaving the restaurant and saying goodbye to the staff, JaMark and Betsy left Mobile and returned to Rosedale. JaMark spent a month in Rosedale before he received instructions to report to a Minor League camp in Arizona to play in the aptly named Arizona Winter League.

CHAPTER 14

The Arizona Winter League was a collection of the best prospects in the lower Minor Leagues who staff, scouts, and team personnel wanted to continue to hone their skills.

A relative unknown among the staff, scouts, and team personnel of teams other than his own, JaMark made his name known after his first appearance. On a hot Tuesday in Tucson, JaMark took the mound and struck out twelve batters and allowed no hits in five innings before his manager took him out of the game. Although JaMark's arm didn't feel pain or weakness, he reached the upper limits of a league-mandated pitch count, and his removal was required.

The next week on a Saturday in Scottsdale, JaMark amazed staff, scouts, and team personnel again by allowing only one hit in five innings. Again he struck out twelve, although he did walk a batter. After four weeks and four appearances of five innings each, JaMark had four victories. He allowed four runs and walked four batters while striking out forty. As the media marveled at the symmetry, fans flocked from across Arizona to follow the phenomenon.

By the end of his stay in the Arizona Winter League, JaMark was accustomed to the hubbub that surrounded his pitching performances. After his first two appearances, JaMark only gave the few reporters reporting on the game the standard quotes about "making his pitch," "getting his pitches to work," and "feeling good on the mound." In the back of JaMark's mind, however, he knew the Devil wanted to hear JaMark give him his due praise.

Following his third pitching performance, JaMark again had to answer the same questions about his achievements. New media personnel who discovered JaMark also asked him to discuss his story and his successes. After hearing the same questions, JaMark looked at the small but dedicated press corps.

"I pitched well. You know, guys, the devil is in the details," JaMark said and walked away. He smiled, knowing he finally had an answer he hoped would please the reporters and, more importantly, the Devil.

When the Arizona Winter League concluded, JaMark traveled back to Rosedale for the remaining months of his offseason. Unlike his previous pitching fame years earlier, JaMark took a more humble approach and laid low. He stayed with his grandmother, saw Betsy, and visited his Uncle Rufus, who was serving six months in the Bolivar County Prison for smuggling moonshine out of a sunroof factory. Although the owner was in the dark, Rufus's idea was brought to light when a co-worker thought one of the boxes felt heavier than the rest. The co-worker opened the box, found several bottles of moonshine, drank one, and called the local police.

JaMark took time to see Rufus, his grandmother, his ex-teammates from the Rosedale semi-pro league, and other long-forgotten friends who heard word of his exploits. The most notable thing about the off season for JaMark however, was that throughout the entire winter, he didn't hear from the Devil.

CHAPTER 15

After a month in Rosedale following his time in the Arizona Winter League, JaMark received a phone call from a member of the St. Petersburg Saints instructing him to report for Spring Training during the first week of February. A few weeks after the New Year, JaMark received a large envelope containing travel arrangements and plane tickets. JaMark followed the arrangements, and after Betsy drove him from Rosedale to Memphis, Tennessee, JaMark took a flight to Tampa, Florida, where he rented a car and completed his journey to the team's Spring Training complex.

JaMark had never been to Florida before. Nor had he ever been to Spring Training. Almost immediately, JaMark stood out, even among the major leaguers. While other pitchers slowly eased their way into their pitching routine, starting with a game of catch, then long toss, then pitching to the catchers at half their normal speed, JaMark immediately began pitching as fast as he could. Unfortunately, the first catcher scheduled to catch JaMark on the first day wasn't prepared for the speed of JaMark's offerings. The unready receiver caught the ball wrong and broke his thumb. After the incident, the Saints pitching coach told JaMark his day was done and instructed him to leave the pitching area and return to the clubhouse to shower, change his clothes, and prepare for the next day.

As JaMark entered the clubhouse, he was stopped by an elderly gentleman dressed in a Saints uniform. He was too old to be on the team, JaMark surmised, unless he, too, had an invincible arm. But JaMark would have heard about a grey-haired pitcher in the Major Leagues if there was one. JaMark concluded the man must be a coach, although he had not seen him talking to any other players in the camp.

"Son, that's a bad way to start the year," the old man said.

"I'm sorry," JaMark said. "My arm feels great, so I just wound up and let 'em go."

"You're going to kill your arm," the old man said. "Happened to me in '53. I had just finished beating New York the year before in the World Series. Struck out Hank McGood on a curve to win the clincher. I came into spring training hot like I was gonna rule the world. I threw three days at top speed. Then 'pop,' the arm blew, and I limped off into the sunset. Gotta take it easy, kid."

"Yes, sir," JaMark said. He knew the common rules of human biology didn't apply to him, but he wanted to be respectful and acknowledge the old man's words of wisdom.

The next day JaMark again threw faster than his peers. Major League veterans and rookies alike all watched JaMark in awe as he fired fastball after fastball to his catchers, who now wore their full gear when catching JaMark. After the third day of spring training, the Saints pitching coach again pulled JaMark aside in the clubhouse, put his arm around JaMark's shoulders, and told him to stop throwing so hard so early. He told JaMark he was concerned not only about JaMark's arm, but he told JaMark the veterans on the team were starting to take offense to being shown up by a rookie few had heard of, no less seen in action.

"Look, kid," the coach said, "you show these guys up and they will look at you sideways and then stare you down. How's the arm, anyway?"

"Arm feels great, coach," JaMark said, avoiding the subject of his velocity. He didn't want to act arrogant, even if he didn't think he was doing anything wrong.

"Well, we are watching you and counting your pitches," the coach said. "We're gonna give you a few days off. Just soft toss the next few days with one of the catchers who caught you last season."

JaMark was disappointed, but he knew he had to follow their process. For the next three days, he played catch with Barry Carusowitz, his catcher in Mobile the season before. Of course,

Carusowitz also was a thrower when he wasn't a catcher and threw the ball to JaMark, who then became a catcher before throwing the ball back to Carusowitz. They were both throwers and catchers for several hours each day.

After his soft-tossing moratorium ended, JaMark pitched in a simulated game against other minor leaguers in the organization. JaMark hurled the horsehide to six batters, including a few former teammates, and struck out all of them. At the request of the pitching coaches, JaMark started throwing his curveball, and similarly to the year before, batters swung their bats feebly or stood and watched the spinning ball rotate through the strike zone.

The next day, JaMark pitched in another simulated game and had the same result, albeit with different batters. After the game, JaMark and several other pitchers practiced fielding bunts, a skill JaMark struggled with. After each pitcher simulated his pitching motion, a coach standing on home plate would roll a baseball to different sides of the pitcher's mound to simulate a bunted ball. No batter had ever tried bunting against JaMark, leaving him completely unfamiliar with the defensive exercise.

Every day for the next two weeks, JaMark worked on his fielding. The idea of improving a part of the game he was weak at helped distract him from putting his all into every pitch during daily pitching practice, simulated games, and during exhibition games against other teams.

JaMark pitched only twice during Spring Training against batters wearing uniforms bearing different logos and city names than his own. His debut came during the bottom half of the eighth inning in a game against Boston in Fort Myers, Florida. Facing five batters hoping to make the major league club or solidify their own spot on a higher minor league team, JaMark pitched well, striking out two, walking one, allowing one hit, and getting the fifth batter to hit a slow-rolling ball to the first baseman, who stepped on the base before the batter could.

In the second game, JaMark pitched against the Washington team in the town of Jupiter, Florida. On the bus ride to Jupiter, JaMark overheard two teammates questioning the origin of the town's moniker. The first, a young cherub-faced infielder JaMark had seen only twice during the spring, asked why the town was named after a planet. He was answered by a tall, lanky pitcher JaMark shared time with in Wyoming, who stated Jupiter the town was named after Jupiter the god, not Jupiter the planet. The infielder then asked if Jupiter the planet was also named after Jupiter the god. When he was told yes, he stated that if Jupiter the planet was named after Jupiter the god, and the town was founded after the planet was discovered, who's to say the town wasn't named after the planet if they were both named after the god. The lanky pitcher who attempted to correct the infielder shook his head in forfeit, granting the youngster the benefit of understanding through obfuscation.

JaMark shook his head and counted down the miles to Jupiter, the town.

In the top of the fifth inning of the game played in the town named after Jupiter the god, JaMark took the mound again in relief of the starting pitcher. In JaMark's two innings, he struck out two, walked one, but gave up two runs, as after he walked a batter, the following batter hit a towering home run. JaMark dropped his head after hearing the crack of the bat and didn't bother to turn around to watch the ball fly out of the ballpark. The runs JaMark allowed gave his opponents a five to three lead. Unfortunately for JaMark, following him on the mound was a trio of fellow young minor league pitchers who combined to give up six more runs, and the Saints lost eleven to four.

Following another week of simulated games against players wearing similar uniforms to his, JaMark was summoned to the office of the Saints pitching coach. The office was sparse with furniture, with only a folding table, one office chair, two folding chairs, and a couch. JaMark's pitching coach from his time in the Deep South League and another gentleman were sitting on the couch as the Saints pitching coach sat on his office chair. After the coach waved him in, JaMark walked into the office, shook hands with the three men, and took a seat on one of the two folding chairs.

"JaMark," the Saints coach said, "you have one hell of an

arm and great God-given talent, but we are going to keep you in the minors for another year. You throw fast, but there is no need to rush, so we're going to take it slow. You're going to our top minor league team in Buffalo. It will be cold, so stay warm, keep bringing the heat, and we'll see you soon."

JaMark wasn't surprised by their decision. He stopped being surprised in his life after a man, or rather a supernatural being from the underworld, emerged from the Earth and gave him the ability to throw again. Even then, he wasn't really surprised as he was in a half-awake, half-asleep stupor at the time. So JaMark stopped being surprised even before that. But the day he met the Devil was the day he could point to and say he would never be surprised again.

Following two more weeks in sunny Florida, JaMark traveled to frigid Buffalo in late March. The snow in Buffalo was still piled in corners across the city, and most people still bundled in at least three layers when JaMark arrived. JaMark, unfortunately, didn't have the time nor the ability to shop for heavy garments in Florida prior to his flight. Without the necessary garments, he felt the cold, Buffalo breeze almost immediately after getting off the plane.

Unlike his delayed arrival in the Deep South League, JaMark was a day early reporting to the Buffalo team. Although he knew the location of the stadium, he left Florida without contact information for his new manager or coaches. After checking into a motel near the ballpark and with time to spare, JaMark visited the local mall to buy some much needed cold weather attire.

After buying a jacket and a few other essentials, JaMark left the mall and visited a small local bookstore. As his eyes went down the titles and he went down the aisles, he found the sports books section. He glanced at the stories of famous athletes and wondered if any of them traveled the same road as he did. Or at least some of the same journey, as he didn't think too many athletes made a deal with the Devil on a dirt highway outside of Rosedale, Mississippi.

At the end of the long row of baseball books, JaMark

saw a book with the title "100 Minor League Prospects to Know". Although he was told in Spring Training to never pay attention to the media, he was curious to see if he was listed as a "prospect to know." He also wanted to know what the book would tell readers about him as he doubted any reader would actually know him from reading a book. He thought they would be better off going to one of his games, saying hello, and engaging in conversation if they wanted to get to know him.

JaMark flipped through the pages, stopping momentarily to read about players he played against in Wyoming, Arizona, and in the Deep South League. He never realized some of the impressive accomplishments achieved by batters he faced or those who were his teammates. He wondered if it was proper etiquette to mention to any teammates or opponents that he read about them in a book.

In the "R" section of the book, JaMark was pleasantly surprised to find his own profile. He was humbled he made the book, and happy he made the author's list of one to know.

"Former high school star. Recovered from near-career ending injury. Signed by the Saints off the semi-pro fields of Mississippi. Posted big numbers in Wyoming and the Deep South League. Pitched first truly perfect game in the history of baseball. Blazing fastball, unhittable curve. When on, pitches like a man possessed."

The last sentence in the profile almost made JaMark drop the book. His hands trembled as he put the book on the shelf and walked out of the bookstore without looking back or even engaging in any customer small talk. He just wanted to leave.

Following his time at the mall and other establishments needed to acquire the necessary necessities for life in Buffalo, JaMark again found the best motel he could afford on the budget of a minor league baseball player. He signed for the room, called Betsy, and then went to sleep, trying to clear his head of anything related to the Devil.

The next day, JaMark returned to the ballpark. This time, his new teammates, coaches, and manager were present. Although most of his teammates were new and JaMark recognized them only from their time together in Florida, there were several former teammates from the Deep South League who resumed their roles as teammates, as they too were promoted to Buffalo.

JaMark's season in Buffalo started as his season in the Deep South League ended: with good pitching, but little hitting from his teammates. During his first few weeks with Buffalo, JaMark was frequently matched against the best pitchers of the opposing team. Although he had little problem shutting down the best offenses in the league, his teammates hardly mustered any offense of their own during his appearances. After a month, JaMark had only one win and three losses, despite giving up only six runs in his four outings. Statistically, he pitched thirty innings, struck out forty batters, and walked only four. Whereas the cold weather and dry air made throwing curveballs difficult for most pitchers, JaMark's long fingers and unique grip kept his curveball curving even in the most arctic of conditions.

Not long into the season, the fans of Buffalo, hearing JaMark's curveball carried local names in other places, gave the pitch their own nickname. They called it "Hagwe", short for "Hahgwehdaetgan" – the Destroyer Spirit of the Iroquois. Like its spiritual ancestor, JaMark's Hagwe continued to destroy the spirits of batters throughout the league. By the time the weather warmed, so too did the bats of JaMark's teammates. JaMark's teammates started to score more runs, and JaMark started to get credited with wins to go along with his league lead in strikeouts, innings pitched, complete games, and shutouts.

As he did in Arizona, JaMark continued to sneak in credit to the Devil during his postgame comments. Along with his often-used phrase of "I pitched well, but you know the Devil is in the details," JaMark also started to use "sometimes there is the Devil to pay" after his team followed up a loss with a win. He made sure to mention the Devil with a smile and always convey an "aw, shucks" type demeanor to reporters. Most of the time, they bought it and walked away happy to get a quote.

On May 8th, on his twenty-fourth birthday, a year after signing his first contract to play professional baseball, and three years after meeting the man with the black suit, tie, and matching top hat under a tree on a dirt road in rural Mississippi, JaMark put on his uniform and took the mound in Durham, North Carolina. Despite the cool May air, which contained just a tinge of North Carolina humidity, JaMark felt warm and clammy from the moment he got out of bed. The feeling stayed with him every moment throughout the day, through breakfast, lunch, his trip to the ballpark, and his pre-game routine.

The evening contest against Durham was a match-up of two of the best pitchers in the Minor Leagues, with JaMark taking the hill for Buffalo and Pete LaGib pitching for the home team. LaGib was a nineteen-year old prospect who, in his second season in the Minor Leagues, had only allowed one run. He didn't pitch as often as JaMark, as his coaches were much more sensitive with his young arm, but he was just as effective.

As close as the two pitchers were in result, their differences on the mound were stark. JaMark threw a blazing fastball and a dazzling curve, while LaGib was already a master at the ancient art of knuckleballing, having come from a long line of Hungarian trick-pitching, gypsy circus performers. LaGib's uncle taught him every trick pitch in the book, but it was his knuckleball that made him unhittable during his four years of high school in South Central Los Angeles.

Reliford versus LaGib was everything baseball fans expected.

CHAPTER 16

Despite feeling ill earlier in the day, JaMark felt great on the field that night in Durham. For the first three innings, he struck out every Durham batter with fleet fastballs and crisp curves. He knew he had his work cut out for him, however, as LaGib frustrated the Buffalo batters with an array of befuddling, fluttering floaters. Even though the pitchers would never face each other face-to-face, JaMark knew he was in for a challenge. He also told himself he wasn't going to leave the game without a win.

In the fourth inning, both pitchers issued a walk, and the baserunners for both teams stole second. The Buffalo runner, however, advanced to third when a LaGib knuckleball knuckled too much and skipped past the Durham catcher. From third, the runner scored by tagging up on the next batter's fly ball to center field, only the second run LaGib had allowed all season.

It was only one run, but JaMark was set on trying to make it count.

Although their pitching styles were drastically different, they were still pitchers. They were great pitchers able to dominate hitters who were not as great of hitters as the pitchers were great pitchers. As evidence, neither pitcher allowed a hit through the first seven innings. Even the home Durham crowd began cheering JaMark's strikeouts. While JaMark had fourteen strikeouts on 106 pitches through eight innings, LaGib was much more economical, throwing seventy-four pitches and only striking out two. With Reliford's pitch count growing and LaGib pitching farther into a game than he had before, both managers were starting to get nervous.

Still one to nothing in the bottom of the ninth, JaMark was optimistic he could end the game and secure the win. But the umpire diminished JaMark's optimism when he called "Ball Four" to the first batter on a pitch JaMark thought was strike three. The next batter hit a short fly ball into right-center field. The Buffalo rightfielder ran left, squared himself under the round ball, and made all the correct motions to catch the ball, but the ball bounced out of his glove and rolled to the centerfielder.

JaMark watched as the runner on first base rounded second base and arrived at third base. Fortunately for JaMark, the batter, after arriving at first base successfully, was unsuccessful in his attempt to reach second base. The Durham team had a man on third without a hit and the league's leading hitter, Damien Ignachio, coming to bat.

Ignachio hit well in every minor league level he played in. His father was renowned fencing gold medalist Claudio Ignachio, and Damien was as skilled with the bat as his father was with the sword. While Damien would practice hitting baseballs with his father's swords, his father's sparring partners were thankful Claudio never practiced using Damien's bats.

In the ninth inning that night in Durham, the younger Ignachio proved better in the bout. After parrying two JaMark fastballs into the crowd, he thrusted JaMark's curveball into right field for the first Durham hit of the game.

After the hit, and with JaMark nearing 120 pitches, the Buffalo manager attempted to visit the pitcher's mound to see how his ace was feeling. JaMark saw his manager take his first steps out of the dugout and scowled. The Buffalo manager saw the look on his ace pitcher, executed a near-perfect military about-face, and walked back into the dugout.

Yet to reach the popular minor league taboo total of 100 pitches, Pete LaGib went to the mound in the top of the tenthinning. He was happy fate had given him another chance to pitch his team to victory. He floated knuckleball after knuckleball, with each pitch dipping, diving, and driving the Buffalo batters bonkers. From the perspective of the fans, he was throwing no faster than a little old lady, but from the perspective of the batters, there was no way of predicting the pitch's trajectory. They could see it, they just couldn't hit it.

The Durham batters, on the other hand, still couldn't catch up to JaMark's pitches. In the bottom of the tenth, JaMark was still throwing curveballs that curved and fastballs that were fast. And he still felt great, despite throwing nearly 130 pitches. Before JaMark struck out his seventeenth batter for the final out of the tenth inning, he overheard his manager say to his pitching coach, "I'll be damned if this isn't already one of the greatest games I have ever seen, but I bet it's the one that gets me fired. God, I hope this kid's arm doesn't fall off."

JaMark hid a smile, knowing he would probably also be damned if his arm fell off. At least he would know someone there in the fiery afterlife.

CHAPTER 17

Welcome back to the Durham baseball broadcast. Folks, if you have been listening to this entire game, I applaud you. You are a hardcore baseball fan. We are running commercial-free for the rest of the game as we would normally be off the air by midnight, but we are far past midnight tonight.

It's been a long night, so let's recap.

We're here in the top of the eighteenth inning, it's 2:10 in the morning, it's dark, and I am wearing sunglasses. A little Blues Brothers reference there. But JaMark Reliford and Pete LaGib are still on a mission from God, pitching a miraculous game. They have each allowed one run and nothing else. While JaMark has struck out plenty, LaGib is baffling the Buffalo lineup with an array of dancing knuckleballs.

You know, we started this game with over 5,000 fans in attendance. After the clock hit 11 pm, hundreds of them went home instead of staying to witness baseball history. And with good reason, many of them probably have work in the morning.

But for those who have stuck around, they've outlasted most of the players on each team. The Durham manager began replacing his players in the fourteenth inning. By the seventeenth, the entire lineup turned over except for LaGib and Mac Dawson, his catcher. And we know LaGib and Dawson have a special relationship as Dawson is the only catcher on the roster who catches LaGib. But eighteen innings on a catcher's knees has to hurt.

On the Buffalo side, according to what's left of my scorecard, only JaMark Reliford and his catcher remain from the Buffalo starting nine.

Folks, think about how amazing it is that these pitchers are still in the game. LaGib just passed his 170th pitch in the seventeenth inning, and Reliford is closing in on pitch 250. Yet each team only has one hit and one run. This is like an old Western showdown, and no man is backing down. If you look in the dugout as I have, since the twelfth inning, each *manager has attempted to ask their pitcher how they felt, only to be turned away. These guys are out to finish what they started.*

And now JaMark Reliford takes the mound in the top of theeighteenth inning. Up to face him is the number four hitter, the second third baseman of the night for Durham, Turner Mayer. Mayer is 0 for four since entering the game in the ninth inning.

Reliford's first pitch of the eighteenth is a strike on the outside corner. The scoreboard said that pitch was ninety-four miles per hour. He must have some kind of God-given talent to have this kind of stamina.

And the next pitch from Reliford is a ball outside. Mayer steps out of the batter's box for a moment, rubs some dirt on his hands, and re-enters the box, ready to hit.

The pitch ... and Mayer taps it towards first base. The first baseman steps on the bag, and one away.

Now batting, the number five hitter, number fifty-five, the shortstop, Omar Benitez. Benitez was one of the many Durham players who entered the game in the twelfth inning. He was recently promoted to Durham, so I am not sure if this is the type of start he had in mind.

Reliford's first pitch is a fastball for strike one. Benitez took a mighty hack, but you can tell the game is wearing on these players. That swing wasn't as mighty as those earlier in the contest.

Reliford winds and the pitch is another fastball, this time on the inside corner. Benitez gave a glance back at the home plate umpire but didn't give an argument. The way Reliford is pitching, I don't think Benitez has much of a claim. And besides, this umpire probably wants to go home just as much as anyone else.

Benitez steps out of the box, rubs some dirt on his hands, and steps up to the plate. Reliford looks in to his catcher. He winds up. And here's the pitch.

That was one of the nicest curveballs I have seen Reliford throw all night. A beautiful 12-6 curve that started at Benitez's chest and ended at his knees. The poor kid had no chance. That's strikeout number thirty for Reliford.

Folks, our stats guy just informed me — first of all, I didn't know our stats guy was still here — but he just informed me that Reliford has tied the Minor League Baseball record for strikeouts in a game with thirty, set in 1941 by Clarence "Hooks" Iott, who pitched for the Paragould Browns in Paragould, Arkansas. We could see some history here tonight.

Well, with two down, here comes the sixth hitter in the Durham lineup, the leftfielder, Tim Nieto. Nieto came in the game in the 15th inning, and this is his first at-bat. Nieto is a left-handed hitter who has been with the club all year but hasn't seen much playing time.

Reliford looks in. He winds and delivers a fastball that rides in a bit on Nieto. The man behind the plate calls it strike one. That was ninety-five miles per hour, according to the gun.

Nieto takes his place back in the box. And he squares to bunt. Reliford fires another fastball, and Nieto fouls it off. Not a bad strategy there, just trying to get on base with a bunt. But with two strikes, let's see if Nieto tries again.

It doesn't look like he is bunting. Reliford delivers. A third fastball, right on the outside corner. Nieto took a feeble swing but couldn't make contact. That's strikeout number thrity-one for JaMark Reliford, setting a new professional baseball record. And the scoreboard just announced the record. The remaining fans are giving JaMark a standing ovation. Congrats to the young left-hander."

CHAPTER 18

As JaMark walked back to the dugout following his record-setting strikeout, he looked to the stands and tipped his cap to the enduring patrons. Before sitting down on the bench, he caught a glimpse of a tall, lanky man in a black suit, tie, and matching top hat. The man looked at JaMark, smiled, and tipped his hat in return.

After the bottom of the eighteenth inning, at 2:38 in the morning, after LaGib threw six pitches and made three Buffalo batters hit three groundballs to the second baseman who each time threw to the first baseman who stepped on first base for three outs, the voice of the tired public address announcer spoke to the exhausted masses who remained in the crowd. Due to a curfew, the announcer stated, the game would be considered a temporary tie and would be continued at a date later in the season. In a lapse of judgment caused by exhaustion, the announcer also stated the game should have ended earlier, but both managers had fallen asleep on their respective benches and forgot to pull their teams off the field by the city curfew. Those still awake in the crowd laughed, as many of them had also napped during the game.

Following the announcement, as the players began to file from the dugout to the clubhouses, the crowd rose to their feet to applaud. A chant started from a few college-aged kids in the right-field bleachers and spread through the stadium.

"Reliford, LaGib," the crowd chanted in a sing-song rhythm. "Reliford, LaGib. Reliford, LaGib."

Hearing the adoration of the crowd, the players on both teams pushed their respective pitchers out of their respective dugouts to acknowledge their standing ovation. As they emerged to the sight of the spectators, they both doffed their caps to the remaining masses, walked towards each other, and shook hands near home plate. An enterprising young photographer by the name of Bradson Merkel snapped a picture of the two hurlers acknowledging each other's accomplishment. Merkel ran upstairs to the pressbox, loaded the image on his laptop, and emailed it to several prominent sports media outlets along with a short story on the history made in the early Durham morning. By sunrise, the entire sports world was abuzz with the names JaMark Reliford and Pete LaGib.

Although his arm felt fine, JaMark was physically and mentally drained by the end of the game. Seeing his star pitcher fight fits of fatigue in order to shower and change out of his uniform, the Buffalo manager closed the clubhouse much to the chagrin of the doggedly determined press, many of whom also caught catnaps during the game. Unbothered by the media, JaMark was able to dress, clean up his locker, and prepare for the drive back to the hotel. Before he walked out of the clubhouse, his manager congratulated him on his performance but told him he would not pitch for several days so his arm could heal. Too tired to argue, JaMark agreed and left the ballpark.

CHAPTER 19

The next afternoon, after sleeping nine hours, JaMark finally awoke. His legs were sore, but his arm still felt as if he could throw another 200 pitches and eighteen innings. As the previous night's starting pitcher, he didn't have to arrive at the ballpark until moments before the evening's game. He didn't have to run, catch fly balls, work out in the gym, play catch, or anything else associated with being a baseball player. According to the team rules, he could even skip taking the team bus to the ballpark and opt for a cab as long as he arrived before the national anthem.

After drinking a protein shake and getting himself ready for the day, JaMark went out into the sunshine and hailed a cab. He asked the cab driver to drive him to the best lunch establishment in town. Five miles and four dollars later, the driver stopped at a local sports bar. When they arrived, the driver told JaMark the sports bar served the best water in town and that JaMark should also try the barbeque. JaMark exited the cab, paid his fare, and thought perhaps the driver mixed up his words when he suggested water.

JaMark walked through the interior of the North Carolina-sports themed sports bar, with its college basketball pennants and panoramas of the city's historic minor league ballpark, and found a table and a seat on the sports bar's outside patio. He angled his seat to watch one of the many televisions the establishment had positioned outside, and nodded at a server. She acknowledged his presence with a smile and raised a finger. JaMark didn't know if her finger raise was to indicate one moment or one minute, but he sat, watched television, and waited for either.

While JaMark watched the latest episode of the local

sports highlight show, a few patrons from inside the sports bar approached him, asked if he was the Buffalo pitcher who pitched the night before, shook his hand, and asked for a few autographs. One of the patrons even confessed to being at the game but admitted they left in the eighth inning. After engaging in some small talk with the tall pitcher, the patrons wandered off, leaving JaMark to wonder why people left baseball games before the final out.

A few minutes after the server again walked by JaMark's table, gave him a smile, and raised a finger for a second, yet untold reason, another visitor came to JaMark's table. Awkwardly sensing someone nearby, JaMark broke his gaze from the report of the local junior high soccer tournament and looked up. His newest visitor was the tall, slender man with a black suit, tie, and matching top hat from years earlier in Mississippi and the previous season in the Mobile hotel.

"May I join you?" the man asked, looking down at JaMark with the same sly smile he used at the old tree at the crossroads.

"You may," JaMark replied.

The Devil sat in the seat across from JaMark, placed his hat on an empty seat beside him, and looked out at the passing traffic. He reached into the front pocket of his jacket, pulled out a pack of cigarettes, took one out, lit it, and took a long drag.

"Do you want one?" the Devil asked JaMark.

"No, thanks," JaMark replied. "I quit a few years ago."

"Oh, yes. I remember," the Devil said with a smile. "Smoking is a terrible habit. I really should quit myself," he said before taking another long drag.

As the Devil finished his cigarette, the server arrived at their table. She was a short, middle-aged woman with shoulder-length, brown hair who looked like she was all business in the most southern hospitality way possible.

"Hey y'all, what'll it be?" she inquired with a deep southern accent. JaMark received the impression that she didn't want to be taking tables outside as she frequently looked inside at her interior tables.

Chapter 19

Despite her unsaid objection to being their server, JaMark decided to give her his order. "I'll have the water and a barbeque pork sandwich. I heard you guys have the best water in town."

"Yes, sir," the server said with a forced smile. "We've been voted best restaurant water six years running by the local newspaper. Our barbeque isn't bad, either."

She looked at the Devil, dressed in his black suit in the middle of the spring North Carolina day.

"Hun, do you want water as well?" she said to the Devil. "You gotta be hot wearing black in the sun like that. You want something to eat as well?"

"I am always hot," the Devil replied as he glared at the server. "It's my cross to bear." He paused for a moment to look over the menu. "I'll have the Buffalo wings, hot. And a sweet tea."

The server took another long look at the Devil before giving him an awkward smile and walking back towards the kitchen. As he watched the server quicken her pace as if something was wrong, JaMark wondered what she thought of the Devil's peculiarities. Having known the Devil for a few years, he had almost gotten used to the supernatural being's attempts at appearing human. JaMark wondered to himself if this human form was the devil's eternal state. Did he walk the Earth permanently, looking for people to send to Hell? Was the Devil a twisted shepherd for the underworld?

JaMark thought to ask the Devil the questions in his head, but the Devil spoke first.

"Quite the game last night," the Devil said.

"Thank you," JaMark replied.

"I really admired that LaGib kid," the Devil said. "Such God-given talent on that one. He's gonna be good. And the picture in the news was spectacular. That photographer kid is going to be big as well if he keeps taking pictures like that. Have you seen the picture of you and LaGib from last night?"

"No," JaMark answered. He remembered a photographer on the field after the game, but he was so exhausted, few details stood out.

"You really should," the Devil said as he stared intently at JaMark. "People will know you because of it. They'll look at it and immediately hold you and Pete LaGib in high regard. They'll think you epitomize all that is great in baseball again. They'll buy magazines just for the picture, no matter what the cost. They'll hang your picture on their walls next to pictures of their children. They'll look at that picture and believe in sportsmanship again. They'll believe in camaraderie again. The innocence of baseball will return to their souls, and they will forget about contracts and labor deals and free agents. Baseball will again be the game they loved as children. A game ended every summer evening by their mother calling them in to dinner, as they shook hands with the kid down the block and arranged to continue the contest the next day, bright and early. They'll remember that friend. And they will remember the good in baseball. Because of you."

JaMark looked at the Devil dumbfounded. He had no idea what to say. He knew his gift from the Devil meant he would be able to play again, but he never thought he would be the torchbearer for the purity of baseball. He considered the irony of a man with Devil-given gifts being a symbol for good.

He also considered the Devil fabricated the whole speech and wasn't actually serious.

"You're welcome, of course," the Devil said, interrupting JaMark's thoughts.

"I'm sorry?" JaMark asked. He knew what the Devil said, but he was shocked at the audacity of the Devil to turn what was a very selfless observation into an ugly, ego-based statement.

"For making you famous," the Devil said with a smile. "It was all my doing, and I want you to know that. I mean, I know you do, but I still like to hear a 'thank you' every once in a while for my hard work."

"Thank you," JaMark answered.

"You're very welcome," the Devil said. "Anytime."

A moment later, the server arrived at their table with the two lunches. She placed the food on the table, asked if they had all they needed, and when they acknowledged in the affirmative, she walked quickly to the safety and security of her other tables.

As soon as the food was in front of him, the Devil grabbed a chicken wing and started eating. JaMark looked at his food for a moment and then took the opportunity to question the Devil.

"So what brings you to town?" he asked.

The Devil pulled the remaining bone from his mouth, wiped the hot sauce from his lips and fingers, and looked up at JaMark.

"I come here often," the Devil said. "Beautiful city and nice people. I'm a big college basketball fan. I made a deal with a coach here years back, and now I can't remember his last name. I told him his teams would be great, and he would be loved, but at the sacrifice of his player's professional careers. Young men would become great professional basketball players from many other schools, but his kids were cursed as long as he wanted to win. He agreed, and we have met ever since."

JaMark dug into his food using his hands, careful not to get barbeque sauce on his fingers. The water was as advertised – the best water JaMark had ever tasted. It was cool, crisp, and refreshing, without being overpowering. JaMark thought the barbeque sandwich was also good, but not as good as the water. He was surprised by the taste of the water and was also surprised to a lesser degree by the taste of the barbeque, which used a Carolina mustard-style sauce instead of the Mississippi-style sauce he was used to. He was also careful not to wash down the food with the great tasting water, but to swallow the food, then get the full effect of the tasty water.

Both men ate in silence for four minutes and several seconds. Then the Devil looked up from his near-finished meal.

"I never could figure out why they call them Buffalo wings. Nothing in Buffalo is hot. You know what is hot? Hell. I think the guy upstairs convinced them to not name these things after me. Devil's Wings. How does that sound? Instead, I got a cake. And not even a good cake. Not as good as angel's food cake. Imagine that. Me, less than an angel. After all, I was once an angel. I've been there, done that. Tried to overthrow God and lost my wings. Hence the predilection for eating wings. There is something psychological there, I'm sure. Maybe it's a complex."

JaMark sat in awkward silence, trying to finish his meal with as little conversation as possible. Although he knew the Devil's peccadilloes, he was still cautious of what he considered the Devil's erratic moodiness. As JaMark took the last few bites of his sandwich, ate the last few french fries, and sipped the last of the amazing water, the Devil pushed his plate aside and lit another cigarette.

A few moments later, after she noticed the two men were finished with their meals, the server returned with their respective bills. She handed the Devil his bill first but paused before giving JaMark his.

"Sir, I have a question for you," she said to JaMark. "Are you a baseball player? Are you the guy in the baseball picture everyone is talking about today? Because if you are, my manager told me to tell you your meal is free if you would sign a copy of this picture for us."

JaMark looked at the server, then looked at the Devil and smiled. The Devil leaned back in his seat with his arms crossed and reciprocated the smile. JaMark looked at the waitress again.

"Yes, ma'am, I am a baseball player," he answered, "and I am in a picture from what I hear. And yes, I'd absolutely sign a copy of the picture for you."

The server took the Devil's payment and the two bills and went inside the restaurant to get the picture for JaMark to autograph. She returned less than a minute later with the Devil's change and a printed page-sized lithograph of JaMark and Pete LaGib, shaking hands at home plate. As JaMark looked at the picture, he realized the Devil was correct – it was a great photo.

JaMark took the server's pen and signed his name below his photographed pose. The server smiled and collected the autographed picture, wished JaMark and the Devil a good day, and returned inside to tend to her other customers.

"You're welcome," the Devil said. "Yet again."

"Thank you," JaMark replied, trying not to be curiously annoyed at the Devil's need to be thanked.

Chapter 19

After one last sip of sweet tea, the Devil stood up, put on his hat, tipped the brim towards JaMark, and walked towards the parking lot. JaMark sat for a few moments, pondering the situation he found himself in.

CHAPTER 20

Compared to his eventful lunch, the rest of JaMark's day was calm. A few hours after lunch and an hour before the Star-Spangled Banner, JaMark arrived at the ballpark and met with his teammates. Most were still tired from the night before, and their play reflected their physical alertness. They committed four errors on the field and made several uncounted base running snafus in a twelve to three loss.

For the next few weeks, however, the Buffalo players played much more awake than they did in the game following their eighteen-inning game. They used their alertness as a key ingredient to winning games, along with good hitting, good defense, and good pitching, led of course, by JaMark. By mid-season, the Buffalo team was in first place, and JaMark was leading the league's pitchers in wins, innings pitched, and strikeouts. In all other positive pitcher measurements, JaMark was a close second to Pete LaGib while everyone else was either a far third, a distant fourth, or further.

By all accounts, the Devil was right about JaMark's picture with Pete LaGib. The Merkel Photo, named after the man who took it, grew to near epic proportions as it circulated through major sports media channels. The moment, frozen in time, became timeless.

During the months that followed, everywhere JaMark went, he was asked about the game and asked if he could sign a copy or two of the popular photo. While on the team bus after a game in Indianapolis, JaMark told his teammates he thought he signed more copies of the photo on any given night than there were fans remaining in attendance in the final inning of the now-classic game. With so many autograph seekers, JaMark had to set a personal rule that he did not sign autographs nor talk about past games on days he was pitching. He liked keeping his mind in the present during his pitching days so he could focus on creating history instead of reliving past memories.

And creating more history was exactly what he did. Every few weeks he added another incredible performance to the track record of JaMark Reliford, minor league legend. There was the game in Columbus in mid-June, where JaMark pitched seven innings and struck out twenty batters, the day in late June in Rochester when he started and pitched the first five innings of both games of a doubleheader, and the July 4th game in Buffalo in which, although he did not pitch, he did hit a pinch-hit home run to win the game in the eleventh inning, his first hit in his first at-bat since his days in the Rosedale semi-pro adult league.

Through his exploits and accolades, JaMark became a minor league phenomenon and the center of the Buffalo sports universe. The games he pitched became cultural events as even the shopkeepers closed their places of business to go watch him, television stations not carrying Buffalo baseball broadcasts went off the air rather than bother with counterprogramming, and "Sorry, I am going to see JaMark Reliford pitch" replaced "I have to wash my hair" as the number one frequently used line for women trying to avoid going on a date.

The affair between JaMark and the City of Buffalo was short-lived, however. On September 1st, the day most rookies are summoned from the Minor Leagues to assist Major League teams during the last weeks of the season, JaMark got "The Call". At the age of twenty-four, after nearly two seasons in the minors, JaMark was told by the manager of his Buffalo team to get ready for the big leagues.

CHAPTER 21

When he arrived at his first big league stadium late in the evening on September 1st, the St. Petersburg Saints, JaMark's new Major League team, were in the midst of an epic pennant race. Of the fifteen teams in the league, nine were still in competition for four playoff spots. The Saints were in second place in their division and holding the final playoff spot, attempting to hold off the four teams whose respective players, coaches, managers, and fans wanted them to be in the playoffs.

JaMark joined his new team not long after talking to his minor league manager, but long enough after to call Betsy and his grandmother, pack his bags, arrive at the airport, board the airplane, fly, exit the plane, depart the airport, check in to a hotel, and then hail a cab to the stadium. Like his previous arrivals at minor league stadiums, the personnel at the major league stadium knew JaMark was on the way and had a locker, uniform, and equipment ready for him when he arrived. As he was too late to participate in the September 1st game, he only wore the uniform but did not use the game-playing equipment.

Although he traveled alone, JaMark was not alone in his journey from the minors to the Saints. From his time with other teams in the organization, he knew several of the other players who got "The Call" – some were even his teammates in Buffalo. He was most surprised to see Barry Carusowitz, his former catcher in Mobile, on the big league team. After a brief exchange of pleasantries, JaMark learned Carusowitz didn't make the big leagues as a player. The former catcher told JaMark that after realizing his playing career wasn't going further than the low minor leagues, he took a position as a coach, instructing catchers throughout the organization. According to his former teammate, now coach, the Saints brought him to the big leagues for the final month to learn from the major league coaches, better understand the organization's philosophy, and watch how the team wanted its players to professionally behave at the major league level.

Despite being a starting pitcher in Buffalo, Mobile, and since his earliest days in Wyoming, the Saints had enough proven major league starting pitchers, and his manager decided to start JaMark's big league career not as a starter, but as a relief pitcher. This was a relief for JaMark, who felt that although his arm was ready, starting as a starting pitcher might make him more nervous and cause more butterflies. He was relieved to start relieving and only deal with the mosquitoes of the bullpen area.

During his first six days in the Major Leagues, JaMark warmed up in the bullpen with Carusowitz and didn't see any game action. That changed on September 9th in Pittsburgh, when JaMark not only warmed up in the bullpen but was finally called to pitch in the game. With the Saints leading seven to three in the seventh inning, JaMark was told by the bullpen coach to warm up. After JaMark made several practice pitches to Carusowitz, the muscles in his arm were loose enough to pitch.

"Are you ready, kid?" asked the bullpen coach, a short, stout man with a bulging belly and a hat two sizes too small. During JaMark's short stay in the bullpen, he already learned from the other pitchers that the bullpen coach wasn't ever a player. Rather, he was the winner of a local phone company promotion to answer the phones in the bullpen for the entire 1981 season. According to JaMark's new teammates, the team decided the bullpen phone contest winner did such a good job answering phones they kept him with the team and gave him the title of "coach" sometime in the 1990s.

"I think so," answered JaMark. JaMark watched as the gate from the bullpen to the stadium slowly opened, revealing the field, thousands of screaming fans, and a pitching mound far in the distance where several of his new teammates stood, awaiting his arrival.

As he made the walk towards the infield, JaMark looked up at the thousands of fans packed in the stadium. The view of the crowd from on the field differed greatly from the view of the same people from in the bullpen. From the field, JaMark felt as though he was in a circular echo chamber of the screaming Pittsburgh faithful, the wall of sound and team colors rising far above his head. He knew, as he walked to the pitching mound, that most of these people wanted him to fail.

JaMark arrived at the pitching mound, unable to hide the smile on his face. His smile disappeared, however, when he was greeted by his manager, his soon-to-be catcher, and the rest of the infielders also on the pitcher's mound. Their serious looks on the crowded mound told him the time for personal significance was over. With the Saints leading by only four, the Pittsburgh squad was threatening to score with the bases loaded and one out. JaMark's new manager, who barely spoke a word to him since his arrival, said only one word to him on the mound. As he handed the ball to the rookie left-hander, the manager said "strikeout" in a deep, authoritative tone. JaMark was sometimes confused as to whether "strikeout" was one word or two, but despite his grammatical dilemma, the meaning came through clear as day on the cloudy Pittsburgh night. The Saints wanted JaMark to succeed.

After the manager, the infielders, and his soon-to-be catcher left the mound, JaMark stood on the small pitcher's hill and took a deep breath. He took one last look into the crowd. He knew his job was to silence them and to ruin the fun they were having at the ballpark. He was correct for all but one fan. In the upper left-field stands, far from JaMark's vision, stood the man with the black suit, tie, and matching top hat.

CHAPTER 22

Hello, fans, and welcome back to Pittsburgh here on Saints' radio. The Saints are up seven to three, but Pittsburgh is threatening in the bottom of the seventh inning. In an unusual move, the skipper of the Saints put rookie reliever JaMark Reliford in the game for his major league debut. It is not often you see a pitcher make his debut in such a high leverage situation in a pennant race.

But we have heard a lot about Reliford. The scouting report on him is that he is primarily a two-pitch pitcher with a fastball in the upper 90s and a big curveball that gets a lot of strikeouts. And I am sure that is what the Saints are looking for here, a strikeout or two to get out of this inning.

JaMark is a good-looking fella out there. Tall, lanky kid with a good pitcher's build. If half of what we have heard is true, he will be a good one in the big leagues.

Reliford is finished with his warm-ups, and he takes a slow stroll off the mound. Can't blame the rookie for taking a look at this capacity Pittsburgh crowd. It is loud here tonight. He climbs back on the mound and toes the rubber.

The first pitch from Reliford to Greg Liges, the Pittsburgh third baseman, is a strike. A ninety-seven mile an hour fastball on the inside corner. Liges took the first pitch from the rookie, but now he is down 0 and one. Reliford looks in, winds up, and throws another fastball inside. This one fouled off by Liges down the first base line. Like most rookies, Reliford is throwing exactly what his catcher wants. It looks like this kid has good control, and is giving it to the catcher exactly where he wants it as well.

Liges gets back in the batter's box, and Reliford comes from the stretch. The pitch is a dandy of a slow curve that had Liges frozen in his tracks. That pitch must have dropped at least six inches right on the outside corner. I don't think Liges read the report on Reliford because there was no doubt he was coming with his strikeout pitch in that situation.

Two away, and here is the number three hitter in the Pittsburgh *lineup, centerfielder Mike Dawson. Dawson has been in a slump of late, hitting only .125 in his last ten games, but JaMark still has to be careful. Dawson is a fastball hitter who can feast on an inexperienced rookie.*

The left-handed Dawson digs in against the left-handed Reliford. Reliford delivers. A fastball low and away for ball one. Dawson typically hits left-handers pretty well, and this season is hitting almost .300 against them.

Reliford toes the rubber and gets his next sign. He comes from the stretch and delivers. Fastball up and away for ball two. Two and 0 now on the dangerous Dawson. JaMark looks a bit nervous now, and the catcher gives him the hand signal to slow down. This kid definitely has the stuff, but at this level, the mental half is 90%, as the great Yogi Berra used to say.

Reliford takes a quick breath and looks at the runners – they are not going anywhere. His pitch is a high fastball that Dawson fouls off. Ninety-nine miles an hour for strike one. Dawson didn't look like he had a good bead on that fastball. A little bit too much movement for him to hit it squarely.

Reliford comes from the stretch again. Another fastball, this time on the inside corner and the umpire calls it strike two. Reliford went from being down two and 0 to evening the count. I wonder if he will bring a fifth fastball or give Dawson the same curve he gave Liges.

Reliford looks in. He winds, and the pitch. And Dawson goes down swinging on a big slow curveball that started at Dawson's chest and nearly ended up in the dirt. Wow. And Reliford gets out of the inning with two strikeouts in his major league debut. A fantastic performance by the rookie left-hander.

To the eight inning we go with the Saints still leading Pittsburgh seven to three."

CHAPTER 23

Although his manager was impressed with the ability of his new hurler, he removed JaMark from the game after the completion of the seventh inning. JaMark took the exit in stride, realizing that at the Major League level he would need to put his ego aside more than ever for the good of the team.

The next night, JaMark was again called upon to pitch in the seventh inning against Pittsburgh. This time he was able to pitch the entire inning and get all three outs, despite not striking out anyone and giving up his first Major League hit followed by his first Major League walk. Three days after, JaMark pitched in the seventh inning for a third time, this time against Cleveland, striking out all three batters he faced. By the end of September, JaMark had earned the trust and confidence of his Major League manager. While pitching entirely in relief, he was able to hold leads and ensure key victories, playing a big role in securing the Saints' playoff berth and holding off the respective players, coaches, managers, and fans of the other four teams who wanted their team to make the playoffs.

Through the first two rounds of the Saints' playoff journey, JaMark continued to impress, at one point pitching ten innings without giving up a hit. He also struck out batters at the same rate he did on the semi-pro fields of rural Mississippi, the lonely mountains of Wyoming, the humid hotness of Mobile, and the cool calmness of Buffalo. This time, however, those shaking their heads in disbelief were among the best in the world.

JaMark wasn't used as often in the championship round of the baseball season, but he was still called upon to get two strikeouts in two key situations, once in the second game and once in the final sixth game of the World Series. JaMark succeeded in both attempts, earning a pat on the butt by his manager, the less touchy admiration of his teammates, and after each post-game interview, the distant approval of the Devil.

With his picture with Pete LaGib still lingering in the hearts and minds of baseball fans, the success JaMark achieved on the grand stage of the baseball playoffs made the young pitcher even more of a star. By the end of his first season in the big leagues, numerous sports media outlets featured stories on JaMark. They wrote what little they could find about his background, they detailed his Minor League accomplishments, and they even analyzed the unique way his long fingers affected his curveball.

With his relative anonymity, blazing fastball, and humble demeanor, JaMark's emergence was considered by many as one of the best sports stories of the year. Most Major Leaguers don't hail from a local semi-pro team near Rosedale, Mississippi, and most baseball players from a local semi-pro team near Rosedale, Mississippi, don't strike out batters in the last game of the World Series.

The week following the World Series was a whirlwind of celebrations, parties, and exuberant bacchanalia for the St. Petersburg Saints. JaMark and many of his teammates stayed in the same hotel for a week, partying each night as they waited for their scheduled championship parade on St. Petersburg's main streets on the first week anniversary of their championship win. The beat writer for the team claimed the Saints painted the town red, although no brushes or cans of paint were found.

For JaMark, the celebrations and shindigs brought an unfortunate reminder of his dismal days of depression. Years after he took his last sip of alcohol under the oak tree at the dirt highway crossroads in rural Mississippi, JaMark again let a sip of fermented nectar slip through his lips during a hotel party. As he did the last night he drank alcohol in Mississippi, JaMark again felt nauseous and disgusted as the spirit made its way down his throat and to his stomach. He excused himself from the party, made his way to the restroom, walked past the sink attendant, and vomited.

CHAPTER 24

JaMark went home to Rosedale after the World Series celebrations and festivities. Hiding out from fans, media, and other admirers was more difficult compared to his previous offseasons. In the small town where he had gone from hero to failure, he was again put on a pedestal of fortune and glory. Even those who did not follow baseball knew about JaMark. They also knew about the plethora of reporters who descended upon Rosedale to ask questions about the then-and-again-famous pitcher.

Although he still lived with his grandmother, JaMark spent much of his free time with Betsy. Betsy was among the few people not enamored by JaMark's new fame. She did not answer questions nor make any statements to the media regarding JaMark's past. She attempted to convince JaMark's family to do the same, but she couldn't control JaMark's Uncle Rufus, who was quick to tell several reporters that he had been the one to convince JaMark to start playing baseball. Uncle Rufus also told any reporter who would listen the story of how JaMark strengthened his arm throwing strawberries on his farm. Uncle Rufus did not mention the trouble he got into for instructing JaMark to throw the strawberries on the farm of Monsignor Hiram Laggums and Uncle Rufus's ensuing charges of agricultural espionage.

JaMark's increased fame and popularity made several Rosedale residents uncomfortable. They still remembered him either as the cocky, arrogant teenager from his high school years or as the drunk troublemaker of his post-high school days. Although the television told them he was a better baseball player since his days of drunken debauchery, they had no way of knowing whether or not he was a better person.

Realizing their attitudes towards him were still off-putting, JaMark attempted to reconcile with the townsfolk. Every week he put on his Sunday best and went out with Betsy for strolls of Rosedale, speaking with people they crossed paths with, and even those they walked parallel with or walked in the opposite direction of. JaMark reintroduced himself to many of the local shop owners, bantering at barber shops and gabbing at grocery stores. He also visited his old elementary school, junior high, and high school to talk to children, teenagers, and young adults, some of whom were too young to remember the times when he was tormenting Rosedale, first with his fastball and then with his fast life. JaMark told anyone in his audience about his newfound lessons in humbleness and the idea of putting the team first; he even advised them that by hard work and determination, they too could be the best they could be.

To the children of Rosedale and the surrounding area, JaMark had become a hero. He was someone they looked up to, metaphorically, and literally, because he was nearly double their height. JaMark was someone the children could aspire to be, even the little girls of Rosedale, who believed after listening to JaMark they could be the first female baseball player in the big leagues. After each speech, however, JaMark felt slightly guilty. He felt like a fraud telling children not to take shortcuts when he, in fact, had given up on his life, and only succeeded after accepting supernatural assistance to return to his chosen career path. But he figured supernatural assistance might not be available for everyone, so the children would need to know how to succeed on their own.

The lessons were not limited to the children. During a high school visit, the students taught JaMark something he had never known before. They told him that contrary to common thought, JaMark was not the first baseball player to hail from Rosedale, Mississippi. According to the research done by the class, JaMark was only the first in over one hundred years. They told JaMark that from 1886 to 1888, a Frenchman and Rosedale native named Earl Le Orlay played what was then considered Major League baseball. Orlay played for the New Orleans River

Captains, a squad of wealthy southern landowners who took up baseball as more of a political statement rather than a recreational endeavor. Orlay only played two years, the students told JaMark, because he lost his fortune investing in an early model telephone that used letters instead of numbers as the basis to connect a call. When phone companies found the proposition of letters more difficult than numbers, Orlay lost his money and his position on the River Captains.

Over one hundred years later, JaMark used the goodwill of the children from his former elementary, junior high, and high school in an attempt to change the public's perception of him and be as victorious in winning the hearts and minds of the people of Rosedale as he was in winning the World Series. JaMark tutored children, helped coach the local baseball teams, and appeared at charity events. Despite his efforts, many in Rosedale remained unsure about JaMark's character.

While JaMark's relationship with the town of Rosedale was on the mend, his relationship with his grandmother grew stronger. He began to see his grandmother as more than a gossipy authority figure – he began to see her as a friend. And the more his grandmother saw Betsy, the more she liked the love of JaMark's life as well. After his morning training regimen, which usually consisted of a six-mile run and numerous push-ups and situps, JaMark and Betsy often took his grandmother to lunch. And every Thursday, they accompanied her to an evening bingo contest.

CHAPTER 25

The week before Christmas, bingo night started as many bingo nights had since JaMark started attending with his grandmother and Betsy. They arrived at the Rosedale Baptist Church bingo hall fifteen minutes before the first game was scheduled. They looked for seats near the caller's table where JaMark's grandmother could best see the board listing the announced numbers. While JaMark purchased the cards, Betsy and JaMark's grandmother found seats at the long folding tables facing the caller's table. When he joined the two women, JaMark sat to the left of his grandmother, as Betsy was already sitting to the old woman's right.

In the four weeks prior to that night, no one had sat to JaMark's left. That night, however, a young man JaMark had never seen before took the seat next to JaMark. Once the young man was settled in his chair, JaMark and the young man exchanged pleasantries. At the end of their pleasantries, JaMark noticed the man was wearing a t-shirt with the face of Gertie Dupree, the bingo player JaMark watched on television the night the devil visited him in the hotel in Alabama.

"I've seen her on TV," JaMark said, pointing to the young man's shirt.

"Gertie Dupree was a legend," the man said with an accent that JaMark realized was definitely not from Mississippi. "She passed away three months ago. She was the best bingo player in the world for over forty years. Sometimes it seemed as if she had the ability to see what numbers were going to be called before they were even called. Some say she had a God-given talent to be the best bingo player the world had ever seen."

"Did she inspire you?" JaMark asked, curious why a young man would take such a keen interest in an elderly bingo player.

"I am inspired to beat her," the man said, his tone growing serious. "My grandmother was the world champion before Dupree's rise. She raised me to be the best bingo player possible so that I might reclaim the title for our family. I wear Gertie Dupree's shirt to keep myself focused on my goals."

"What brought you here?" JaMark asked, curious why the battle for worldwide bingo supremacy would cross the small town of Rosedale.

"For years, my grandmother and I have traveled the country to bingo halls in an attempt to re-assert our family name," the man explained. "We heard there was bingo here, so we figured we would visit and assert our dominance."

JaMark looked to the side of the man but did not see anyone who would resemble his grandmother. "Is your grandmother here?" JaMark asked.

"She is over there," the man said, pointing to an elderly woman in a wheelchair by the front door of the bingo hall. The young man's gray-haired grandmother looked far older than JaMark's grandmother, and unlike JaMark's grandmother, the woman in the wheelchair sat with her eyes closed with little idea of anything going on around her. Although she looked frail, JaMark could see she was still a tall woman and guessed that in her prime, she might have been an imposing figure in the bingo world.

JaMark was interrupted in his admiration of the long-ago bingo legend by an announcement that the current game was starting. As the game progressed, JaMark watched his young friend struggle valiantly to achieve bingo. The young man had eight cards spread in front of him, and JaMark saw several spots on each that were marked on his, his grandmother's, or Betsy's cards and should have been marked on the young man's. But the aspiring bingo master did not lose hope, shaking his head at every missed call and tapping his heart with the side of his fist to keep focus. JaMark watched as the young man was so busy trying to keep up, he missed the caller's announcement of the last number he needed for a bingo winner.

After the first game, the young man was finally able to catch his breath. Seeing his neighbor's disheveled demeanor, JaMark offered to buy him a soft drink as he was going to buy refreshments for himself, Betsy, and his grandmother. The young man took up the offer and joined JaMark in a walk to the concession stand in the back of the bingo hall, not far from the entrance and near the young man's elderly grandmother.

JaMark and the young man finished buying their concessions and were sipping their sodas when the young man suggested JaMark meet his stationary grandmother. The young man explained that although his grandmother looked distant, she liked when people walked close enough to meet her. JaMark agreed to meet the woman, although he didn't think he would garner many reactions from a woman who had barely moved in the hour she had been in the bingo hall.

He was wrong.

The young man led JaMark to his seemingly catatonic grandmother. He signaled for JaMark to lean in close to his grandmother and say hello. JaMark was hesitant, as he doubted even the closest hello would render a response. But he followed the young man's instructions.

As he leaned in, the odor of hotel soap pierced his nose. The thought that she was washed comforted JaMark for a moment.

"Hello, ma'am," he said. "Hope you enjoy your stay in ....."

Before JaMark could finish his greeting, the woman's eyes sprung open, and she immediately straightened her posture in her wheelchair.

"Ahhhhh!" the woman screamed. "It's the devil!"

The old woman, who had just been still for over an hour, thrashed her arms wildly at JaMark, knocking his sodas to the ground and forcing him to move back several feet.

"Go away! Go away, devil! I smell Satan on you! You devil!" she yelled, staring at JaMark and wildly pointing.

The young man couldn't calm his frantic grandmother as she almost toppled from her wheelchair in an effort to get away from JaMark.

"Please, leave me alone!" she screamed as she leaned her torso out of her wheelchair. "Devil!"

The woman's screaming caught the attention of everyone in the bingo hall. Many in attendance turned to see the commotion. Within moments, organizers and an on-scene medic re-established the woman in her chair despite her continuing ruckus. As the young man continued in his attempt to calm his frantic grandmother, JaMark quietly backpedaled as far from the scene as he could go, trying to increase the distance between himself and any mention of the Devil. He walked almost halfway back to his seat when he noticed Betsy walking towards him.

Betsy looked at JaMark as she stood next to him. They walked to the end of their table but paused before returning to their seats near JaMark's grandmother. JaMark knew Betsy saw the fear on his face, and he knew she saw the shaking in his hands. With the woman's screams still echoing throughout the bingo hall, he felt slightly comforted when Betsy put her arms around him and hugged him before taking his hand and walking with him to their seats.

Several minutes after JaMark and Betsy sat, the bingo organizers at the caller's table instructed all participants to take their respective seats. Although the young man's grandmother had stopped her theatrics and resumed her semi-catatonic state, the pair were asked to leave the Rosedale Baptist Church bingo hall.

The remaining months of JaMark's offseason were calm and tranquil. Following the bingo incident, JaMark took caution in what public events he attended. He still went to his former schools and continued to coach youth teams when he could, but most of the second half of his offseason was spent at home with his grandmother or with Betsy watching movies, making dinners, and playing games of "Go Fish".

After a quiet New Year's celebration, JaMark began increasing his preparations for the upcoming baseball season. After a month of focusing on individual work-outs, on February 2nd, JaMark said good-bye to Rosedale again as Betsy drove him to the Memphis airport so he could fly to Tampa, Florida, and his second Spring Training.

CHAPTER 26

Unlike the previous spring, when JaMark was an untested minor leaguer unaware of the rigors and challenges of the Major Leagues, he arrived for his second Spring Training not only as a prized prospect but also a near-lock to make the Major League Opening Day roster. JaMark was also much smarter than the year before, especially in regards to Spring Training etiquette and protocol. He remembered, for example, not to throw at full strength during the first days of practice as he did the year before, even though he knew he still could.

Due to his short stint with the Saints the season before, JaMark was treated like a big leaguer at the Spring Training complex. While many of his former minor league teammates still ate fast food and drank water from faucets, JaMark now ate specially designed food made by specially designed trainers in specially designed kitchens and drank the purest water from the purest mountain springs delivered in the purest plastic bottles. JaMark tried to hide his new life of luxury when he crossed paths with his old teammates, but his attempts at humbleness were nixed when his manager told each big leaguer to empty a bottle of water in front of a minor leaguer in order to motivate the younger ballplayers trying to rise up the ranks. Some of the minor leaguers were fired up at this show of class warfare, but most of the players JaMark talked to after the event failed to see the point, as the grounds crew had just watered the field hours earlier.

On the field, JaMark again amazed his coaches and teammates with his ability to be in mid-season form in the first week of training. Although few on the team could throw as fast as JaMark at any point in the season, the pitchers who could throw as fast were not throwing as fast as JaMark at the beginning of spring. Nearly all of them asked JaMark about his offseason training regimen and laughed in disbelief when he told them he spent the offseason playing bingo and Go Fish with his grandmother and girlfriend. One pitcher even offered him five hundred dollars to share with him the secret of his elastic arm. While he laughed it off, JaMark didn't think the offer was anywhere near what it would cost him to tell the truth.

Two weeks into Spring Training, on a fair spring day in the Tampa Bay area, JaMark and a Saints backup catcher were on a secondary all-grass field doing their daily workout while the rest of the team took batting and fielding practice on the complex's main field. As JaMark was purposefully not pitching to his utmost ability, an elderly gentleman approached the pitcher. JaMark remembered the man as the same person who talked to him the year before during Spring Training. Like JaMark, the old man was a year older, and like JaMark, he also again wore a baseball uniform.

Instead of striding toward JaMark, as many others who were athletic enough to don a baseball uniform did, the old man waddled, as age and an overweight physical form stole what athletic gait the old man might have had. He stood near JaMark, crossed his arms, and watched the young pitcher.

"You are holding back this year, I see," the old man said.

JaMark caught the return throw from his catcher and turned to face the old man. "Yes, sir. I am," he replied. "I figured there is no need to burn myself out so early. Best to keep pace with the rest of the crew."

"Smart," the old man said. "You may just last after all."

JaMark turned from the old man and signaled to his catcher to resume the catcher's position. Once he saw his catcher set, JaMark executed his pitching wind up and threw another fastball at less than full strength.

"I saw you during the series," the old man said. "You looked good. A lot like me in '52."

JaMark received the ball again from his catcher, wound up, and threw another not-so-fastball.

"I think you will do well at this level, kid," the old man

said. "You have a good make-up."

"Thank you," JaMark said as he received the ball yet again from his catcher.

The old man looked at JaMark one final time. "As long as you know who to put first," he said.

The old man's statement caught JaMark by surprise. But by the time JaMark could ask the old man to repeat himself or to explain his statement, the old man was waddling away towards the complex's main field to watch the rest of the players.

JaMark caught his last return throw from his catcher and walked towards his teammate.

"Do you know who that guy was?" he asked the catcher, pointing in the direction of the old man.

"Yeah, you don't?" JaMark's catcher replied. "That's Dusty Polichardo, the greatest pitcher in the history of our team. He had a few amazing seasons in the '50s, but then it all fell apart. Some said it was an arm injury, some said he partied too hard, and others even said he hung out with some strange people. When I first got here, one of the coaches told me Dusty couldn't deal with the fact that he couldn't play anymore. After his career, he got weird."

JaMark listened to his catcher as he watched Dusty waddle behind a practice field backstop on his way towards the indoor training facility.

"I'm surprised he talked to you," JaMark's catcher said. "From what I've seen, he hardly talks to anyone and he especially never talks to young players. He tends to stay only with the people he knows and fans. He talks to a lot of fans. He signs a ton of autographs. I got one from him when I was a kid. He signed it 'White Lines', which probably had nothing to do with baseball."

JaMark saw Dusty Polichardo a few more times during Spring Training, but he didn't exchange any words with the former big leaguer. Dusty's comment of who JaMark should put first remained on JaMark's mind, but, like the Luciferic linguists of his minor league manager, he regarded his interaction with Dusty as a coincidence.

Besides the mystery of the old pitcher, JaMark's Spring Training was otherwise uneventful. The day before games against real opponents began, JaMark's pitching coach told him he was scheduled to pitch in three exhibition games a week. JaMark was also told his appearances could either be in relief, as he pitched last season at the Major League level, or as a starter, as he pitched last season at the Minor League level. No matter what, his pitching coach said, three times a week, JaMark would be in the game.

"A pitcher could stand on the mound after the game is over and maybe even throw the ball past home plate, but he wouldn't be contributing anything, and he might as well go home and collect a paycheck. He should be on the mound during the game. That's where you get the best bang for your buck," JaMark's pitching coach concluded. JaMark laughed at his coach's attempt at humor.

The first game JaMark pitched during Spring Training was in relief in Daytona, Florida. Having just won the World Series, the Saints drew hundreds, if not thousands of their fans to opposing team's Spring Training ballparks. Wherever they went, the Saints usually played to full stadiums. A Tuesday day game in early March in Daytona was one of few exceptions.

In front of a small gathering of only two thousand retirees and early spring breakers, JaMark entered the game in the fourth inning and proceeded to strike out the next fifteen batters on only forty-five pitches, as effective and efficient as he was during his perfect game in Wyoming two summers earlier. Unfortunately, JaMark didn't have a chance to strike out any more batters as the Saints only had to pitch eight innings, failing to score enough runs in their nine innings of hitting to necessitate any pitches in the bottom of the ninth inning.

Two days later, JaMark pitched again. And then two days after that and two days after that. Finally, after seven relief appearances in which he struck out twenty-seven batters in thirteen innings while only allowing four hits and one run, JaMark was given the ability to start a game on the pitcher's mound. Two days later, in front of a sell-out crowd sitting in an outdoor stadium in Winter Haven, JaMark outpitched his competition. During the game, JaMark's manager was so confident in the ability of his young pitcher that he relieved himself more than he thought of relieving his moundsman. Although JaMark was on his own on the mound, while their manager was in the bathroom, JaMark's teammates helped him by scoring eight runs, five more than the three JaMark allowed during his nine innings on the field.

After his complete game performance, JaMark was told he made the Major League team. He was also told he would be part of the Major League team's starting pitching rotation. Then he was told to take a few days off and relax his arm.

On his first day off, a clear day with only a few scattered, high clouds and an easy cooling wind, JaMark visited a beach near St. Petersburg. After walking on the sand for a while, he wandered into a small bar. The bar was decorated in an island motif with tikis scattered throughout, and several surfboards hung on the walls. A blackboard by the cash register listed the day's tide conditions and the time for sunset. There weren't many people in the establishment, JaMark noticed, except for a few locals and a group of spring breakers JaMark assumed were looking for a "townie" experience.

As JaMark stood near the centrally located bar drinking a diet cola, he introduced himself to a middle-aged woman with stringy, long, blond hair. She stood at the bar, wearing a tie-dye shirt, a casual dress, a gaggle of colored beads around her neck, and introduced herself as Debbie Sue. After exchanging a brief greeting, JaMark watched her scamper from the bar to the stage to introduce the next musical act: a tall, lanky man with similarly long, scraggly hair and a tie-dye shirt that shared the style, but not the color, of the woman's shirt.

Instead of the typical beach bar guitar JaMark was expecting, the man carried a French horn to the stage. For the next hour, the man played the French horn with an elegance and grace JaMark had never heard from any instrument, no less an instrument as out of place as a French horn in a beach bar. JaMark contently listened to the mellow notes of the horn player as he switched from classical pieces to meditation music to jazz and back to classical standards without missing a beat or a note.

When the man abruptly finished his lengthy jam, he followed Debbie Sue to the bar near JaMark. Although the man was only slightly taller than JaMark, he had much more hair and also a bit more weight around his stomach, which JaMark attributed to a life of laidback days on the beach. The French horn player stared at JaMark for a moment as if he was examining him. Without saying a word, the horn player stuck out his hand. JaMark and the French horn player shook hands. The French horn player then released JaMark's hand, smiled, and walked past him towards the exit, leaving with Debbie Sue and his French horn.

Upon his return to the team, JaMark pitched in three more games, all in relief and only for one inning each time. He allowed three hits in those three innings, with three strikeouts and three walks, but only one run. After his final spring performance, many in the sell-out crowd gave him a standing ovation, except those who were already standing. They clapped louder.

CHAPTER 27

J aMark's first full season in the Major Leagues started where his first partial season left off. While his role changed from relief pitcher to starting pitcher, he still struck batters out at a high rate and did not allow many runs. After a spring in which they did not score runs often, the Saints batters started hitting the ball, putting more runners on base, and scoring more runs. For the first month of the season, the runs the batters scored during the game exceeded the runs JaMark allowed, giving JaMark an undefeated record through the month of May. Following the tradition of fans throughout his Minor League career, a local fan gave JaMark's curveball yet another nickname. In St. Petersburg, a Seminole medicine man dubbed JaMark's curve "The Stikini", a Seminole Indian monster that fed on the hearts of men.

JaMark was not the only rookie pitcher impressing the baseball community and frustrating batters. In the other of the two leagues that comprised the Major Leagues, Pete LaGib was also enjoying his first season and frustrating hitters with the same array of knuckleballs and trick pitches that made him successful in the Minor Leagues. Although LaGib's manager in the Minor Leagues occasionally hinted at pitch counts, his Major League manager was a stickler for pitch counts, especially for rookies, regardless of how slow or fast they threw. The resulting restrictions left LaGib far beyond JaMark in statistical categories such as games pitched, innings pitched, complete games, shutouts, and wins.

For the first months of the new season, both JaMark and Pete LaGib were their league's rookie sensations. While LaGib continued his success in June, JaMark's fortune began to change. On June 1st, JaMark lost to New York. Although he struck out eight and walked only one, JaMark allowed six runs in five innings, including yielding his first grand slam. In his next start, a day game at home against Detroit, JaMark again did not fare well, allowing four runs in five innings, despite striking out six and walking no one.

The next week, JaMark took the mound in Oakland for his third start in June. He arrived at the ballpark earlier than usual, thinking a change of schedule might lead to a change in results. But he didn't know what to do with himself while he waited for the rest of his team to arrive. He spoke briefly with some of his teammates, but they were busy preparing themselves for the game. He even spoke with the Oakland clubhouse attendant, who heard about JaMark's recent struggles and wished him good luck.

JaMark didn't think he needed luck. He just needed to get outs.

CHAPTER 28

Good afternoon fans, and welcome back to Oakland and Saints baseball. It is a beautiful Sunday here in the Bay Area. Our Saints take on Oakland in the last of a three-game series. The Saints and Oakland split the first two, and after last night's extra-inning win, they hope they can rest the bullpen a bit with JaMark Reliford pitching today.

JaMark has hit a bit of a rough patch the last few weeks. The young left-hander cruised through April and May, but June has been a struggle. He has lost two in a row, and given up an eye-popping ten runs in his last ten innings.

Before the game, I had a chance to speak with the manager of the Saints, who assured me JaMark is as healthy as can be. He just has to work his way out of his first professional slump. This is a pitcher who blew through the Minor Leagues like a man among boys. Now, here at the big league level, he is facing adversity for the first time.

After the Saints failed to score in the top of the first, let's see if JaMark can get back on track.

Leading off for Oakland is their centerfielder, the very speedy Russell Mack. The left-handed-hitting Mack is a first ball, fastball hitter who usually jumps on the first thing he sees. That's gonna be trouble for JaMark if he can't hit his spots today.

JaMark winds, and the pitch. Mack smacks a fastball into short left field for a single. Not a good start for Reliford to have Mack on base after one pitch. Mack led the league in stolen bases last year with seventy-one. He was only caught ten times. He can be a distraction on the basepaths.

Coming to the plate now is the Oakland first baseman, Renaldo Hernandez. Hernandez has some pop, with eight home runs already this year. But he is struggling against lefties this season, hitting only .213 against southpaws.

JaMark looks over at Mack, and deals from the stretch. The first *pitch to the right-handed-hitting Hernandez is a strike at the knees. JaMark hit ninety-eight on that pitch, and that fast in that spot can be very tough to hit.*

JaMark looks in and gets the signal from his catcher, again looks over at Mack, and deals. Another fastball, and Hernandez couldn't catch up for strike two. Reliford blew that one right by Hernandez, ninety-nine miles per hour right down the middle.

Hernandez gets back in the batter's box. JaMark looks in, checks Mack on first, and makes the pitch. Hernandez hits a curveball to deep left field. High, hard, and uncatchable. And the Saints are down two to nothing on the home run by Hernandez. JaMark tried to get the curveball past Hernandez, but the Oakland first baseman was all over it.

Not the start JaMark Reliford was hoping for."

CHAPTER 29

Bottom of the second inning here in Oakland, with the Saints still down two to nothing. After giving up a home run to Hernandez, JaMark got out of the first untouched. Not one of the next three batters put the bat on the ball. It is rare to see a pitcher get so unhittable so quickly.

Let's see if the young lefty can get back on course and hold down this power-hitting Oakland lineup in the second. Leading off the inning for Oakland is their rightfielder, number 31, Chris Bass. Bass came over from Boston in a trade in the offseason and is another one who can bring some pop.

The first pitch from JaMark is a fastball for strike one. Bass couldn't catch up with the gas as JaMark again hits ninety-eight miles per hour. Reliford gets the ball back from the catcher, watches Bass get set in the batter's box, winds, and deals. Another swing and a miss by Bass on a fastball for strike two.

JaMark gets the ball back, gets back on the mound, and looks for the sign. Bass is ready. And the pitch by JaMark is a curveball, and Bass goes down swinging. That's one out for Oakland, and JaMark Reliford's fourth consecutive strikeout in six batters faced.

Now batting is the Oakland catcher, Creighton Cruz. Cruz is a second-year player who didn't get much playing time last year but Oakland has high hopes for him. He faced JaMark a few times in the Minors with little success.

JaMark winds and pitches. A fastball and Cruz laces it into left field for a base hit. JaMark left the fastball up, and Cruz jumped on it. One on and one out for the Oakland second baseman, Rory Kalljoy. Kalljoy has gone three for fourteen so far this series with a game-winning hit in the first game.

The first pitch to Kalljoy. A fastball inside for ball one. JaMark tried to jam Kalljoy but it ran inside a bit too much.

JaMark winds, and the pitch is a fastball low for ball two. JaMark is just off on his command these last two pitches. They were close, but Kalljoy is showing patience and making JaMark work. JaMark looks in again, checks Cruz at first, and delivers.

Kalljoy hits a fastball to right centerfield, but it is caught. The Saints knew exactly how to play the Oakland second baseman. They were shifted slightly to right, and the Saints centerfielder barely had to move to catch that one. Two down now for the number nine hitter, Oakland shortstop Jose Zalen. Zalen, a product of Argentina, was signed in the offseason by Oakland to shore up a defense that led the league in errors last year.

JaMark winds and delivers. The first pitch to Zalen is a high fastball that Zalen tried to catch up with but missed. Strike one. Cruz on first, two down, and now 0 and one on Zalen. The Saints trail two to nothing here in the top of the second.

Here's the pitch by Reliford. Zalen swings and pokes it into left for a basehit. Cruz heads to second and now Oakland is threatening again. Reliford put that fastball over the plate, and Zalen slapped it into the outfield. The swing didn't need much against the ninety-nine mile an hour heater, but Zalen hit it where they ain't.

Batting now is the Oakland centerfielder Russell Mack. He singled in his first at-bat. He hits in as low of a crouch as anyone I have seen since Pete Rose. The Saints have to be wary of the bunt with Mack as well. He can lay it down on occasion. But with two out and two on, we'll see if Oakland would risk the bunt.

The first offering by JaMark is a fastball outside for ball one. Nothing seems to be coming easy for the young lefty today.

The pitch, another fastball. Mack takes a weak swing and fouls it off. One and one to the Oakland batter. Reliford doesn't even seem to notice either of the runners as both have big leads on the basepaths. For a catcher, Cruz does have decent speed, and Zalen has been known to take an extra base. He is not the fastest, but he is a smart baserunner.

The one and one pitch to Mack is inside for ball two. Reliford tried to put the fastball on the inside corner, but it just missed. I've noticed with Reliford, when he is off, he is just off. I don't think these umpires are going to give anything free to the rookie. He is going to have to earn his strikes.

Two and one to Mack. The pitch is another fastball low. Ball three. Three and one to Russell Mack. Reliford walks off the mound for a moment, rubs the ball, and wipes his brow. The weather today is pleasant, but Reliford is looking like he is starting to labor a bit through this Oakland lineup.

The pitch. Another fastball and Mack fouls it off. Three and two now to Mack. Reliford needs to bring this pitch. He doesn't want to load the bases for Hernandez, who took him deep last inning.

Reliford from the stretch, winds, and delivers. A rare curveball that Mack takes a half swing at. The ball started at the belt and dropped into the dirt. But did Mack swing? The home plate ump looks down to the first base ump who says Mack checked his swing. That's ball four, and the bases are loaded for the Oakland first baseman Renaldo Hernandez.

Reliford thought he had Mack, and you can see the disappointment on his face. He wanted to be out of this inning. He threw the pitch he wanted, where he wanted, and almost got the result he wanted. But baseball is a game of inches, and Mack held his swing just enough for the first base ump.

Now Hernandez steps in. You have to wonder if JaMark will go back to the curveball after Hernandez deposited the last one he saw into the left-field bleachers last inning for his ninth home run of the year. Bases loaded, two outs, top of the second. Reliford is in a jam and needs to get an out here.

Reliford winds and delivers. And that ball is crushed. Another shot into deep left field. No chance for the Saints leftfielder as he just watches it go. A grand slam for Hernandez, and now Oakland leads six to nothing.

A really bad day at the office for JaMark Reliford. He didn't even turn around to watch that hit. The moment Hernandez hit it, Reliford just hung his head. The kid is struggling out there, and here comes the Saints manager with a call to the bullpen.

You can see the dejection in the body language of Reliford as he hands the ball over to his manager. He is walking back to the dugout slowly with his shoulders slumped. Despite the strikeouts, he knows he is not getting Major League batters out when he needs to.

Six to nothing, Oakland over the Saints in the top of the second inning. And we will be right back after these words from our sponsors."

CHAPTER 30

After his manager pulled him from the game following his third poor pitching performance, JaMark walked into the dugout with his shoulders slouched and head down. A few teammates tried to offer words of encouragement, and JaMark listened and nodded his head, but even as they talked, his mind raced with worry.

After the game, JaMark raced through his post-game routine of showering and changing into street clothes. He then ran out of the stadium to his car and drove to the hotel. He parked, went to his room, and called Betsy. Although nearly midnight in Rosedale, Betsy answered the phone.

"Betsy, it's gone," JaMark said to her, almost interrupting her initial greeting.

"What's gone?" Betsy asked.

"My ability to pitch and get people out," JaMark said. "It's gone. Everything I throw has been hit hard the last few weeks. I don't know what to do."

JaMark was beginning to panic. He never faced failure on a baseball field. He listened as Betsy tried to calm him as much as she could, despite her being in Rosedale while he was still in Oakland. She offered consoling phrases such as "it will be alright" and "it's ok, I'm here for you," none of which addressed the problem but did make JaMark feel a little better.

JaMark continued to relay his problems to Betsy for a third time when she interrupted him excitedly.

"JaMark," she said. "Does your arm hurt?"

"Ummm …. No," JaMark replied. "Not at all. It feels like it always feels."

"If the Devil took away your ability to throw, shouldn't your arm hurt?" she asked. "Shouldn't it go back to how it was before?"

JaMark paused for a moment, realizing Betsy had a point.

"Maybe," he said. "It doesn't hurt. As a matter of fact, my arm feels great. No pain at all."

JaMark heard Betsy let out a deep breath and realized although his girlfriend wasn't completely sure if she was correct in her hypothesis, he knew her guess was correct, and he was thankful he would still be able to play.

"Good," she said. "I'm glad you are ok. Don't all pitchers allow runs every once in a while?"

JaMark calmed as the conversation progressed. "Yeah, they do," he said. "Even the best ones get hit. Maybe the hitters are just on to me. I've been pitching against different batters since I started. This is the first time I've faced the same batters a second time."

"Well, you know I don't know much about baseball," Betsy said, "but there is someone here with me who might be able to help."

JaMark wondered who Betsy might have in her vicinity who could possibly help him.

The familiar voice surprised JaMark and brought a smile to his face. "Hey boy, what seems to be the problem there?" Uncle Rufus asked. "Why you gettin' hit like that?"

"Not sure," JaMark answered. "I'm still throwing hard, but they're hitting it. And hitting it hard."

"Son," Uncle Rufus began, "what did I tell you when you first started playing? Do you remember? I told you baseball was a thinking man's game. I told you baseball was like chess. When was the last time you did some thinking on the mound?"

JaMark never thought on the pitcher's mound. At least not about baseball. Maybe on occasion when he did think on the mound, he thought about the fit of his mitt or the tightness of his cleats, but never about the game. In high school, he thought about cheerleaders and pretty girls and how he would party after a win; on the semi-pro team, he thought about his arm and how lucky he was to be able to throw again without pain; in the minors, he didn't think at all – he just threw. He never thought about baseball on the baseball field. He brought a philosophy of non-thinking to the Major Leagues. According to Uncle Rufus, that was the problem.

"Son," Uncle Rufus continued, "you need to be thinkin' on the mound. You need to be outthinkin' those hitters. Put the ball where they don't think it's gonna be. Surprise 'em. Son, I ain't no big leaguer, but I do know that."

JaMark realized Uncle Rufus was right. He could still throw fast and he still had a great curveball, but he needed to be smarter. He realized he was facing the best hitters in the world, hitters who had seen the fastest of fastballs and the curviest of curveballs. Those things were not unusual to them. What would be unusual would be a pitcher with those skills who could also outthink them.

The next day, JaMark woke up refreshed and without any of the malaise that surrounded him since his struggles began. Although the Saints had a night game against Los Angeles, JaMark arrived at the stadium early in the afternoon and waited outside his pitching coach's office, ready and eager to learn the finer points of pitching.

For the next few days, JaMark studied the batters of Cleveland, the next team he would be facing. Burying his eyes in the video database the team had of every batter in every situation, JaMark created his own reference book of how he thought his skills could be best brought to bear against the Cleveland hitters. He asked other pitchers what they had done to be successful, inquired with the Saints catchers for their opinions, and even asked the three players on the team who had played for Cleveland in recent years what would work against their former teammates. He wanted to leave no stone unturned when he stood on the finely-combed, dirt mound at the center of the Cleveland baseball infield.

CHAPTER 31

Four days after the Oakland batters embarrassed him and sent him to an early shower, JaMark took the mound in Cleveland. In his head, he had notes on every hitter in the lineup, except one, a rookie JaMark faced when he pitched for Buffalo.

Following the top of the first inning and a three-run scoring outburst by his teammates, JaMark took the mound in the bottom of the first inning in front of a sparse Cleveland crowd. As he stood on the mound, JaMark looked around the stadium and was surprised at the lack of attendees. What he didn't know was the Cleveland team had planned a Latin Night promotion aimed at Cleveland's large Hispanic population. Due to a marketing mix up, however, commercials for the game were not broadcast in the correct language. Instead of being broadcast in Spanish, the ads were written and broadcast in Latin, resulting in mass confusion and attendance by only a few traditional Catholics in the Cleveland area.

In front of those most devout Catholics, JaMark began to work on the hitters of the Cleveland lineup. With a mind full of plans, JaMark began to execute, throwing pitch after pitch exactly where he wanted the ball to go. With seven perfectly placed fastballs and two perfectly placed curveballs, JaMark struck out the first three Cleveland batters. After the first inning, JaMark returned to the dugout feeling better than he had in weeks. He felt like a real big league pitcher, using his brains as well as brawn to beguile batters and flummox opponents.

The second and third innings went as well as the first, with JaMark throwing his fastball and curveball up and down and left and right within the strike zone. He even sometimes purposefully pitched outside the strike zone in an attempt to get a batter to swing his bat at a pitch JaMark knew would not generate good contact. During the third inning, JaMark saw his pitching coach smile at JaMark from the dugout. JaMark smiled back, symbolically saying 'thank you' for the hours of video and other tips and tricks JaMark learned in the previous week.

After he watched the Saints score two more runs, JaMark went back on the pitcher's mound and struck out every batter in the fourth inning and one more in the fifth. JaMark felt his confidence return with every Cleveland batter he got out.

Through the seventh inning, the plan he and his catcher devised was working perfectly. JaMark's month of insecurity seemed like a distant memory. Coincidentally, as his confidence increased, so too did his distance from his teammates. With every inning, they moved farther away, attempting to honor the ancient baseball tradition of not talking to pitchers when they are throwing no-hitters.

Many moments of silence later, JaMark went through the eighth inning, continuing to pitch to plan and also not allowing a hit. His offense aided him further by adding another run, making the score six to nothing. Despite walking two batters and throwing nearly 120 pitches, JaMark was on pace for his first Major League no-hitter. There were only three batters in his way, all of whom he had reports for and all of whom he had gotten out at least once before.

CHAPTER 32

*I*t is the bottom of the ninth here in Cleveland, and JaMark Reliford is pitching a magnificent game. He has walked only two and not allowed a hit through eight innings. He has attacked these Cleveland batters with a vengeance, topping out at ninety-nine miles per hour and striking out ten so far. He has been in total control on the mound today. It is a welcome sight for Saints fans considering his last few outings were nothing short of a disappointment. But the rookie seems to be on a historic course today.

You can see the joy on Reliford's face as he takes the mound here in the ninth. Looks like he had to step off the mound for a moment to regain his composure. Can't lose focus here. The Saints catcher got up and started to walk to the mound to check on Reliford only to be waved back to his spot behind the plate.

Talking to the Saints pitching coach earlier today, he told me Reliford had a plan for every Cleveland batter. In the ninth, he has to face the ninth, first, and second batters in the Cleveland lineup. Let's see how well he executes and if he can finish this game.

Leading off is the Cleveland centerfielder, Ken Wigginton. Wigginton is 0 for two with a strikeout. The first pitch to Wigginton is a strike on the inside corner. A ninety-six mile per hour fastball for strike one.

Reliford is still strong out there, despite throwing over 120 pitches so far. One thing we have learned about this kid is he has a really durable arm. He definitely has the physical ability to be a successful Major Leaguer.

The second pitch to Wigginton is another fastball strike on the inside corner. Wigginton has yet to take the bat off his shoulders and is now down 0 and two.

Reliford winds up and delivers. A fastball and Wigginton wildly whiffs. One down here in the ninth. That pitch was a few inches off the outside corner. A definite ball. But Wigginton tried to slap it with that swing and came up empty. That's Reliford's eleventh strikeout of the night.

Now batting for Cleveland is the leadoff man, shortstop Nomar

Rodriguez. Rodriguez is one of the few Cleveland batters who has not struck out today. As Rodriguez comes to the plate, the Saints catcher goes to the mound to talk with Reliford on their approach to Rodriguez. Rodriguez does lead the league in on-base percentage, so he is a risk to JaMark's attempt at history."

CHAPTER 33

As Rodriguez walked to the batter's box, JaMark's catcher jogged to the pitcher's mound and told JaMark to pitch the batter "backward." JaMark initially thought pitching backward would be ineffective as he might not be able to see the batter if his back was to the plate. He told his catcher he never tried pitching backward, although he once tried pitching upside-down while standing on his head in the bullpen in Wyoming. The Saints catcher waited until JaMark was finished offering suggestions, then informed JaMark exactly what "pitching backward" was, which was not, in fact, turning himself backward. As the home plate umpire approached to break up the meeting and resume the game, the catcher returned to his spot behind home plate.

At the catcher's insistence, JaMark started Rodriguez with a curveball, a pitch he typically threw at the end of an at-bat. Expecting a fastball, Rodriguez stood with the bat on his shoulder and watched the pitch curve through the strike zone as a good curveball does.

JaMark received the ball back from his catcher, assumed his position on the mound, and looked in for a sign of what to throw. His catcher indicated another curveball. JaMark threw, and again Rodriguez stood and watched, perplexed at JaMark's out-of-sequence offerings.

For the third pitch, JaMark's catcher gave him the signal for a fastball, completing the opposite pitch sequence from the order JaMark typically used. JaMark wound up and threw a fastball low and inside to Rodriguez. A third and final time Rodriguez failed to remove the bat from his shoulders. As soon as the ball hit the catcher's glove, the umpire signaled strike three, and JaMark was one out away from a no-hitter.

From the dugout appeared the only batter JaMark did not have notes for, but someone he had faced in the past. The batter coming to the plate was the same Major Leaguer who struck out for the final out in JaMark's Minor League no-hitter in Wyoming. At the time, Dustin Pershing had been rehabbing an injury, but now, he was healthy and back in his Major League element. Pershing stood in the batter's box, familiar with JaMark and again looking to ruin his date with history. JaMark knew Pershing, now a pinch-hitter extraordinaire, would be looking for a fastball and would be eager to swing. JaMark also knew Pershing was familiar with his curveball and would be ready to hit that as well.

The drama and JaMark's apprehensions were short-lived, however. On the first pitch, a fastball on the outside part of the strike zone, the once-rehabbing-now-healthy Pershing hit a short fly ball to the second baseman. As the second baseman squeezed the shallow pop up in his glove for the final out, JaMark's catcher and other infielders swarmed the mound to congratulate JaMark.

Following JaMark's dominant performance in Cleveland, his confidence grew, and he rediscovered his groove on the pitching mound. In July of his first full season, JaMark was told he was selected to the annual All-Star Game. With his World Series-victorious manager at the helm of one half of the all-star competition, JaMark learned his manager requested him personally to fill the role of late-game emergency relief pitcher, in case the game went ten innings or more. JaMark was humbled and tried to stay grounded as everyone asked him about his place among the stars of baseball. He was especially humbled when told he was the first all-star from Rosedale, Mississippi, something the ancient Earl Le Orlay never accomplished.

Unfortunately for JaMark, he did not see action in the All-Star Game, despite being named to the team and wearing the uniform of an all-star. As a late-game emergency relief pitcher, he was not needed. The All-Star Game only went the regular length of nine innings, and there were no emergencies for him to relieve.

The second half of JaMark's first full season in the Major

Leagues was as successful as his first half. Although he was credited with a few losses, he was credited with more wins, thanks to his combination of getting opposing hitters out and his teammates' ability to score more runs than JaMark allowed. JaMark was also aided by the relief pitchers his manager brought in to relieve JaMark, and their ability to keep the leads JaMark left securely in place.

While JaMark's first full season was similar to his partial season the year before, the second half of the Saints' season was also similar to their previous season. Once again, there was a battle between five teams for four playoff spots and once again the Saints were among the qualifiers for the playoffs.

There would be no championship during JaMark's second season, however. Although they won both of the playoff games JaMark pitched, the Saints failed to score more runs than their Seattle opponents in the three games JaMark did not pitch, and the Saints were eliminated in the first round of the playoffs. JaMark watched from Rosedale with Betsy and his grandmother as his Seattle opponents then lost in the following round to a Boston team who lost in the World Series to the team from Los Angeles.

Despite the lack of a championship, JaMark considered his first season in the Major Leagues a success. He proved to himself he could be a Major League pitcher, a position he dreamed of since the days of throwing strawberries on his Uncle Rufus's farm. Being a Major Leaguer was his dream in high school, when he thought he was close to achieving it, and haunted him through his drunken injured years, when the nightmare of his life made the dream seem impossible. Being a Major Leaguer was the reason he put his soul in the hands of the Devil.

CHAPTER 34

One month after his season ended, the sportswriters of America agreed with JaMark on the success of his first year by awarding him the league's Rookie of the Year award. While excited and humbled about winning the award, JaMark also felt a sense of dread as he knew he would have to credit the Devil in his acceptance speech without sounding too out of the ordinary. From the moment the team's public relations coordinator called until the moment he had to talk to the press, JaMark worked on a suitable speech. He didn't think the "devil is in the details" line would work well in an award speech, but he was struggling to think of any method of satanic recognition that would not cause people to consider him an occultist.

After working with Betsy, JaMark decided on a way to include the Devil in his speech. When the phone finally rang, and the team public relations coordinator asked for a word, JaMark paused for a moment, took a deep breath, and said:

"I just want to thank everyone who has ever supported me. Sometimes there is a devil on your shoulder telling you to throw concern into the wind and pitch with all you got. To go all out and then go for more. Thanks to that voice, I like to think I did that. I gave it everything. I want to say thanks. Thank you to my grandmother, my girlfriend, my teammates, my manager, the organization for taking a chance, and that little voice for helping me to achieve my goals."

JaMark let out a sigh of relief.

"I told you that you had nothing to worry about," Betsy said before kissing him on the cheek. "Now, let's go get dinner, Mr. Rookie of the Year winner."

Winning Rookie of the Year was the highlight of a calm winter for JaMark. He returned to Rosedale and still practiced with the local little leaguers and signed autographs for charities on occasion, but he stayed away from the public eye as much as possible. After a month in Rosedale, he and Betsy traveled often. They drove along the Mississippi highways through the cotton fields of the Mississippi Delta to Memphis several times, including a week-long getaway between Christmas and New Year's Day, in which they took in the sights, the sounds, and the tastes of Beale Street and the surrounding downtown.

After a week in Memphis, the pair traveled to Chicago to visit members of Betsy's family who had left the rural south for the bright lights, hustle, and bustle of the Windy City. Along the way, the pair discovered JaMark's grandfather's original Rosedale home was once owned by a neighbor of Betsy's uncle.

Although Betsy's uncle didn't know anything about JaMark's grandfather, JaMark discovered quite a bit about his girlfriend's uncle. Clifford "Windy" Horseman was a semi-famous jazz musician who migrated to the Windy City from Jackson, Mississippi. He learned to play the trumpet at a young age, although due to a lingering gastrointestinal problem, he passed gas frequently when he took deep breaths. As playing trumpet required many repeated deep breaths, Windy blew out of both ends during many performances. When one of Chicago's most prominent bandleaders of the day heard Clifford's talent, he nicknamed him "Windy", saying the name would be an instant tribute to the Windy City while an inside joke to their inner circle of performers who had to play outside because of Windy.

For the next week, Windy showed Betsy and JaMark the sights and sounds of Chicago. JaMark found it easier to disappear in Chicago than in Rosedale. In Chicago, he was just another athlete enjoying a stroll in the park or a dinner at a well-known steak house. In Chicago, he was recognized on occasion, but people who spotted him gave him a nod or a smile. They sometimes asked for an autograph, but left him alone when he was with Betsy. In Chicago, JaMark enjoyed the ability to go out and be as normal as a person of above-average height who plays professional baseball for a living could be.

Despite the calmness of his offseason and the joy of his vacation, JaMark couldn't shake thoughts of the Devil. He hadn't heard from or seen the Devil since their lunch in Durham a year earlier. The lack of contact scared JaMark.

Even if he didn't cross his path, the Devil often crossed JaMark's mind. Despite Betsy's advice against thinking about the Devil, JaMark often wondered what the Devil was doing when he was not following him. He wondered if there were others the Devil had made deals with. One night after returning to Rosedale, JaMark awoke from his sleep, his face dripping in sweat. He nudged Betsy to wake her. When she came to, he asked her if she thought there was a large soul management system the Devil controlled consisting of different times and different places and different people and perhaps even different dimensions of time and space. When Betsy didn't answer but stared back with a shocked look, he knew he scared her. He tried to calm her as tears rolled down her face. He wrapped his arms around her and told her to go back to sleep.

After his calm winter, JaMark again left Rosedale for another Spring Training. Betsy drove JaMark to Memphis and he boarded a plane and flew to Tampa, where he rented a car and drove to meet his team, just as he did in years prior.

The first few weeks of JaMark's third Spring Training went almost exactly as the first and second year went, as the organization kept on many of the same coaches and the coaches kept many of the same regimens they wanted the players to follow. Among the few changes were new players for JaMark to meet, including three new relief pitchers, two new outfielders, and a new first baseman, Renaldo Hernandez. JaMark was especially happy to meet Hernandez as the former Oakland first baseman was among the most successful in the league at reaching base against JaMark, whether by hit, walk, or error.

Midway through Spring Training, after all the players arrived, but before the exhibition games began, JaMark again encountered Dusty Polichardo, the once-great pitcher turned enigmatic wanderer. On a humid Wednesday in mid-March, just after lunch, but before the usual rain clouds of the Florida spring rolled in, JaMark was long tossing with one of his new teammates when Dusty waddled towards him. JaMark noticed the former pitcher put on a few pounds and was looking rounder than he did the previous spring. JaMark guessed Dusty was five foot four or so, and with his extra weight, bald head, and round glasses, he reminded JaMark of a penguin or a bowling ball or any other spherical orb-shaped thing that rolls to and fro.

When Dusty finally reached JaMark, the former pitcher stood still and blankly stared at the current pitcher. JaMark caught the ball from his new teammate, glanced at Dusty, gave a smile and a nod to the old man, and then threw the ball back to his teammate. His teammate caught the ball and threw it back, ignoring the guest next to JaMark. JaMark caught the ball with ease and noticed Dusty was still standing in the same position and still intently staring at him. JaMark slowly turned to the round old man in the baseball uniform and said hello.

Without warning or provocation, Dusty fell to his knees and threw his arms out, bending forward. He lifted his upper body up and down off the ground several times as if in prayer. He mumbled several incoherent words JaMark couldn't understand. JaMark tossed his baseball glove to the side, bent down, and lifted the old man by the arms, forcing him to his feet. When he stood again, Dusty stared at JaMark with a look of awe. JaMark didn't know what caused the old man to look spooked, but his actions scared JaMark. Still holding the old pitcher's arms, he gave the old man a slight shake in an attempt to wake him. In response to JaMark's slight shake, Dusty's eyes shut, and his head fell forward as if he had fallen asleep.

As his teammate watched, JaMark stood in horror, holding the old man for almost a minute, although to JaMark it seemed as if time stood still. He hoped Dusty would wake up and go about his business. JaMark again shook Dusty's arms in an attempt to wake him. As quickly as they had closed, Dusty's eyes opened, his head sprung up, and his eyes grew wide.

The bald, short former pitcher looked directly at JaMark for a moment before letting out a loud blood-curdling scream. The noise made JaMark let go of the old man's arm and jump backward. Dusty screamed again, garnering the attention of everyone in the immediate vicinity, from ballplayers to fans to the grounds crew. They all watched the short, round, old man with the baseball jersey scream at JaMark. Then, nearly as soon as the screaming started, Dusty was quiet again. He stared at JaMark for another moment before slowly turning his back on the young pitcher. The portly former pitcher then ran as fast as his overweight body could take him off the fields and towards the Spring Training facility's office complex.

JaMark stood motionless, not sure how to comprehend what had just transpired. His new teammate walked up to him and asked him if he had any clue what happened.

"I have no idea," said JaMark.

That night, JaMark sat alone in his team-paid condominium and thought about Dusty Polichardo. JaMark didn't know why Dusty acted the way he did, but the former player's blank stare and sudden scream reminded him of the actions of the old woman at the bingo hall the year prior. But according to veteran teammates and other personnel who had been with the Saints for years, Dusty Polichardo had a history of acting irrationally. Maybe he was having an episode of some sort, JaMark thought to himself. JaMark hoped Dusty would get the help he needed.

Besides the incident with Dusty Polichardo, JaMark had a calm and effective Spring Training. He pitched twice a week and grew to accept his manager's insistence of pulling him out of the game after the third inning. Instead of arguing, JaMark realized the insignificance of the exhibition games and knew it was better for the overall success of the team if his teammates got their practice in before the season. After the first week of games, in which he pitched his first three-inning appearance and struck out every batter, JaMark even campaigned to not pitch at all for the rest of spring. He told his manager the less batters saw him, the more effective he would be during the regular season.

Unfortunately, JaMark's manager had another line of thought. He told JaMark that the less the fans saw JaMark, the less employed the manager would be. JaMark understood, as every game he pitched was packed with a stadium full of fans wearing his jersey, wanting to see him, and applauding every strikeout. JaMark knew fans paid good money to see him pitch, and owners liked fans who paid good money, and owners liked managers who made them good money, and managers had to play good players who made good fans visit the ballpark and pay good money.

CHAPTER 35

By the beginning of his third season in the big leagues, JaMark had amassed a list of amazing professional accomplishments. He was known in baseball for his Minor League eighty-one-pitch no-hitter, his eighteen-inning battle with Pete LaGib, his championship pitching performances, and his Major League no-hitter. But JaMark's story and his ascent to the upper tier of sports from the lowlands of the Mississippi Delta made him a sports celebrity. He became a household name even known in apartments, condos, and timeshares.

Two weeks into the new baseball season, a reporter informed JaMark that he was nominated for the award of "Best Sports Newcomer" by a cable television sports channel. The reporter also told JaMark he was the favorite to win over the other candidates: a fifteen-year old who set the new world record in the fifty-hectometer run, a blind gold medal winner in ping-pong from Uzbekistan, and a college basketball player who "brought it back to the old school" by shooting his free throws with a two-hand underhand style.

Cable sports awards were only the beginning of JaMark's newfound celebrity. By the end of May in his third season in the Major Leagues and fifth overall in professional baseball, JaMark also appeared on a national talk show, made four national magazine covers, and received an offer to act in his first movie, playing the role of a baseball player. JaMark did well on the talk show, did better on the magazine covers, and told the movie people he would only be available for filming after the season as he didn't want any unnecessary distractions. The director understood, but because filming was on a schedule, the movie found an actor to fill the role.

On the field, JaMark picked up where he left off the previous season. Using his strategy of studying batters on the other team prior to his pitching appearances, JaMark dominated opposing lineups from his first start on Opening Day. He shut out the lineups of Boston and Toronto, and only allowed one run to New York on May 8th, JaMark's twenty-sixth birthday.

After his birthday, JaMark continued his success and only allowed one run each to the lineups from Detroit, Minnesota, and Seattle. Through the first three months of the season, JaMark led the league in almost every positive pitching category, from most innings pitched to lowest opponent batting average. He allowed the least baserunners of any pitcher who started games and had yet to allow a home run. He felt good, and more importantly, his team was winning. By July 1st, the Saints had the best record in their division and were in first place by a wide margin.

In the middle of July in his third Major League season, JaMark was selected to start the All-Star Game for his league. Although he pitched seven innings the day before the beginning of the All-Star break, JaMark accepted the offer to represent his league.

Wearing a special red and white jersey and donning a special blue hat, JaMark was introduced as a member of his second All-Star Game roster. Whereas he did not pitch in the previous year's game, in his third season in the Major Leagues, JaMark started the game and threw the first pitch for his league. And the second. And the third. And the fourth, fifth, twelfth, and eighteenth. All for strikes. And none of the batters who received these pitches made contact.

CHAPTER 36

We are back here in New York for the bottom of the fourth inning of the ninety-fourth annual All-Star Game. It is such a thrill to see the best of the best from every team. And the best of them all thus far has been young JaMark Reliford of the St. Petersburg Saints. The starting pitcher for his league, Reliford has now completed three innings throwing only twenty-seven pitches and striking out nine. I do not know what is more miraculous — that Reliford has not thrown a pitch out of the strike zone or that these batters, possibly the best in the world, have not hit any of his pitches in fair territory. The only two batters to make contact hit a foul ball each in the second inning.

We have seen some amazing performances in All-Star Games, and I have announced a few of them, but this may be among the best already. And Reliford takes the mound again in the bottom of the fourth inning facing the top of the lineup. Let's see if these hitters can make contact now that they have seen JaMark once already.

Leading off is Cincinnati shortstop Diego Cabrera. The switch-hitting Cabrera, hitting right-handed against the lefty Reliford, struck out in his first at-bat. Cabrera leads the league in walks, hits, and on-base percentage. He and fellow all-star Maddox Bozeman make up a very dynamic middle infield for Cincinnati.

The first pitch by Reliford is a called strike on the inside corner. Reliford is throwing extremely hard, averaging ninety-eight miles an hour on his fastball tonight. That fastball was only ninety-seven.

Reliford winds and delivers. The pitch is a curveball on the outside corner of the plate for strike two. Cabrera made an attempt to swing but missed that one. I don't think he was expecting a curveball from Reliford there. That's one big difference for Reliford this season over his first few. He is mixing his pitches much better as he learns the league. He remains a two-pitch pitcher, but he used to only rely on the curve for strikeouts, now he throws it at any time during an at-bat.

Reliford delivers and another curve, and Cabrera is down swinging. That curve started around the chest and nearly dropped into the dirt. A beautiful 12-6 curve by Reliford. And now the first ten batters have gone down on strikeouts on three pitches each. Amazing.

Now batting is the New York left fielder Brock Whitson. An eight-year veteran in the Majors, Whitson finished second in MVP voting last year. This year he already has fifteen home runs and seventy-five runs batted in. New York signed him in the offseason, and he is already paying dividends.

Reliford looks in to his catcher and gets the signal. He winds, and there is the pitch. Whitson swings at a high fastball and can't catch up to it. Strike one. Whitson looked completely overmatched on that pitch.

Reliford gets the ball back from his catcher and looks in for the signal. The pitch, another fastball, and Whitson again swings and misses. That was ninety-nine miles an hour low and away. Whitson, a left-handed hitter, has had trouble with that pitch in the past.

Whitson takes a step out of the batter's box to readjust his batting gloves. You can hear the jeers from the crowd, many of whom are still angry Whitson left one New York team for the other. Even though it is in his city, this is far from a home All-Star Game for Whitson.

Whitson steps back in the box, and Reliford is ready. The Saint Petersburg pitcher winds and delivers. Another fastball on the inside corner for strike three. Whitson must have been looking for a curveball because he didn't even swing. Strike out number eleven for Reliford on pitch number thirty-three. The amazing thing is that not one batter has yet to dispute a call by home plate umpire Gregg Dent. Dent is typically known for his big strike zone, but we haven't seen any hitters yet give even a look of protest.

Up next is Pittsburgh first baseman Mike Scrubbings. Scrubbings leads the majors in home runs and was one of the top vote getters in this year's All-Star balloting. A three-time all-star hailing from New York, Scrubbings has family in the crowd tonight, as his wife, kids, and parents are all in attendance. We saw his kids last night at the All-Star home run derby.

Scrubbings steps in, and Reliford with the pitch. Fastball right down the middle and Scrubbings swung and missed. Strike one. Reliford seemed to be saying, "hit this, big guy" with that fastball. The scoreboard said Reliford hit 100 miles per hour with that pitch. That is the second-

fastest pitch ever in a Major League All-Star Game.

Scrubbings steps back in the box with the count 0 and one. Reliford winds and throws another fastball. This one a little higher and Scrubbings again swings and misses. Strike two. Let's see if Reliford breaks out that big curve or comes with another fastball, maybe a little higher.

The pitch, and that is exactly what Reliford does. Another fastball, a bit higher than the last pitch. Just as fast, again at 100 miles an hour. And again Scrubbings swings and misses. Three fastballs, each a little higher than the last, and each at or near 100 miles per hour. Reliford continues to pitch a historic game at the ninety-fourth All-Star Game here in New York. To the top of the fifth, we go."

CHAPTER 37

When JaMark walked back to the dugout after the fourth inning, after he had thrown unhittable pitch number thirty-six to end the inning, he asked the Boston manager if he would be coming off the mound and ceding pitching duty to another All-Star pitcher. The manager looked at the faces of the other players in the dugout and asked if any other pitcher wanted to take the mound. Although they were all all-stars and competitive by nature, not one pitcher stood up, raised his hand, or made any demonstrative motion to acknowledge the manager's inquiry. The manager asked again, fully offering any willing volunteer the chance to relieve JaMark and make an appearance in the All-Star Game. Again, no one stood up or announced any desire to take the mound. Before the manager could ask a third and final time, the oldest and most frequently-named All-Star pitcher, a tall left-hander from the Seattle team, stood up. Before the manager could approach the veteran hurler, the pitcher addressed the manager and the team.

"Skipper, no one is going in the game," the veteran pitcher said. "This young man is doing something magical out there and none of us is going to take that away from him. This is history right here."

The manager acknowledged the veteran's decision and nodded his head to JaMark, letting JaMark know the game was his and his only.

As he did through the first twelve batters, JaMark completed the fifth and sixth innings without a hit and without a batter making fair contact with a pitch. He struck out every batter on three pitches and only allowed three foul balls – two to the opposite league's number six hitter in the fifth inning and one to the number nine hitter in the sixth. Only the last foul ball was nearly fair, a groundball that skirted to the foul side of the third baseline. On the following pitch, the number nine hitter promptly struck out as did the rest of his teammates.

In the seventh inning, JaMark faced the top of the lineup again. He struck out the first two batters, Cabrera of Cincinnati and Whitson of New York, again on three pitches each. After Whitson became his twentieth strikeout, the crowd stood and applauded JaMark as he not only completely surpassed the record for strikeouts in an All-Star Game but also tied the Major League record for strikeouts in any game. And he still had seven batters to face.

With the crowd on their feet, JaMark took the mound to face batter number twenty-one, Pittsburgh's Mike Scrubbings, former most valuable player, hometown hero, and one of the most productive offensive players in professional baseball. JaMark took his position on the mound and looked to the catcher to see what pitch the catcher thought would be most effective. JaMark saw the signal for curveball and nodded in approval. The tall, lanky left-hander gripped his long fingers around the ball, wound up, and released a pitch that had a slight imbalance in the equilibrium allowing for the unequal air current to move the ball slightly downward and to the right as it flew through the air. Scrubbings took a mighty swing, whipping his bat through the strike zone, and hoping to strike the pitch with a mighty force. Unlike any previous batter during the first six and two-thirds innings of play, Scrubbings made fair contact, grounding the ball weakly back to Reliford, who threw to the first baseman for the final out of the seventh inning.

With the inning over, JaMark walked off the mound to the thunderous applause of a standing ovation, as each of the over 55,671 people in attendance, all of his fellow Major Leaguers, the groundskeepers, and even the media rained cheers and praise on the young left-hander. Even the other team and those rooting for them yelled, whistled, and clapped in approval of JaMark's historic feat. JaMark heard their applause, made a slight bow to the opposing dugout to acknowledge his opponents, and tipped his cap to the crowd as he exited the field.

With his historical effort ended, JaMark was replaced on the mound by another pitcher in the eighth inning, as the manager attempted to showcase the abilities of the rest of his all-star roster.

CHAPTER 38

Whereas his similar pitching performance in Wyoming years earlier was witnessed by a few hundred and made him known as a Minor League prospect, JaMark's performance in the ninety-fourth All-Star Game, witnessed by thousands in attendance and the millions in homes, pushed him beyond baseball and into the rare air of celebrity athletes. The day after the All-Star Game, JaMark's name was known from Christmas Island to Easter Island and everywhere in between. National news shows that normally focused little on sports featured him on their broadcasts. Overnight, his rise to the Major Leagues went from a sports story with a humanistic flavor to a human story with a sports seasoning. National reporters from all major news channels, magazines, and other outlets tread the same path to Rosedale that sportswriters took a year and a half earlier when they first told the story of JaMark's rise from anonymity.

The second time the mass media descended into JaMark's hometown, the residents were more than eager to talk about their first-ever baseball all-star. When JaMark's fame grew, so too did the citizens of Rosedale's eagerness to talk.

When they saw news trucks from each of the major cable news stations, many Rosedale residents told stories about how they knew JaMark, how they saw him develop into the pitcher he was, and how they thought the world of him. They talked about his visits to the highschool he used to attend and how he inspired the students, they talked about how he helped coach local little league teams, they talked about their relationship with him, and they never failed to mention their input into his life. According to the amalgamation of stories, JaMark was raised by a village of caring, compassionate souls, he dominated the high school ranks, went on to become a great pitcher, and came back to be a perfect community member. There was no mention of alcohol, arrogance, or aggravated assault. Any hint of a question that Rosedale used to have about JaMark's change in character was dropped in favor of a moment in the spotlight, and proximity to his greatness. The national media swallowed the story and regurgitated it to the masses on every channel, in every magazine, and on every website.

Although JaMark followed the advice of baseball veterans and ignored stories about himself, the team, or baseball, Betsy read everything she could that mentioned JaMark. During his first years in the Minor Leagues, she kept a scrapbook, and following his achievement in the All-Star Game, she had an entire closet full of magazines, newspapers, web articles, and other printed mentions of her man. Betsy even requested the Saints send her any program or team yearbook that featured articles on him.

As she read the comments of JaMark's neighbors following his All-Star Game performance, Betsy expressed her disappointment to JaMark.

"They are clinging on to your coattails," she said. "They all say they were so important to your success. One gym owner even said it was because of his fitness center that your arm is as strong as it is. JaMark, that gym just opened two months ago. I expected that kind of hogwash from your Uncle Rufus, but not the rest of the town."

Betsy's comment hurt JaMark and reminded him of Uncle Rufus's latest debacle. A week before the All-Star Game, JaMark learned Uncle Rufus was back in jail and behind bars serving six months for literary kidnapping. Despite the work Betsy did as Rufus's community agent and caseworker, he decided to take a bookmobile for an unauthorized joy ride around town. Because the judge was a friend of Betsy's, Rufus wasn't charged with stealing the bus, only holding the books hostage, which came with either jail time or a late fee to the library for as long as he had the books in his possession, which came to fourteen hours and thirty-two minutes multiplied by the over 200 books in the bookmobile at the time. Following Betsy's advice, Rufus took jail time.

"Betsy," JaMark began, "don't worry about it. You said they didn't say anything about the bad times I went through. That's good. They painted a good picture of me, albeit with their own interests in mind. I'm not upset at all. Besides, after the season, I want to buy a new house, and I want you to move in with me, and find somewhere where we can both be happy."

From her silent pause, JaMark knew his idea made Betsy happy. He thought about moving from Rosedale but didn't yet have a plan. He knew getting Betsy involved would speed up the home search, which he found difficult with his constant baseball-related travels. The only places JaMark usually saw on the road were hotels, the ballpark, and an occasional restaurant. Only on a few trips did his routine differ. During his trip to Chicago, for example, he met with Betsy's uncle Windy and sat through a few jazz performances. But JaMark didn't have family in every city, and he didn't enjoy going to bars and clubs with his teammates. On most road trips, he chose to stay away from temptation and anything that might return him to a life of vice.

CHAPTER 39

With the media covering JaMark's every move and as he became a household name, companies wanted to use his face to endorse their products. Two weeks after his historic performance at the All-Star Game, JaMark received a phone call from the makers of Colonel Crispy's Frosted Sugar Bombs. The representative asked if JaMark would be interested in starring in a commercial for the famous cereal. Colonel Crispy's Frosted Sugar Bombs contained three times the sugar content of the average children's cereal and contained enough powdered caffeine extract for over nine hours of energy. Despite the lack of health value, the cereal was JaMark's favorite as a child. Every morning through his youth, through high school, and through his difficult times, JaMark ate a bowl of Colonel Crispy's cereal. The cereal's rapid high and resulting excitableness was a comforting feeling for a young man who often felt bored and isolated when off the pitcher's mound.

JaMark didn't need long to think about pitching for the Colonel Crispy team. Without a second thought, JaMark accepted the offer to star in a commercial for Colonel Crispy's Frosted Sugar Bombs. Although the company offered nearly a million dollars in endorsement money, JaMark refused any financial compensation, accepting only a lifetime supply of Frosted Sugar Bombs. JaMark's enthusiasm and willingness to perform the commercial for a unique compensation caused the CEO of the Colonel Crispy Corporation to call JaMark and express his gratitude personally.

During their phone call, the Colonel Crispy CEO told JaMark his company had actually already known that JaMark was a fan of Colonel Crispy's cereal. The CEO explained that he decided to present the pitcher the offer for the commercial after seeing a picture of JaMark in Food Fan Magazine, a magazine dedicated to informing readers what food their favorite celebrities enjoy. Between photos of Michael B. Jordan enjoying sweet potatoes and Dwayne Johnson eating falafel was a grainy candid shot of a young JaMark Reliford smiling in front of a bowl of Colonel Crispy's Frosted Sugar Bombs.

"You are definitely the right person for us, JaMark," said the CEO. "We have big plans to expand the Colonel Crispy product. We see brand development. We see horizontal and lateral growth. We see worldwide market penetration. And we want you to come with us. The Saints will be in New York next week. That's where we film. Will you have personal time off?"

JaMark didn't understand most of the CEO's business terminology, but he appreciated the call and told the CEO he would be available the following Wednesday afternoon before the Saints game against New York. JaMark was excited at the thought of being on television. He had never been on TV for anything other than playing baseball, post-game interviews, baseball-themed talk shows, or general entertainment talk shows. JaMark realized the cereal commercial would be the first time he ever needed to memorize lines for a camera. That scared him.

The next Wednesday, JaMark arrived in New York City with the Saints. After checking in to the hotel with his teammates, JaMark took a taxi to Colonel Crispy's corporate headquarters in Manhattan. Colonel Crispy's corporate headquarters was the most extravagant headquarters in the cereal business. The building stood over fifty stories tall in the middle of the financial district. The architecture surrounding the first ten stories flared out as if it was a giant cereal bowl. As the other forty stories extended upwards, a spigot on each side of the building poured fountains of white liquid down toward the bowl-shaped architecture. The entire building was designed to provoke thoughts of cereal, from the architecture to the several spoon-shaped antennae on the roof.

JaMark entered the building in a state of awe. He had never seen such a shrine to cereal, no less his favorite cereal. After exchanging brief hellos and signing a few autographs for the staff, he was escorted to a small room lined with what he concluded to be soundproof material. Having seen film set-ups on television, JaMark was not surprised to see a green screen pulled down behind a mock kitchen table. There was enough room behind the kitchen table for a person to sit, and a bowl on the table was accompanied by a box of Colonel Crispy's Frosted Sugar Bombs. JaMark assumed he would be the person to sit at the table and eat from the bowl filled with cereal from the box.

JaMark's assumption was proven correct. Moments after JaMark arrived, a tall man with a head of red dreadlocks, a reggae concert shirt, jean shorts that barely reached his knees, and a pair of Converse sneakers entered the room. He did not enter quietly; instead, he immediately began pointing directions and telling people on the set what to do and how to do it. A crew member standing near JaMark saw JaMark's confusion and told him the outlandish and eccentric man yelling directions was famous foreign commercial director Lutherus Condere. According to the crew member, this was Condere's first American commercial, but he was well-known in Europe for his pre-paid phone card commercials. Despite airing in different languages, the commercials were known for their accurate re-creations of historic events such as the birth of Christ, the fall of Rome, and World War I. The commercials featured international comic Felipe Khan, who often walked through the event talking on a pre-paid cell phone. The crew member told JaMark that both Khan and Condere won several awards for their work. JaMark was very impressed and hoped his commercial would be as epic and inspiring.

The dreadlocked director concluded his instructions to the crew and turned his attention to JaMark. He shook hands with JaMark and exchanged brief pleasantries before excitedly telling JaMark how he was going to be part of what Condere called "a magnificently epic old-fashioned cereal ad." According to Condere, the first twenty-three seconds of the commercial would feature JaMark talking to a camera and telling the world how much he loved Colonel Crispy's Frosted Sugar Bombs. That would be followed by three seconds of JaMark digging into the bowl of prepared cereal and smiling while he chewed. Condere told JaMark the commercial would then fade to a picture of the cereal box and a voice-over stating how Colonel Crispy's Frosted Sugar Bombs were part of a complete breakfast. According to the dreadlocked director, all JaMark had to do was sit at the table, eat the cereal, say his lines, and the crew would take care of the rest.

Before JaMark could sit down, however, he was told by a short woman with short blond hair to put on attire that would let the audience know he was a baseball player. Because the Colonel Crispy's Cereal Corporation did not have licensing rights for Major League Baseball, JaMark couldn't officially represent the Saints, and he was told to wear a generic blue baseball hat and a generic blue baseball jersey.

As he sat at the small table, JaMark noticed there was something missing from the table. He had a bowl, he had cereal, he had a napkin, he had orange juice, and he had all the other parts of a complete breakfast, but he was missing a spoon. He alerted the surprised staff to his lack of a spoon, and in a few moments, JaMark had his missing utensil.

JaMark struggled with the scene as he was not an actor, and so was not familiar with reciting lines. By the time he memorized the words he had to say, he was too wired on spoonfuls of Frosted Sugar Bombs to say his part slow enough. While his first five takes were hindered by nerves, his next fourteen takes were sabotaged by the cereal's massive amounts of sugar and caffeine. As he ate several spoonfuls each take, each attempt became further marked by JaMark's uncontrollable shaking, rapid voice, and even faster heartbeat, which, by the twelfth take, was so loud that it could be heard through his microphone.

Not until JaMark followed the suggestion of a crew member and ran up and down each of the 53 flights of stairs at Colonel Crispy's Corporate Headquarters was he finally calm enough to perform. Unfortunately, the run made JaMark forget some of his formerly memorized lines. After thirty more minutes of practice, and six more takes, JaMark finally pronounced each word with the correct inflection, tone, and timbre, leading to a collective sigh of relief by Condere, the staff, and camera crew.

Twenty minutes after Lutherus Condere called "cut" and the filming ended, the director's assistant took JaMark to a small room several doors down from the film set. In this small, closet-sized room sat several computers, a tower of hard drives, servers, and other technological equipment, and a small balding man who introduced himself as "Bill, the lead editor." After standing up to shake JaMark's hand, Bill sat on a chair marked "Bill's chair" in front of the computer marked "Bill's computer." JaMark could see Bill was watching the scene they had just created. Bill hit a few keys on his computer, reset the program, and reminded them that much work needed to be done, and what they were about to watch was far from a final product. JaMark didn't say anything but thought Bill's comment was quite obvious, considering the green backdrop was still in the scene.

JaMark and the assistant director huddled in front of Bill's monitor and watched the commercial they just filmed. "Hi, I'm JaMark Reliford, big-league baseball player. I've eaten Colonel Crispy's Frosted Sugar Bombs since I was a kid. They are the best. I'd do anything for the great taste of Colonel Crispy's Frosted Sugar Bombs. And they are great for you. Look at me. I am a Major League baseball player because of the energy and spark I get from my Frosted Sugar Bombs. They can make your dreams come true!"

JaMark wasn't impressed with his performance and thought his lines sounded forced and choppy. JaMark looked at the assistant director and saw the same lack of confidence. Bill looked at the faces of both men and reassured them he would work magic and "through hell or high water" there would be a commercial on the air in thirty days.

After finishing his business at the Colonel Crispy Headquarters, JaMark returned to the team in time to engage in the usual pre-game rituals. Although his manager knew, many of his teammates were not aware of his commercial endeavor. JaMark wanted to keep it that way. There were already a few players questioning his focus after he was featured on so many media outlets after the All-Star Game. JaMark didn't want to add to their discontent. JaMark also figured the commercial would be a pleasant surprise to the teammates who wanted to follow along in JaMark's commercial exploits and enjoyed playing on the same team as a national celebrity.

CHAPTER 40

Weeks passed, and JaMark forgot about the commercial. The summer days were heating up, and so was the pennant race. Again, teams were jostling for playoff positions, trying to squeeze into the limited spots available. JaMark, again, was doing all he could to get his team into a playoff spot. On the final day of August, JaMark remained at the top of almost all positive pitching performance measurements and was running away with the standard statistics of wins, strikeouts, and average earned runs allowed per nine innings. He even led the league in the least home runs allowed to left-handed hitters on Tuesday with runners on first and third. Only the most hardened hometown-biased reporters failed to call him the best pitcher in the league.

Unfortunately, JaMark's efforts were not enough. On the final day of the season, in the final game, during the final inning, a Saints relief pitcher acquired at the final hour of the trade deadline allowed a game-losing home run to a Boston second baseman who had not hit a home run all season. The game-winning home run for Boston and the game-losing home run for the Saints propelled Boston into the playoffs and ended the Saints' season.

Three weeks after the Saints season ended, after all the baseball had been played, JaMark sat on the couch watching Betsy's favorite primetime drama. Just before the television lawyers finally put the fictional criminal in jail, JaMark received a call from the Saints' public relations director. The PR director informed JaMark he won the "Pitcher of the Year" award and would have to follow strict etiquette and protocol for a speech he would be required to give. As she continued to give JaMark directions, Betsy let out a joyous squee and pointed at the television. JaMark followed Betsy's finger to the screen, where his own visage stared back, except instead of holding a phone, the JaMark on the screen held a spoonful of Colonel Crispy's Frosted Sugar Bombs. JaMark quickly ended his phone call with the PR director in time to hear the baritone voice-over inform the audience that Frosted Sugar Bombs were part of a complete breakfast.

As soon as the commercial was over, JaMark's phone rang again. JaMark answered without looking at the caller ID screen, leaving the caller's identification to the fates.

"JaMark," the voice said, "this is the CEO of the Colonel Crispy Cereal Corporation. Did you see it? It was wonderful. Such grace. Such beauty. Such power to convince people to buy Frosted Sugar Bombs. You nailed it, kid."

"I saw it, sir," JaMark answered, stretching the truth by twenty-three seconds. "It turned out great."

"You bet your bippy it did, son," said the CEO. "We bought airtime during primetime every night for the next three weeks. Your face will be everywhere: billboards, bus panels, basketball courts, the moon. You name it, you will be there as the pitching pitcher for Frosted Sugar Bombs. Market domination, here we come. Gotta go. Ciao!"

Before JaMark could put the phone down, nearly a dozen text messages appeared. He scrolled through, reading several variations of congratulations from friends, family, current teammates, and former teammates. JaMark wondered if he would receive more congratulations for his commercial appearance than he would for his upcoming Pitcher of the Year announcement.

As the Colonel Crispy CEO foretold, JaMark's commercial aired every day during primetime hours for weeks. Although JaMark thought the commercial would be limited to the channel he originally saw it on, he and Betsy saw the commercial on many other channels. It was on food channels, children's channels, news channels, and even on the sports channel following the news of his Pitcher of the Year award. Betsy even claimed to see the commercial on a Spanish-speaking channel with a Spanish voice-over instead of JaMark's voice. JaMark agreed that this must have been the case, as he did not speak Spanish.

JaMark was interviewed several times after winning the Pitcher of the Year award, but otherwise lived an uneventful offseason out of the spotlight as he usually did. Although he and Betsy both talked about eventually moving out of Rosedale and were both actively house-hunting, JaMark considered the town's secluded nature an advantage. Everyone knew him in Rosedale, and they generally left him to his business, and after his public image repair, he believed the people of the town generally liked him. At least he didn't think otherwise. Even his former teammate, the bartender whose face JaMark smashed with a pitcher of beer several years earlier, asked for an autograph and gave JaMark a smile. JaMark considered that a fair trade.

CHAPTER 41

In the safe seclusion of Rosedale, JaMark rarely encountered fans, and by spending most of his days and nights inside Betsy's house, he saw very few people other than his family. A week before Christmas, however, JaMark heard a midday knock on the front door. When he answered, he saw the same tall, slender, well-dressed man in a black suit, tie, and matching top hat who visited him in Mobile, in Durham, and under the old oak tree at the crossroads just outside of Rosedale.

"Hello, Satan," JaMark said.

"Hello, JaMark," the Devil answered. "It is good to see you again. I was in the neighborhood and thought it well for me to stop by. You know, you've done far more with your talent than I ever thought you would. I am impressed, and you should be proud."

"Thank you," JaMark answered. "I try to work hard and stay humble. I try not to let anything go to my head."

"That's good to hear," said the Devil. "May I come in?"

Although he thought it odd to let the Devil into Betsy's house, JaMark was not going to refuse his guest. JaMark knew Betsy would not consent to the Devil in her home as she remained a very pious woman. JaMark knew his relationship with the Devil was a strain on her. But JaMark also knew that if he did not allow the Devil to enter, he could jeopardize his very tenuous relationship with the ancient demon.

JaMark was comforted slightly as the Devil acted like a gentleman in Betsy's house, even acknowledging a collection of glass angels Betsy kept in a wooden menagerie in the living room. After passing the menagerie and the entranceway of the home, the Devil removed his hat and jacket and walked side-by-side with JaMark into the living room. The Devil took a seat on the couch, and JaMark sat on the room's loveseat.

"You failed me again, JaMark," the Devil said calmly after the two men were comfortable. The Devil leaned forward on the couch. "I thought you would be the one, JaMark. The one who would see past the false idols and the one who would give me the undying credit I deserve. But, no. Now you failed me for the last time."

JaMark looked at the Devil. He was confused and had no idea what the Devil was talking about. After he figured out how to mention the Devil, he always gave him thanks in speeches, post-game interviews, and whenever else he was quoted.

"I'm not sure I know what you mean," JaMark said defensively. JaMark sat upright on the edge of the loveseat, uncomfortable on what he considered the most comfortable piece of furniture in the house.

"Who is Colonel Crispy?" the Devil asked. He placed his hands on his knees, as if ready to pounce. "Who is this man you said you would do anything for and who made you into the baseball player you are today?"

The Devil's accusation caught JaMark by surprise. "That was a commercial," the young pitcher answered, "I had to say the lines in the script they gave me."

The Devil stood up and walked towards JaMark, standing over the pitcher, who still sat on the loveseat, parallel to the couch where the Devil was sitting a moment ago. Whereas JaMark thought he was slightly taller than the Devil, as long as he remained seated, the Devil had a height advantage.

"Do not lie to me. Who is this man you gave credit to, JaMark?" the Devil yelled, leaning forward towards JaMark and forcing JaMark to lean back in the loveseat to avoid a collision. "Who is this man you would put in front of me?"

JaMark swallowed his fear and tried to breathe confidence. But the Devil's imposing figure and increasing anger smothered the air and stifled his attempts to gain the upper hand. He found it difficult to even try to reason with the man from the crossroads. JaMark could not prove it, but the Devil appeared to be growing taller and larger by the moment, filling every inch of

JaMark's vision.

After moments of feeling the Devil's eyes and anger peering down on him, JaMark watched the Devil turn his back on JaMark, walk to the jacket he left on the couch, pull out a pack of cigarettes and a lighter, and walk outside, presumably to have a smoke and let out steam. At least JaMark hoped the Devil would let out steam.

Through Betsy's living room window, JaMark watched the Devil finish his cigarette. The Devil then let himself into Betsy's house, walked to the couch he was sitting on, collected his jacket and hat, and turned towards JaMark.

"I am taking back all that I gave you," the Devil said calmly. "You have proven to be a poor choice. But because you did well prior to turning into an epic disappointment, I will make another deal with you, and I suggest you be wise enough to take it."

JaMark looked at the Devil, but could say nothing.

"One day, I will return," the Devil continued as he put on his jacket. "On that day, baseball man, you will pitch for your soul. If you strike me out, our deal is over, your soul is yours, and I walk away. If you do not strike me out, your soul is mine for eternity. I think that's fair."

The Devil placed his hat on his head and walked out of Betsy's house. "Good day, JaMark," the Devil said, tipping the brim towards JaMark and closing the door behind him.

JaMark sat on the couch, petrified, thinking about what just happened. The Devil's entire visit occurred in less than twenty minutes, but JaMark replayed every moment in his head at least three times. He couldn't believe the Devil was upset over his Colonel Crispy commercial, he couldn't believe the Devil claimed to take back his gift, and he couldn't believe he let the Devil in Betsy's house. He was in shock, unable to move, and barely able to breathe.

Over an hour later, JaMark still sat transfixed on the same spot on the same loveseat. He thought of his entire career and all the fame, acclaim, and financial gain that came with it. He had achieved more than he could have ever imagined or even dreamed of. All because of the Devil. JaMark cried as he realized he could lose everything he loved to do and everyone he loved to be with.

Daylight slowly disappeared, and dusk settled on Rosedale. Soon dusk grew to evening, and light vanished from the house, leaving JaMark in the dark.

After sitting in the dark for some time, JaMark forced himself off the loveseat. He wiped his tears and turned on a small lamp on an end table in the living room. The light flickered before illuminating the room. At the same moment the light lit the room, Betsy's car pulled into the driveway.

JaMark was glad he wiped his tears when he did. He considered whether or not to tell Betsy about the Devil's visit. He wanted to, but didn't know if he had the strength. He thought perhaps Betsy would see the trouble on his face and give him the emotional support he needed without her knowing what was wrong. JaMark knew Betsy was good at drawing out his emotions and making him talk about his problems. He liked that about her.

As she entered the house, Betsy didn't notice anything in JaMark's demeanor, in his eyes, or on his face. She had a look of joy and pushed forward her own positivity, not even asking JaMark if anything was wrong.

"JaMark," she shouted as she bound through the door and walked towards him, "I found the perfect house! It's beautiful and I want us to live there and be happy there and raise a family there and it's perfect!"

JaMark knew Betsy was normally well-composed. Her rapid speech gave away her excitement almost as much as her rapid heart rate did when she embraced him. JaMark knew the house she found must be special for her to be so emotional. He smiled as she told him all about the single-family home she found in the suburbs of Chicago, approximately an hour from her family. He nodded as she told him all about the rooms, the bathrooms, the ceilings, the floors, the neighborhood, the schools, and how the house was empty and was waiting for a buyer. He was happy to hear her excitement about the house, not only because it was about their future, but because he didn't

immediately have to tell Betsy about the Devil.
He decided to wait for a better time.

CHAPTER 42

A better time never came.

The new house was an ongoing topic until the couple traveled to Chicago and made a down payment shortly after Christmas. In mid-January, less than a month after JaMark was visited by the Devil, he and Betsy moved into their first home. For the rest of the offseason, JaMark spent most of his time unpacking and helping Betsy arrange their new home. Once they were settled, JaMark invited his grandmother to live with them, but she declined, saying Chicago was too far north for her bones. JaMark guessed that besides the weather, his grandmother would miss the familiarity of Rosedale, where she knew everyone, and everyone knew her.

Uncle Rufus, on the other hand, offered to live in the couple's spare bedroom after completing his latest prison term. Betsy counter-offered and suggested Rufus stay under the guidance of another Rosedale community advisor with the intent of keeping him in Mississippi, as she had her fill of Rufus's exploits. But Rufus insisted he stay associated with her, which meant moving to the Chicago area. Relocating Rufus also meant Betsy had to complete and submit paperwork stating she would be responsible for moving a convicted terrorist, smuggler, and kidnapper from Mississippi to Illinois. She also needed to cite how she would help him move and propose what he would do once in Illinois. Seeing her stressed over the administrivia, JaMark thanked her for going through the trouble. Although she could do without Rufus, he enjoyed his uncle's company, and JaMark wanted a family member of his own nearby, as they now lived closer to Betsy's family. Betsy's rebuttal was that JaMark didn't have to live with Uncle Rufus once baseball season began, and she did.

In February, shortly after Uncle Rufus moved in, JaMark again traveled south to begin training for the new season. Instead of leaving from Memphis as he had for the last few years, this time, his journey began in Chicago. Betsy drove him to the airport, where he said his good-byes and boarded his plane for Tampa. He landed in Tampa, rented a car, and arrived at his team's Spring Training complex a day before many of his teammates. On his first day, without the pressures of other teammates in the area, JaMark met with the Saints' new manager, Hiroki Montana, the first manager in the Major Leagues to hail from the Japanese Professional Baseball League. As one of the team's all-stars and a valued member of the organization, JaMark wanted to talk with his new manager about some of the plans and strategies for the new season.

JaMark spoke with his new manager for over an hour, and discovered Montana was a stern but fair baseball man who came from a long line of Japanese baseball legends. Montana reminded JaMark of Joe Shelter, his manager in Wyoming. Despite their different backgrounds, JaMark and Montana shared the same desire to win. JaMark ended his discussion with his new manager on a personal note, telling his new boss about his new house and how despite the move and the packing, unpacking, and homemaking, he still maintained a semi-rigorous workout schedule.

The next morning, JaMark left his room in the team-arranged local condominium and drove to the Spring Training complex. He heard the sounds of baseball as he pulled into the parking lot – the crack of wooden bats, the pop of baseballs hitting baseball gloves, and the chatter of his teammates, some old, some new, and some he had yet to meet. JaMark exited the car, grabbed his gear from the trunk, and walked into the locker room to prepare for the day on the field.

JaMark's first day at Spring Training was the same as the first day each year, save for that first year when he didn't know to start out slow. He learned quickly, and since then spent the first week only soft-tossing, running, stretching, introducing himself to new teammates, and catching up with teammates he hadn't seen in months.

Starting his fourth year in the Major Leagues, and third spring as a big leaguer had some perks. JaMark was one of the senior veterans of the pitching staff and the most accomplished. Under a new rule by new manager Hiroki Montana, JaMark was given a Minor Leaguer of his choice to carry his bags, shine his shoes, tie his shoelaces, or perform other menial tasks. JaMark thought the concept was foolish, but Montana thought it would help young players learn the "way of the Major Leaguer."

JaMark's liege was a Texas teenager named Beau Kesey. Kesey was a stocky kid with an All-American build and a short military-style crew cut. He was the Mobile minor league team's starting catcher in the previous season and was a rising star, a power hitter who won Most Valuable Player in each of his first two seasons in the Minor Leagues. JaMark knew other Major League veterans would probably try to humble the kid and break his back, but JaMark wanted a personal catcher, and if the kid was that good, JaMark thought perhaps he would be catching at the big league level soon. It would be better to give the kid experience catching a Major League pitcher than picking up jockstraps, JaMark decided.

On the second day of Spring Training, JaMark did more running, soft-tossing, and conversing with teammates. Near the time he and the other veterans typically broke for lunch, their new manager emerged from the training complex headquarters and yelled that he wanted to see his pitchers in action before they left to eat. Montana ordered that each pitcher was to throw twenty-five fastballs to a catcher so the manager and his staff could see what shape his pitchers were in at the onset of Spring Training.

Although the veterans groaned with displeasure, they complied with their new manager's demand. Most grumbled that their arms were not fully stretched out, but their new manager told them to do what they could. JaMark found a mound and waited for Kesey to put on his gear and assume his crouch behind the plate. JaMark told the kid to be ready as he might be faster than the average pitcher on their second day of Spring Training.

The former Mobile catcher took his position behind the second home plate in a row of five home plates and pitcher's mounds in the pitcher's warm-up area. As other catchers took their spots parallel to each other and other pitchers mounted pitcher's mounds, JaMark walked slowly up the slightly inclined regulation-sized smoothed pile of dirt sixty feet and six inches from Kesey and the home plate.

As he did thousands of times before on dozens of pitching mounds across the United States, JaMark wound up and let a baseball fly from his left hand as hard as he could. On this day in February, however, the baseball failed to fly as fast as it had thousands of times before. Whereas he could throw nearly 100 miles per hour on a typical day, none of JaMark's twenty-five fastballs to Kesey topped eighty-two miles per hour, according to the pitching coach's radar gun.

When the pitching coach told him the speeds of his pitches, JaMark stood on the mound with a look of disbelief. Years earlier, he broke a catcher's hand on the first day of Spring Training, and now according to the team radar gun, he was throwing slower than any other member of the pitching staff. Luckily, none of the other pitchers made a big deal over their first spring performance, so JaMark didn't make a big deal of his. He decided his lack of speed was due to the impromptu nature of his new manager's request. Perhaps like the others, JaMark thought, he just wasn't stretched out enough.

After lunch, the rest of the second day of Spring Training was much of the same. JaMark ran, soft tossed, and lollygagged around the complex, chatting with teammates and signing the occasional autograph for fans. JaMark didn't understand why fans were interested in watching him run slowly, throw slowly, and talk amicably, but they were. In exchange for their interest in him, JaMark signed his name on whatever they put in front of him.

Following the afternoon drills, JaMark returned to his team-arranged condominium, made dinner, talked to Betsy on the phone, and went to sleep. The next morning, as the sun broke through the horizon, hours before his alarm was due to ring, JaMark awoke to a feeling he hadn't felt in years.

Pain.

JaMark's left shoulder screamed in a rage of silent pain. JaMark grasped his shoulder with his right hand, biting his lip to stifle his own verbal expression. He lunged from the bed and struggled to the bathroom, hoping to find anything to ease his pain. With his left arm held tight across his body, he threw open cabinets and pulled open drawers with his right hand, searching for any pain-relieving medication or muscle soothing cream. As the team-sponsored condo was empty before he moved in, his search also came up empty.

Frustrated and still in pain, JaMark grabbed a handtowel, walked quickly from the bathroom to the kitchen, wrapped several handfuls of ice in the handtowel, and placed the towel against the muscles of his still-hurting left shoulder, hoping the coolness would constrict the blood flow to his shoulder and numb the pain.

He looked at the clock. It was barely past six o'clock.

Three hours later, JaMark was still icing his arm. By noon, an hour before he needed to report to the Spring Training complex, the pain had subsided and JaMark felt as well as he did the day before and the day before that and for years before that. As he drove to the complex, he made the decision not to tell anyone on the coaching staff what happened with his shoulder. If they asked why he was so exhausted, JaMark decided to blame a leaky faucet, throwing the condominium management under the proverbial bus.

But JaMark also couldn't shake the feeling that he knew who was really to blame for the pain in his shoulder. He hadn't thrown a ball or exerted himself since the Devil visited him the week before Christmas. He tried not to think that his Devil-given gift of an impervious arm was gone. He buried the thought deep in the back of mind, focusing instead on the upcoming day at the ballpark.

Whatever the cause of his newfound pain, JaMark was

going to keep it to himself. Not even Betsy could know.

After arriving at the field, JaMark found Kesey standing near his locker and reading a schedule that was posted on each player's locker by their new manager. According to the paper, the third day of Spring Training included more running and more soft-tossing in the morning, and occasional hard-tossing and long-tossing drills in the afternoon. JaMark and Kesey walked out to the field and started throwing. As he practiced, JaMark didn't feel the pain that seared his left shoulder earlier in the morning. But he stayed cautious nonetheless, throwing as soft as possible during the soft toss. He was happy he paired with a rookie instead of a catcher who was more experienced with his velocity. JaMark knew a more familiar catcher would have noticed his difference in approach.

JaMark teamed with Kesey again for the pair's long tossing drill, and JaMark's shoulder withstood the exercise. But as he did the day before, JaMark's hard-tossing performance was less impressive than in years past. Again, he failed to come close to his previous speeds, barely registering over eighty-two miles an hour on a pitch he threw with all the energy he could physically muster.

After another underachieving day, JaMark had another night of pain. His second night of pain started much earlier than the first, nearly the moment he walked into his team-sponsored condominium. Fortunately, he had time to visit a local pharmacy to buy pain relievers. Discreetly purchasing the pills was difficult as JaMark saw one of his teammates at the pharmacy. Luckily for JaMark, his teammate was too distracted by his evening purchase of condoms and cheap beer to notice JaMark's bottles of pain pills. Still, JaMark let out a sigh of relief when his teammate exited the store.

JaMark returned home with the pills after buying dinner at a local sandwich shop. He sat on the couch and tore open the bottle of pain relievers and took two pills before unwrapping his sandwich and turning on the television. As he finished his dinner, the searing pain in his shoulder grew worse, distracting him from the television show about policemen and the people they arrest.

JaMark tried to keep his mind off the pain by imagining himself in the show. But his thoughts were interrupted by the notion of a mugger continuously stabbing him in the left shoulder.

As the night went on, JaMark continued to suffer. He felt slightly better after taking two more pills two hours after he took the first two. Two hours after he took pills three and four, he took pills five and six in an attempt to numb the pain and sleep. When he awoke nearly ten hours later, his arm felt well enough to leave the bottles at home and drive to the ballpark.

JaMark was relieved when he learned there was no hard-toss practice that day. Instead, he and the other pitchers practiced fielding, throwing only to the bases surrounding them. JaMark did well in the fielding drills and caught a break as first, second, and third base were manned by minor leaguers who were not used to JaMark's arm strength. He knew even his throws to bases did not have the same velocity the fielders who usually manned the bases were used to. Although there weren't any long throws or pitching practice, JaMark's shoulder again hurt from sundown to the moment he laid to sleep. Again, he numbed the pain with several pain pills.

After two weeks, JaMark's tolerance for pain pills decreased, and the pain in his shoulder increased. On the field, he had yet to throw a ball over eighty-two miles per hour. JaMark started to worry that he would never regain his old velocity nor go a night without his shoulder causing him excruciating pain. He wasn't the only one worrying either, as teammates started noticing his odd behavior and asking each other if they knew why their best pitcher wasn't throwing as hard as he had in the past. With the acquisition of a new all-star third baseman and two former all-star bullpen pitchers, there was a consensus throughout the organization, from the players to the upper management, that they expected to win more games than most teams, make the playoffs, and possibly contend for another World Series championship. But that conclusion was made with the assumption of a healthy JaMark Reliford.

On the morning of the first day of the third week of Spring Training, the day before exhibition games versus opposing teams began, JaMark was approached by his former catcher and teammate in Mobile, Barry Carusowitz. After a year managing the Mobile team to a Deep South League championship, Carusowitz was promoted to manage Buffalo, the best minor league team in the organization, and only one step below the Major League level. Although the Saints front office had faith in Hiroki Montana, the organization thought highly of Carusowitz's baseball strategy and people skills, and let him work with both minor leaguers and major leaguers.

"Hey, JaMark," Carusowitz said as he approached JaMark by the pitcher's locker. Practice hadn't started yet, and the players and coaches were in their respective offices and locker rooms putting on their uniforms and other articles of baseball attire.

"JaMark, can I talk to you for a second?" Carusowitz asked.

JaMark paused tying the laces of his left shoe for a moment and looked up at his former teammate.

"Sure, what's up?" the pitcher replied.

"I need to see you in the manager's office," Carusowitz said. "Just us."

JaMark finished tying his shoe and nodded his head. He wondered if anyone could see what he was trying to hide. He figured if anyone could tell something was wrong, it would be his old teammate and one of the few people who had known him since he entered professional baseball.

His old teammate stood at JaMark's locker watching him tie his shoe, then slowly led the way to the Major League manager's office. JaMark followed his former catcher through the door. JaMark hadn't been in the manager's office since his new manager took the position. The walls were lined with pictures of Montana. There were pictures of him during his playing days and pictures of him during his managing days. There were also pictures of Montana during his playing nights and managing nights. Unique to the new manager, however, were two samurai swords mounted above his desk. Both had Japanese script etched on their handles. JaMark didn't read Japanese but imagined the swords were gifts, perhaps from his former players. The positioning of the pictures, the swords, and other decorations instilled a professional, no-nonsense feeling to Montana's office, which matched the impression JaMark received from the man.

"Please close the door," Carusowitz said as he sat on the manager's couch along the back wall of the office, opposite the manager's desk.

"JaMark, take a seat. I want to talk to you about what's going on this spring," JaMark's former catcher said as JaMark sat on a chair facing the manager's desk, turning it around to face his coach. "You know we have a new manager and new Major League coaching staff. They are still trying to see what they have and evaluate the talent. And I think your personal training with Kesey is making that difficult."

JaMark knew most of the team was scheduled to travel to Daytona the next day to play their first exhibition game of the year against an opposing team. Throughout the previous week, many of the pitchers pitched in simulated games against minor leaguers or teammates. But JaMark had not, choosing only to work in private with his pitching coach and Kesey, his new catcher.

"We are going to take the kid with us to Daytona," JaMark's former catcher said. "We want to give him some playing time in the later innings to see what he does against different types of pitchers. We have no doubt his bat is ready, but we want to make sure the defense and the maturity of a big leaguer are there. So you won't have a Minor League apprentice anymore. Is that alright?"

"Sure," JaMark answered. "He needs experience. He is going to be good. He has a good head on his shoulders."

"Thanks, JaMark," Carusowitz said as he got off the couch and walked to the door to open it for JaMark. "He is going to be my catcher in Buffalo this year. At least for a while. I want to see what he's got."

JaMark nodded as he too rose from where he was sitting. He knew players could never be the last ones out of a manager's office, but he still appreciated Carusowitz's gesture of opening the door for him. JaMark took a quick glance at his former teammate before walking back into the locker room.

"Oh, JaMark," Carusowitz said, "one last thing."

JaMark turned to face Carusowitz.

"You are pitching tomorrow in Daytona as well," the minor league manager said with an unsuspecting smile. "Possibly even to Kesey. I thought you might not mind."

A sudden fear struck JaMark. He was afraid that after weeks of training in the shadows, his suddenly weak arm would be exposed, and his slow pitches hit by the bats of the opposition. He knew the Major League team that trained in Daytona had several hitters capable of hitting good Major League pitches. JaMark also knew that with his shoulder in its current state, he was not a good Major League pitcher.

CHAPTER 43

The sun shined bright on the trimmed green grass of the Daytona ball field. The first game of spring drew fans from across the nation who packed the stands, hoping to get an early glimpse of their favorite ballplayers in the casual setting of Central Florida. As the clock ticked closer to game time, the sights, sounds, and smells of Spring Training filled the stadium. Autograph seekers lined the edges of the playing field, hoping to get a signature on a baseball card, magazine, ball, or program. The air carried the aroma of hot dogs and suntan lotion, and vendors practiced their familiar bellows for beer and cotton candy, reacquainting themselves with the familiar steps of the bleachers. All was set for a perfect afternoon of baseball.

As the Saints were the visiting team, JaMark took the mound in the bottom of the first inning. According to his manager, JaMark was scheduled to pitch three innings. Unfortunately for JaMark and the many fans who came to see him, the perfect afternoon for baseball was about to become less than perfect.

With the Daytona fans cheering, and Saints fans in confused silence, JaMark barely made it past the second inning. After allowing four runs in the first two innings, in the third frame, JaMark allowed a grand slam to a Daytona batter on a pitch that registered only seventy-six miles per hour. After the eighth run crossed the plate, Hiroki Montana came to the mound, took the ball from JaMark, and signaled in an unprepared and surprised relief pitcher. JaMark never had a chance to pitch to Beau Kesey, who was put into the game in the seventh inning and hit his first home run off a big-league pitcher. The ball landed in a crowd of several hundred Saints fans who remained to see the heralded rookie.

JaMark didn't stay in the dugout after leaving the game, choosing instead to shower, change, and sit in the locker room. He threw every pitch to the best of his ability and knew it was only a matter of time before his shoulder started hurting. As he packed his gear, he pulled out his latest bottle of pain killers and took double the recommended dosage, hoping it would mask the inevitable pain. As soon as the game was over and JaMark's teammates poured into the clubhouse from the field hanging their heads from their fifteen to four loss, JaMark exited the stadium for the sanctuary of the team bus.

Three days later, JaMark stood on a pitching mound again, this time in front of a capacity home crowd of nearly 10,000 at the Saints' Spring Training stadium.

CHAPTER 44

Welcome to *Saints baseball, fans. Today, the Saints take on Atlanta in their fourth exhibition game of the Spring Training schedule. So far, the Saints have only one win to their name* while *Atlanta is starting off hot this spring with five wins and no losses. Of course, we can't predict anything from the beginning of Spring Training, but it would be good to see the Saints on the winning side.*

Today we have JaMark Reliford on the mound. He did not look sharp in his first game the other day in Daytona. His fastball hasn't come out of winter hibernation and his curveball was not sharp. Usually, JaMark jumps right into that high level of performance from day one. The last few seasons, he was in the zone with that high nineties fastball in his first spring start and kept that excellence all season. So it is a bit rare to see him struggle with velocity. But it is Spring Training, and that's why we are here, to knock off the rust of the offseason.

It is a beautiful spring Florida afternoon. We have a near sell-out today. The Saints have a definite advantage in Spring Training as their fans do not have to travel very far to see them. And with ticket prices typically a bit cheaper for Spring Training, the Saints get a good crowd even on a Wednesday afternoon like today. Also great to see a lot of kids in the crowd today as it is spring break throughout Florida.

The Saints take the field, and JaMark Reliford begins his warm-up pitches. The Saints are playing most of their starters today for the home crowd, including new all-star third baseman Price Adelhoff, acquired from Denver in the offseason. There is a lot of excitement surrounding the Saints this year. After trading three of their top five Minor Leaguers for Adelhoff, the Saints are all in for a championship run.

Leading off for Atlanta is the catcher, Jake Alurns. Alurns was in the Minor Leagues last year and is very athletic for a catcher. There is talk Atlanta might move him to centerfield to save his legs, but for now, he is behind the plate.

The pitch from Reliford is an outside change-up for ball one. That pitch clocked in at seventy-six miles per hour. Reliford didn't throw any offspeed pitches last year, he was strictly fastball and curveball. Perhaps this is a new pitch he is adding to his repertoire and struggling to get control of.

Reliford winds and the next pitch is another offspeed low for ball two. That pitch was only seventy-four miles an hour. If Reliford can bring the fastball in the high nineties, he will definitely get some outs with that offspeed. But we haven't seen the fastball yet this spring.

Here's the pitch. Alurns swings and slaps a base hit into left field. That was yet another offspeed pitch by Reliford. The Saints get the ball back in and now one on and no one out for Atlanta.

Stepping to the plate is the Atlanta shortstop Matt Griffin. Griffin, now in his fifth year with Atlanta, played in 146 games last season. He has been an all-star once in his career, when he played for Boston, but since then has been a steady fixture in the Atlanta infield after joining this ballclub.

Reliford gets set and delivers. A curveball taken by Griffin for strike one. That curveball didn't quite have the bite we have seen in the past from a JaMark Reliford curveball, but it got the job done for strike one.

Reliford gets the ball back from his catcher and toes the rubber. He looks at Alurns on first and tosses over. Alurns gets back easy. Reliford is right to be wary of this young man on first, he did steal thirty-two bases for Albuquerque last season. He has good speed.

The pitch to Griffin is fouled off for strike two. That looked like another one of those offspeed pitches JaMark is working with. That one was in a good spot to the righthanded hitting Griffin, low and away and all Griffin could do was slap it foul.

One on, nobody out and no balls and two strikes to Atlanta shortstop Mike Griffin. Reliford looks in for the signal, gets set, and here is the pitch. Another change-up low and inside to Griffin for ball one. Reliford has now thrown five pitches, and not one of them has been over eighty miles per hour. Very strange for a pitcher who lives by his fastball.

Reliford with the pitch. Yet another change-up, this one too far outside for ball two. Two and two to Griffin. The Saints catcher makes a quick visit to the mound to talk to JaMark. After that last pitch, he pounded his glove as if he wanted JaMark to throw something faster. But Reliford kept going with the change-up. Perhaps there is a misunderstanding *in the signals. While that is not uncommon in Spring Training, you have to think Reliford and his catcher have worked together for a few seasons and should have good communication.*

The catcher returns to his position as Reliford looks in. The pitch to Griffin. Griffin swings at a curveball and hits a groundball to short. The flip to second and the throw to first, and the Saints turn the double play. Reliford put the ball right where he wanted it and got the double play he needed. Two down in the top of the first inning.

Now batting for Atlanta is centerfielder Pedro Beltran. Beltran led Atlanta with a .323 batting average last season. He is hot so far in Spring Training, hitting over .400 in a handful of at-bats.

Reliford gets ready on the mound, winds up, and delivers. The pitch to Beltran is laced into the gap in right-center field. The Saints centerfielder tracks it down and throws it back to the infield, and Beltran is on second base with a double.

Beltran jumped on the first pitch from Reliford. Another change-up. It doesn't take much for opposing batters to see what a pitcher is throwing, and Reliford needs to start throwing his fastball to get these batters off-balance. Mixing in a new pitch in Spring Training is something a lot of pitchers do, but relying on it as your only pitch is something very different.

Stepping to the plate is the Atlanta clean-up man, their rightfielder Luke Withers. Withers, a big righty, hit thirty-three home runs last year. He led Atlanta and was fourth in the league in that category. He has only one hit thus far in Spring Training, a single in Atlanta's second game last week.

The pitch to Withers. A curveball on the outside corner for strike one. Reliford has to be careful with that outside pitch, Withers has those long arms, and he likes to extend them and drive the ball the other way. And when he gets a hold of one, it travels.

Reliford winds and delivers. And Withers crushes it. A high drive to deep right field. Withers got all of that one. A no-doubt home run and Atlanta is leading two to nothing over the Saints. Looks like Reliford tried to throw one past Withers, but he kept the pitch over the plate, and in a bit of unintended foreshadowing, Withers did what he likes to do and extended his arms, and hit that ball high over the right field fence. Reliford can't put offspeed pitches out there like that and not expect them to get hit.

Not the start the St. Petersburg Saints fans were expecting from their ace. In four batters, Reliford hasn't thrown any pitch over eighty miles an hour, and he is trying to baffle hitters with a mix of change-ups and curveballs.

Now batting for Atlanta is first baseman Fred Uzhen. Uzhen, a lefty, played last season for Detroit. In his career, he is one for thirteen against JaMark with six strikeouts. Reliford needs to get out of this inning without any more damage.

Reliford looks in for the sign. He winds and delivers. A curveball inside, fouled off by Uzhen. 0 and one now on the Atlanta first baseman. Reliford appears to also be experimenting with a shorter curve than in season's past. Not quite the big 12-6 slow curve we are used to seeing.

Reliford winds and the next pitch to Uzhen is a change-up in the dirt for ball one. Now one and one to Uzhen. That pitch was barely seventy miles an hour and died before it got to home plate. We are seeing one of the hardest throwing pitchers in the league experiment with being one of the softest throwing and it is certainly an uncanny thing to witness.

Uzhen steps out of the batter's box, tightens his batting gloves, and steps back in. Reliford looks for the sign, winds, and here is the pitch. Uzhen swings and hits a lazy fly ball to center. It is caught, and we go to the bottom of the first with the Saints down two to nothing."

CHAPTER 45

After escaping the first inning, JaMark further struggled in the second frame, allowing two more runs and four more hits. Fortunately, the Saints scored three runs of their own in the bottom of the second to make the score five to three. Although JaMark was scheduled to pitch three innings, Hiroki Montana inserted a relief pitcher an inning earlier than he planned in order to minimize the damage and keep the game close. After a back-and-forth game, promising rookie catcher Beau Kesey delivered a game-winning double in the bottom of the ninth to salvage a ten to nine victory sending the Saints and their fans home happy.

JaMark again avoided any postgame interviews or questions following the game, leaving the clubhouse as soon as possible and driving directly to his team-sponsored condo. Again, he swallowed more than the recommended dosage of pain killers to ease the pain of a shoulder that continued to hurt.

Over the next week, JaMark appeared in two more games where he failed to reach eighty miles per hour on any team radar gun. Following his fourth poor pitching performance, people who watched baseball started to ask if anything was wrong with JaMark Reliford. Although his pitching motion was the same and his arm speed was the same, the ball was not traveling as fast from his hand to home plate as it once had. Even his curveball, which in years prior had an incredible curving motion and exceptional rotation, was far less effective, deceiving only the least experienced batters.

Team reporters and other media who followed the team during Spring Training began to question JaMark's personality changes as well as his ability. Never in his years in professional baseball did JaMark avoid interviews. Team reporters started asking his teammates what they thought was wrong with the all-star, left-handed pitcher. In defense of their teammate, JaMark's teammates told reporters JaMark was rusty and cited timeless clichés that Spring Training results didn't matter, and that JaMark would be ready by the start of the season when games counted. Behind closed doors, JaMark's teammates weren't so sure the reigning best pitcher in baseball would remain so.

A week before Opening Day, JaMark had yet to pitch well. He lasted only three innings once and was pulled from another game after giving up four runs and getting no one out. The commotion over his slow start had grown to a full cacophony with radio talk shows, debate shows, websites, and the rest of sports media postulating and prognosticating over his poor performances.

JaMark knew the worst fears of the fans, his teammates, and the team were true. Although he wouldn't say it, he knew his career was over. He knew the gift he was given years ago under the old tree at the crossroads was taken back by the man in the black suit, tie, and matching top hat. He also knew the amount of pain killers he had to take to sleep through the night was growing. Yet the pain persisted.

On the last day of Spring Training, on a day most of the team and the coaching staff made their final road trip to Fort Lauderdale, JaMark convinced Hiroki Montana to allow him to stay behind to work on "personal issues." The Saints manager and coaches were out of ideas on what was wrong with their ace pitcher and allowed JaMark's request.

CHAPTER 46

When he arrived at the Spring Training complex in mid-morning, the Florida weather was already hot and humid. Despite a temperature in the low nineties, JaMark began running around the minor league practice field. He ran three laps along the perimeter of the field from the outfield to home plate before he noticed Dusty Polichardo sitting alone in the first base dugout. JaMark continued running, knowing the old pitcher was watching him.

JaMark ran two more laps around the field before slowing down between home plate and Polichardo's dugout. JaMark saw the old pitcher stand up and walk towards him. After his experiences with Polichardo the previous two springs, JaMark didn't know what to expect from the eccentric ex-player, but he knew it would be rude if he didn't at least acknowledge his presence.

"Hey, Dusty," JaMark said cautiously, as he wiped the sweat from his forehead.

Polichardo approached with his usual waddle, his head down and his hands in the pockets of his uniform pants as he approached JaMark.

"He won, didn't he?" the enigmatic veteran asked, still looking at the ground.

JaMark looked at the old man with a puzzled look. "Who won?"

"You know who," the old man replied, his eyes still focused on the dirt and rocks of the infield. "He found a good one in you. I was impressed. I only lasted one season. But eventually, he takes it away from everyone. Then your soul is on his time."

JaMark looked at Dusty. He didn't know whether to be

confused or surprised.

"I knew it was only a matter of time," Dusty continued. "You hung in there longer than I expected. I was impressed with your smarts. You did well."

JaMark looked at the short round man in front of him. Polichardo still hadn't looked up at JaMark. JaMark wanted to keep denying anything was wrong, tell Polichardo he had no idea what he was talking about, and walk away. But he had a feeling the old man would see right through the lies.

"You know?" JaMark asked.

"Young man," the old pitcher said, finally raising his head and looking at JaMark, his green eyes connecting directly with JaMark's, "I have always known. You are not the only one who made a deal, you know."

JaMark stood silent, almost in a state of shock. He thought about his earlier encounters with Polichardo and wondered if the man's eccentricity was an act.

"Let's sit," the old man said. "This is usually the toughest time."

JaMark followed as Dusty made an about-face and waddled towards the dugout he was sitting in moments earlier. The old man found a seat in the middle of the bench. JaMark sat a foot away to his left.

"It was bound to happen eventually," Dusty said. "He always collects. First, he gives, then he takes back, then he takes all. The hardest part is the wait after the gift is gone. Knowing he is coming to collect and bring you with him. Knowing one day you will see him again. But you never know when. It will drive you crazy. That's the reason I am how I am. The doctors called it post-traumatic stress disorder because my career was so high and then so low overnight. But it was him. I know the waiting and anticipation made me lose a marble or two."

"How did it happen?" JaMark asked. He was still amazed there were others. Not only distant others, but another who was also a Saint.

"It was the early '50s," the old man started. "I was pitching well in the minors. I played for a team from Houston.

They were a minor league city then. My manager had me pitching so often my arm went dead. Couldn't feel a thing. Nothing. Won a bar bet by hammering a nail into my shoulder and not screaming. I couldn't feel and couldn't pitch. I had to leave my team and go home without ever seeing the Majors."

"I was crushed," Dusty continued. "Devastated. Ever since I was a kid, baseball was all I had and all I wanted. One night, a year or so after my arm went dead, I was sitting in a bar in South Texas, a small, smoky, seedy joint near my hometown. I was from a poor, small border town. Maybe you've been. Maybe not. Anyway, this bar was not the type of place for women and children, nor was it where professional baseball players should be. It tried to be a jazz bar, but too many bad seeds took root there. I was a regular. It was a good place to forget things. One night, a man said he recognized me and started buying me drinks. Whiskey, beer, more than one tequila shot. The next thing I knew, I was wandering the streets drunk as a skunk and as wasted as yesterday's diapers."

Dusty smiled as he tried to pass a bit of humor into his story, but JaMark listened too intently to return the smile or appreciate the humor.

"I must have passed out in an alley," Dusty said, "because I fell asleep in a pile of garbage. When I woke up, or rather when I was woken up, I saw the face of the man I will never forget. He was a tall, pale, skinny white man, and very well dressed. He wore an all-black zoot suit, a string tie, and an all-black hat. Never seen anyone like him before. He was very out of place for my town. He asked me one question. One question I never should have answered. *¿Quieres lanzar la pelota otra vez?* – 'Do you want to throw the ball again?'

"I never should have said yes. But I did."

"What happened then?" JaMark asked. He was hanging onto Dusty's every word, noting how similar their experiences were.

"Everything I wanted happened," Dusty answered. "I pitched the next year in the Mexican League and won the MVP. The season after that, when Major League Baseball recognized the Mexican League as a legit Minor League, the scouts came flying down in droves. I couldn't pitch a game without seeing ten or more scouts. They were all there. They all saw me. I didn't even pitch half that season in Mexico before a man from New York City gave me my first contract. I played for Minor League teams in Denver, San Francisco, Amarillo, and New Orleans in my first year before I made it to the Saints.

"But when I was in New Orleans, he visited me. He always wore that sharp zoot suit with the black hat. I'll never forget that. He told me to praise him. For him to be *mi dio*. I liked how you used his name in interviews. I just pretended I didn't speak English, which wasn't completely a lie as my English wasn't very good back then. But I could have thanked him.

"I pitched that season in the Minors, then in Mexico again over the winter. Then in March, I went to my first Spring Training. No one knew I was going to make the team. Not even me. But I did. I had a great year. Rookie of the Year, All-Star Game. Pitched in the World Series versus New York – Games one, four, and then in relief in Game seven. I was smokin'. Struck out Hank McGood to end it. Highlight of my life."

"But also my worst day."

"We drank a lot after the game. Partied all night. I had a few too many drinks and talked to a reporter I adored. She asked me about being a champion. I told her it felt great. She told me my story was incredible and asked who I would thank the most. I was so drunk I didn't even think. I named everyone in my family, my friends, even a priest I hadn't talked to in years. But not the man in the zoot suit."

JaMark could see Dusty's eyes tearing up as he continued.

"Just before Christmas that year, he came to visit. He likes to do that. Visit around Christmas. Told me it makes him feel better to take his gift back before we get gifts from family. That's what he did to me. He took it back. My arm hurt just like I bet yours does every night."

JaMark looked at his left shoulder. He was so entranced by Dusty's story, he forgot about his arm and his nightly pain.

Dusty continued, telling JaMark about his failed attempts to play baseball after he lost his talents. He talked about his own horrible Spring Training, his eventual release, and his attempts to resurrect his career in Mexico. For JaMark, the story was too real.

"Five years later, by the time I was thirty-two, I was out of baseball," Dusty finished. "It was a horrible time for me. Baseball was all I knew. Until I found drugs. From the late-'60s to the mid-'80s, I was into one drug or another. Sometimes more than one. LSD, PCP, angel dust, acid, shrooms, coke, uppers, downers, roofies, smack, crack, and of course, weed. I was gone to the world. I just wanted the man in the black zoot suit to take me. But he never did. And as you can see, he still hasn't. For fifty years, he has tormented me."

Dusty's story scared JaMark. Baseball was his life as well. Baseball kept him stable and sane. He thought about the pain killers he was taking. JaMark wondered if they counted as drugs. They weren't as bad as what Dusty said he had done. At least JaMark didn't think they were.

"When was the last time you saw the Devil?" JaMark asked.

Dusty paused for a minute and stared into the empty baseball field. A minute turned into two. Two turned into three, which turned into four. Moments after the four-minute mark, Dusty looked at JaMark.

"It has been a while," he told the younger pitcher. "*El Diablo* used to visit much more often. Once every two years, at least. Just to say hello. I don't think I have seen him in at least five years. But he still haunts me every day."

Dusty wiped the tears from his eyes and turned his attention towards the setting sun beyond the left field fence. They had been sitting in the dugout for hours. Soon, the team bus would return from its trip carrying JaMark's teammates and coaches. JaMark sensed Dusty would much rather keep to himself and didn't want to see the bus and the team inside of it litter the serene setting with hustle, bustle, and noise.

"What about you?" he asked JaMark. "When was the last

time you saw him? Was he still wearing the zoot suit?"

JaMark took a deep breath. He still hadn't told Betsy about the day in Rosedale before the previous Christmas when the Devil came to her door. But he told Dusty about the Devil's visit and his own fear. He not only told Dusty about that visit, but he told the old pitcher everything, from the crossroads to the Devil's bargain.

"He gave you a way out of the deal?" Dusty said. "I am surprised. He must have been impressed with you. I am sure he will be back soon. He will be back for your soul. JaMark, I wish you all the best, but I doubt there is any way you can strike him out. You know that. I'm sorry, JaMark, I really am. If you are lucky, he won't make you wait fifty years as he has done to me."

Dusty put his hand on JaMark's knee as a sign of comfort, knowing his words offered little. In the distance, the two cursed pitchers saw the team bus arrive in the stadium parking lot, signaling the end of their long talk. JaMark felt relieved at the sight of the bus. He was glad he talked with Dusty, even if the conversation ended on a depressing note. He was also glad he was not alone. There were others. Unfortunately, if they were all like Dusty, they were scarred with paranoia and distress. JaMark didn't want to be that way.

After exchanging an embrace and farewells, the two men with the same dark secret went their separate ways. As he left the field and walked towards his arriving teammates, JaMark wondered if he would ever see Dusty Polichardo again, and more importantly, he wondered if the old man would ever find peace.

CHAPTER 47

Despite his horrible spring performances, JaMark was on the Saints roster on Opening Day. When asked, his teammates wrote off his early struggles to "spring rust" and were confident he would be back to all-star form by the first game of the regular season.

Their confidence was ill-placed. In his first start on the second day of the season on the third day of April in his fourth season as a big leaguer, JaMark allowed five runs and only retired six batters. The symmetry would continue as he allowed six runs in four innings in his second start and seven runs in three innings in his third. Whereas weeks earlier his poor pitching performances were masked by sunshine and the eternal hope of Spring Training, during the regular season, JaMark's lack of velocity and effectiveness were exposed for the whole world to see.

Six weeks into the season, JaMark had yet to pitch well, losing almost every game he pitched in. As a result, Saints manager Hiroki Montana demoted JaMark to the bullpen where he would pitch in relief when called. Although he hadn't been a relief pitcher since his rookie year, JaMark took the demotion in stride, knowing his removal from the starting rotation was best for the team.

In the second month of his fourth season in the Major Leagues, JaMark continued to struggle. He lost his first relief appearance, giving up a game-losing hit to Philadelphia. He also nearly lost his second.

In the second week of May versus last-place Texas, JaMark came in during the seventh inning with a thirteen to four lead. He finished the game for the Saints but allowed six runs in three innings for a final of thirteen to ten. In a post-game interview, he thanked every deity except for the Devil that the wind was blowing into the stadium and turned what would have surely been a game-winning grand slam for Texas into a deep fly ball to the centerfielder and a victory for the Saints. JaMark celebrated his lone win with the same postgame ritual he had after every other game that season – he took half a bottle of pain killers, chugged a glass of milk, and went to sleep.

On May 8th, on his twenty-seventh birthday, JaMark walked into Hiroki Montana's office before the first game of a long homestand in St. Petersburg. JaMark knew he couldn't keep costing the team runs and knew there were pitchers in Buffalo, Mobile, and possibly even Wyoming who could help the team more. In a league where most teams were nearly even in talent with one another and every year ended in a race for the pennant, JaMark knew the Saints couldn't keep a pitcher who would never get back his fastball.

Like his Spring Training office, Hiroki Montana's regular season office was decorated with several items from Japanese baseball culture. JaMark assumed the "Montana" jersey hanging in the office was from the manager's days in the Japanese League, as the advertisements on the shoulder were not akin to those on an American-style jersey. A samurai sword was mounted above Montana's desk, and a mural of a Japanese stadium hung on the opposite wall.

"Mr. Montana," JaMark said as he sat in a seat at the desk opposite his manager, "I have a problem. It's obvious I have not been pitching well this year. I am letting the team down. The bottom line is that things are going on in my life that I don't know how to explain. I just feel like I've lost control."

Hiroki Montana sat up in his seat as JaMark spoke. He leaned forward, placing his hands together in front of him on his desk.

"JaMark," the manager said, "we know. As a responsible team leader, we wanted you to come to us. We have seen you struggling. I am familiar with your success as I watched you do well when I was in Japan. You are part of the reason I took this job. Now watching you perform poorly is my biggest challenge.

I know you have a pain in your shoulder that you have been hiding. We spoke to Dusty Polichardo after Spring Training. He told us."

Fear suddenly seized JaMark. How much did Dusty tell him, JaMark wondered. He hoped the old pitcher did not tell them about the Devil. JaMark thought their conversation was in the utmost secrecy. But then again, JaMark thought, everyone knows Dusty is slightly off his rocker, and he wasn't sure anyone would believe the eccentric veteran even if he did tell them about the Devil.

"I understand your mind has been elsewhere. This is understandable," Montana continued. "Drug addiction is a horrible weight to have around your neck. I managed a pitcher in Tokyo who overused pain pills until he finally had surgery. His honor kept him pitching until the pain was too much to bear."

JaMark let out a small sigh of relief. He was glad Dusty only told them about the pills. He was actually glad Dusty had mentioned it, as deep down, he did know that half a bottle each night was too much, though he didn't know what else to do. He thought about how miserable he was years ago when he needed alcohol to get through the day. Needing pain killers had gotten almost as bad.

"We have two options," Montana said. "We can either put you on the injured list or send you down to the Minors. The choice is yours. If you have pain, surgery might be inevitable. But many pitchers have come back and been as good, if not even better. Right now, you cannot help us."

JaMark liked Montana's directness usually, but not that day. That day, he wanted a more emotional, caring manager, one who would let him down easy. But JaMark also understood being easy on players doesn't win championships, and Montana's job was to win championships. Knowing neither time in the Minors nor surgery could help him, JaMark didn't even consider the options.

"I need to leave the team for a while," JaMark replied. "I need time by myself. I will see a doctor if it doesn't get better, I promise."

181

Montana stood up and walked around his desk towards JaMark. He placed his right hand on JaMark's right shoulder. Hiroki was tall, slightly over six feet, but was still a few inches shorter than JaMark.

"In my hometown," Montana said, "we have a saying: 'a man is only as strong as his family.' You are strong, JaMark Reliford. Sometimes a man should not fight battles alone. Many samurai did that, but they are all dead. That is why. But if you must walk the lonely road, I wish you good luck and a swift return."

JaMark thanked Hiroki Montana, shook the Japanese veteran's hand, and attempted a small bow before walking out of the manager's office. He wasn't sure the bow was entirely appropriate or correctly executed, but it felt like the right thing to do.

As the Saints players took the field for batting practice and other assorted stretches and limbering activities, JaMark stayed in the locker room and quietly packed his equipment bag, stuffing it with four years of memories and innumerable friendships, cheers, and well-wishes. But the cheering and well-wishing had stopped, and now he wanted to leave as fast as he could.

JaMark nearly finished packing his cleats, socks, and other equipment when he felt a hand on his shoulder. He turned to see the five teammates who had been on the Saints since JaMark's first day in the Major Leagues. Behind them were the rest of his Saints teammates. Each walked up, shook JaMark's hand, embraced him, and wished him good luck. Many also told him they wanted him back on the team soon. Others offered support, telling JaMark to call or contact them if he needed anything. By the end of the line, JaMark was overwhelmed by feelings of family and camaraderie, and a single tear dropped from his right eye.

"Thank you," JaMark said. "After some great years, I have had a very rough time lately. I want to thank all of you for your support, whether on the field or off of it."

His teammates clapped, and many spoke words of

encouragement.

"I guess I should be open and tell you guys the cause of all this," JaMark continued, carefully choosing his words. "During the offseason, I hurt my shoulder lifting furniture into my new house. I heard a pop but didn't think anything of it. When I reported to Spring Training, I was fine. Then I started pitching. Nothing has been the same. The pain in my shoulder has been so bad I started taking pain killers. I'm on them every day now. Needless to say, I have a lot of things to figure out. But I do hope to be back soon."

If only it was as simple as an addiction to pain killers, he thought to himself.

JaMark wiped away the tear.

After the hugs and handshakes ended, JaMark left the stadium. He called Betsy, informed her he was on his way back to Chicago, and told her what happened in the locker room. She knew he wasn't pitching well, and knew about his shoulder and the pain. He had even told her about the Devil's deal, although he did not mention that the man in the black suit, tie, and matching top hat was in her house. As much as Betsy helped and stood with JaMark, the idea that Satan made himself comfortable in her home might be unforgivable.

JaMark also never mentioned his pill habit. That was also too much for him to admit. Betsy never knew him as an addict, and he wanted to keep that side of him away from her.

CHAPTER 48

As JaMark drove from St. Petersburg, Florida, to his new home in the suburbs of Chicago, Illinois, memories of baseball and his success in the game played through his mind. He already missed the teammates, the camaraderie, and the closeness he developed with each group of strangers he shared clubhouses with during his baseball journey. He thought about the people he wanted to stay in touch with, people such as Barry Carusowitz, his first friend, and now a successful Minor League manager. He thought of Dusty Polichardo, a man with whom he had a deep connection and a man he wanted to see again, albeit not under the same negative circumstances.

He also thought a lot of Betsy, their life, their new home, and how he was going to pay the bills. He felt broken, useless, and less than the man he was when he could provide for the people who mattered most.

Immediately after their game that night, as JaMark crossed the Georgia border into Tennessee, the Saints released a statement informing the league, fans, and the sports world their star pitcher was placed on the sixty-day injured list and had left the team for "personal reasons".

The next morning, only six hours after the team's statement, itinerant Minor League baseball writer Jennifer McDavidson, who years earlier wrote the only in-person recap of JaMark's perfect pitching performance in Wyoming, submitted a freelance article for a sports gossip website claiming JaMark's absence was drug-related. The website published the article without question or fact-checking, as JaMark was a celebrity, and his struggles were the subject of many sports conversations. The editorial team knew even if the story was factually incorrect, the website would receive hundreds of thousands of page views and see a boost in advertising revenue.

"Major League Pain Addict: All-Star Pitcher on Pills" the article read.

Since writing about JaMark in Wyoming, McDavidson spent years trying to make baseball writing a career. Although she occasionally submitted articles to the official websites of Major League and Minor League Baseball, she was often forced to freelance for a local deep-sea fishing guide to pay the bills. But with her latest article on JaMark, McDavidson struck gold. While covering Spring Training, she spoke with and quoted a nighttime pharmacist at JaMark's most frequent Spring Training drug store. The pharmacist, in an attempt to grasp fifteen minutes of fame, stated the once-star pitcher was a frequent customer and even gave the opportunistic writer an alleged security photo of JaMark buying pain killers to accompany her article.

Unbeknownst to JaMark as he drove back to Chicago, the sports media machine took the story and churned out rumors, innuendos, theories, and conspiracies about JaMark, his sudden rise to fame, and his even more rapid fall from grace. While McDavidson appeared on nearly every sports talk show, increasing her own fame, pundits proclaimed the discovery marred all of JaMark's accomplishments, while others argued in his defense, asking if anyone knew when he started taking the pills and blamed the Saints overuse of their all-star pitcher for the pain that led JaMark to seek out drugs.

When he finally arrived at his home, JaMark was ambushed by reporters and media types who found his address, but couldn't find him during his drive. Although he wanted to keep his addiction away from her, Betsy continued her habit of reading every article she could about JaMark. After JaMark brushed past the horde of reporters, Betsy was waiting inside to ask why he hadn't told her about his addiction. But JaMark refused to tell her anything of the sort.

Within days, every media member JaMark knew was calling him asking for an "exclusive" interview. JaMark repeatedly refused the media. While some media members fled after JaMark's refusal, two members of the Chicago sports media did not respect JaMark's privacy nor his story. Until Betsy filed a restraining order, they pestered JaMark every time he left his house, making his trips outside difficult and turning his new home into a prison.

Inside the house, JaMark felt lonely, remorseful, and in a general malaise. He stopped playing baseball to prevent his arm from hurting, reducing his need to take pills. But he also stopped doing anything else. He spent hours in front of the television, watching reruns of syndicated sitcoms and recycled reality shows. He barely ate, and when he did, he indulged on cupcakes and breakfast pastries. Occasionally Uncle Rufus, who had taken residence in the couple's basement, would join JaMark to keep him company, but Rufus was often busy with his new place of employment. After moving to Chicago, Rufus found work at The Recycling Plant, a landscaping company that found better places for unwanted or uprooted greenery.

As he became a more permanent fixture on the couch, depression and anger again wrapped JaMark as they had when he first lost his baseball ability after high school. For the first time in their several year relationship, JaMark became antagonistic towards Betsy. After their initial confrontation the day he arrived, Betsy tried several other times to learn why he never told her about the pills. Her efforts ceased a month after JaMark's return, when on an early June evening, JaMark threw a lamp across the living room in anger. Although the lamp landed on the other side of the room far from his girlfriend, JaMark knew he scared Betsy. JaMark also knew he was hurting the woman he loved and that he was quickly losing control. But he was lost and didn't know how to change.

By the end of July, after JaMark passed his second month on the couch, he could sense Betsy's compassion turning to impatience. Like the sports world, she wanted to know what was next for JaMark. Unlike the sports world, she didn't care if it was baseball or something, anything, else. He knew she wanted to help, and she wanted him to be himself again. He also wanted to be himself again, but he felt himself slipping, constantly thinking about the Devil and the downward spiral Dusty warned him about.

After a summer of inactivity, JaMark finally ventured out of the house on the first Thursday after Labor Day. He had not been outside in weeks but decided that morning it was time for a walk. He waited for Betsy to leave for work then dressed himself in a hoodie to cover his face from fans or curious onlookers. With his head hung low, he walked out into the cool, fall, Illinois air. He walked out of his neighborhood to the center of town. He walked past shops and offices and shoppers and officers. He walked aimlessly for hours.

Late in the afternoon, JaMark stopped in front of a local lounge and liquor store. His curiosity piqued as he admired the bottles in the window and the neon signs displaying several selections of beer. He hadn't enjoyed a sip of alcohol since making his deal with the Devil. He remembered his reaction to his last drink but now wondered if the foul taste was the Devil's doing. The allure of a drink or two was too strong to pass up. JaMark entered the lounge, sat at the bar, and ordered a beer. The familiar taste provided a relaxing feeling. His troubles began to melt away as he drank a second, third, and sixth beer.

Hours later, the happy hour regulars began to file in for their evening libation. Not wanting to be recognized, JaMark paid his fare and stumbled out of the lounge before the crowd filled the establishment. He forgot how the comforting numbness of alcohol quickly led to the inhibited stumbling of drunkenness. He had to catch himself on the wall of the establishment after his first few steps out of the bar. After he recovered his motor function, JaMark began the long walk home as sunset, drunkenness, and a lack of direction turned his journey from a saunter to an excursion.

CHAPTER 49

When JaMark returned home hours later, he had mostly walked off the effects of the alcohol. He was more tired than drunk. He opened the door to find Betsy waiting. She was sitting on the same couch he spent days on during the last few months. He saw the trail marks of tears on her face. His emotional fragileness caused a similar trickle of tears to fall from his own face. He walked to the couch, sat next to Betsy, and buried his face in his hands. The weight of depression and the fear of the Devil caused more tears. He felt Betsy wrap her arms around him.

"JaMark, talk to me," Betsy pleaded. "I want to help."

Minutes later, after the tears dried on both of their faces, JaMark removed his head from his hands, pulled slightly away from Betsy, and looked at her. "I don't think you can," he said. "I'm waiting. Then it's over. It's all over."

Betsy pulled him closer as fresh tears began to fall down both of their faces.

"I want everything to be back the way it was," he said. "I want to play again. I don't want the pain. I want us to be happy. Betsy, I am afraid of him. And I am afraid of me. I don't want to be what I was before he came."

JaMark let his tears flow on to Betsy's shoulder. He sniffled a few times.

"I'm afraid, Betsy," he said. "I'm afraid I will fall back to what I was before," JaMark said. "I was horrible."

"This," JaMark pointed to his left arm, "this made me who I am."

Betsy sat up and placed her arms on his shoulders. She stared at him.

"No," she said, her right hand moving to his chest.

"Your heart made you who you are."

Betsy's voice grew in intensity.

"This time you're different," she said as she lifted JaMark's chin with her fingertips.

He looked up at her.

"How?" he said.

"This time, you have me," she replied, "and I don't care about your arm. I care about you."

JaMark tried to smile as Betsy wiped away his tears. He never felt so strongly for her. He knew she was exactly what he needed in his life. But all of his hopes of optimism were overshadowed by his fear that their life together could end. All because of a bad decision he made before they met. He thought that was unfair to Betsy. He wanted to be what he thought she deserved.

"Betsy," he said as he tried to regain his composure, "remember the strange former ballplayer I told you I encountered every spring?"

"Yes," Betsy replied.

"Well," JaMark continued, "I didn't tell you I talked to him this year. There was a reason I couldn't tell you. He…"

JaMark paused, overcome with emotion again. Betsy wrapped her arms around him and rubbed his back.

"Take your time, JaMark," she said. "I'm here."

JaMark took another deep breath, sat up, and grabbed both of Betsy's hands.

"His name is Dusty. He also made a deal with the Devil," he said quickly. He took another deep breath and continued slowly, ensuring he told Betsy every detail. "He told me on the last day of Spring Training. We talked for hours. He said he made a deal with the Devil fifty years ago in Mexico after he hurt his arm. Betsy, his story was just like mine."

JaMark looked Betsy in the eyes and took another deep breath. He could see her eyes were again beginning to water.

"He went mad, Betsy. The Devil has tormented him for over fifty years. I don't want that for me, for you, for us. We can't live like that. I have no idea what to do. I don't know. That's what I was worried about all these months. I was thinking not about me, not about baseball. I was thinking about us."

Both crying, the couple wrapped themselves in a comforting hug.

"We have to do something," Betsy said as they relaxed their embrace. "There has to be a way."

"I don't know if there is," JaMark said, choking back tears. "Dusty didn't know. He said the Devil drove others mad in suspense before he took their soul."

"JaMark," Betsy said moments later with a glimmer of hope and enthusiasm, "I think you should go see a preacher. I found a good one a few weeks ago in a new church downtown by the grocery store. I've been going every Sunday. He knows who you are, and he asked why he never sees you. I think if we talked to him, he might be able to help."

JaMark tried to smile again. "Betsy, that's a good idea," he said. "I'm sure he could help."

Their moment of hope was interrupted by a familiar voice.

"I hate to tell you different, but ain't no Chicago preacher gonna help you with a Mississippi Devil."

The couple turned towards the kitchen, surprised to see Uncle Rufus walking towards them with a rye bread sandwich and a glass of milk.

"Sorry, I came home from work while y'all were huggin'. I heard cryin' and figured something was wrong, so I stayed in the kitchen for a bit after I made my dinner." Uncle Rufus took another bite of his sandwich and a swig of milk.

"JaMark, I had a feeling you went to those crossroads, didn't you?" Uncle Rufus said. "I always thought it, but I never could be sure."

JaMark looked at Uncle Rufus. "Yes, sir," JaMark replied, unsure how Uncle Rufus knew about the crossroads.

Uncle Rufus shook his head.

"When I was young, we used to talk about those dirt highways. Heard all sorts of stories of bluesmen and other wayward souls losing their way there."

"Can you help him?" Betsy interjected.

Uncle Rufus took another swig of milk, nearly finishing his glass. "Ain't but one person can help him," he said. "They say there's a little old woman who lives by those crossroads who knows the mojo hand. They say she danced with the Devil and left him on the altar. Ain't never seen her myself, but I heard she is there. JaMark, you need to go back to those crossroads, and you need to find her."

JaMark shuddered at the thought of returning to the place where his life took an incredible turn. Betsy noticed his apprehension and offered her support.

"I'll go with you," she said as she gripped his hand.

"No, you can't," Uncle Rufus said. "A man put himself in this mess, a man gotta get himself out. He made the deal. I don't know much about the Devil, but I know he don't deal with anyone but the man who made the deal."

JaMark took a deep breath, squeezed Betsy's hand, and stood up for the first time since walking in the house.

"Uncle Rufus is right, Betsy," he said, looking at Betsy. "I put myself in this. I need to get myself out, if possible. If Uncle Rufus is right, this woman can help me. I have to try. I'll start packing tonight and leave for Rosedale after the weekend."

JaMark looked at Uncle Rufus. "Thank you," he said.

"Anytime, my boy. Anytime," Uncle Rufus said before taking another bite of his sandwich, finishing his milk, and turning back towards the kitchen.

For the next two days, JaMark packed for his trip, staying focused and barely speaking. Realizing the emotional toll his situation was taking on Betsy, he made reservations the night before his departure at the finest steakhouse in Chicago. They ate well that night, trying to forget the future and celebrating their time together. Following dinner and the romance reserved for couples, JaMark slept well with his arm wrapped around the love of his life.

At eight o'clock the next morning, on a rainy Monday a week after Labor Day, JaMark's alarm rang, shattering their serenity. JaMark awoke, kissed Betsy on the forehead, and got out of bed. Thirty minutes later, he walked out of the house, put his suitcase in the trunk of his car, and tossed a backpack and an old baseball glove in the passenger seat.

As he made his way around the car to the driver's door, he saw Betsy run out the front door of their suburban home.

"JaMark, wait," she yelled. JaMark paused next to the driver's door as Betsy ran through the rain towards him. When she reached him, she threw her arms around him in a passionate embrace.

"No matter what happens," she said. "I will always love you."

"I will always love you, too," he said as they slowly eased their embrace.

"Here," Betsy said, handing JaMark a small pendant of a cross. "I don't know if this will help, but please take it."

JaMark took the cross pendant and fastened it around his neck.

"Thank you," he said. He gave her one more kiss, opened the driver's seat door, sat in the car, started the ignition, put the car in reverse, and pulled away. From the rearview mirror, he saw Betsy standing in the road, watching him drive away.

CHAPTER 50

JaMark took his time driving to Rosedale. He arrived three days later, just past midnight and barely into Thursday. When he arrived, Rosedale was quiet, and the clouds and humidity still lingered from an evening rain. He timed his arrival in Mississippi well, as he only told his grandmother he was visiting and wanted to keep his visit otherwise private.

As JaMark expected, his grandmother welcomed him and set him up in the same bedroom where he spent most of his adolescent years. The next morning, only two hours after he woke from a much-needed sleep, she asked where Betsy was. JaMark hated to lie to his grandmother, but he had an excuse planned if she asked why he arrived alone. He couldn't tell her the truth about the Devil.

"She couldn't leave Uncle Rufus," JaMark said as he finished his breakfast. "He got in trouble again. Trying to sell 'run-flat' wheels and liability insurance to wheelchair users. The judge didn't throw him in jail, as the tires were fine, but he got another six months probation. Betsy can't leave him unattended."

He knew his grandmother never approved of his uncle's get-rich-quick schemes and adventures. Pinning the blame on Rufus was an easy excuse.

"That rapscallion," his grandmother said. "Always causing mischief. One day, he'll be locked up for good, and we'll all be better for it."

After two days with his grandmother, JaMark packed clothes, his baseball glove, and food and water in his backpack. He set out under the cover of darkness to re-trace his steps to the crossroads. Unlike the last time he left Rosedale, this time, he didn't have rambling on his mind. He had a place to go.

JaMark walked along the back highways of Mississippi throughout the night and into the next day. Although he tried to keep his mind focused on the task at hand, the dusty highways and the overbearing heat brought back memories of the life he used to live – memories of uncertainty and uselessness.

JaMark was surprised at how easy the journey to the crossroads came to him. His legs carried him almost by instinct and told him when to turn down one road, make a left, turn right, and when to carry forward. Despite his inebriated and wandering state during his last journey, each tree, sign, and intersection felt ingrained in his memory.

As he did during his first walk to the crossroads, JaMark walked continuously. Instead of swigging moonshine and smoking cigarettes, during his second trip, he stopped only to sip from a bottle of water, eat a granola bar or snack cake, and relieve himself.

Once again, on the second night of his travels, JaMark arrived at the crossroads. It was the same desolate intersection of the same two weather-worn dirt highways he remembered. Still standing near the intersection was the same large oak tree, seemingly unchanged and unaffected by the power of the crossing it loomed over.

"This was where everything started," JaMark said aloud to himself.

JaMark entered the crossroads and looked at the middle, at the exact spot the Devil emerged from and made his presence felt in JaMark's life. If only he said no, JaMark thought, he wouldn't be back here trying to save his soul. He also knew if he didn't say yes to the Devil's offer, he wouldn't have ever played baseball again. He might have still been a lost and addicted mess, and he might never have met Betsy.

JaMark took a deep breath as he stood in the middle of the crossroads and looked in every direction. He saw no sign of a woman or a house or anywhere else a person could be hiding. There was nothing but trees or fields for as far as he could see. With darkness creeping over the Mississippi Delta, JaMark decided again to sit at the base of the old oak tree and attempt to sleep. He decided to wait until sunrise to continue his quest, vowing to himself to search every waking hour under every tree and through every field for the woman Uncle Rufus told him about. If he failed to find her by the night of the next day, he would return to Rosedale, drive back to the suburbs of Chicago, and spend his life waiting for the return of the tall, slender, well-dressed man in a black suit, tie, and matching top hat.

JaMark tried to ease his mind. After a bit of tossing and turning, he finally fell asleep under the old oak tree.

"Wooooooooo, wooooooooooo!"

Shortly after midnight, JaMark was awakened by a startling noise. A dense fog draped over the crossroads, limiting JaMark's vision to only several yards past the dirt highway intersection. JaMark sat up, struggling to determine the source of the noise.

"Wooooooooo, wooooooooooo!"

The noise grew louder and closer.

"Wooooooooo, wooooooooooo! Wooooooooo, wooooooooooooo!"

The noise sounded eerily like the whistle of a locomotive, but JaMark didn't recall seeing any train tracks in the area.

The noise grew louder and closer.

JaMark stood, walked from the oak tree, looked down the dirt highways in every direction, but saw nothing. He heard the noise again, closer and louder. Nervousness started to overcome him as he eased back to the old oak tree. The air filled with the noise of a locomotive whistle for the third time.

"Wooooooooooo, wooooooooooooo!"

JaMark's nervousness grew to fear as the noise approached the crossroads and he still could not surmise its source.

The loud din echoed through the crossroads once more, so loud JaMark was forced to cover his ears, close his eyes, and lower his head in an attempt to shield himself from the penetrating wail. When he opened his eyes and looked down each road again, he saw the vague outline of a man walking towards the crossroads from the opposite direction JaMark arrived from.

The man slowly progressed towards the dirt highway intersection. When he was closer, JaMark watched the man as he moved his hands to his mouth.

"Woooooooooooooooooo! Woooooooooooooooo!"

JaMark realized the sound did not come from a locomotive, but from a harmonica. The tone began to vary in pitch and tempo.

"Wooooo, wooooooooo. Wooo, wooo, wooo, woooooooooooooo!"

JaMark's nervousness dissipated as he realized the man was no threat. As he neared, JaMark got a good look at the fellow wanderer. He was a small, elderly black man dressed in an all-white suit with a white top hat, a black string tie, and white shoes. JaMark noticed the man's opposite similarity to the Devil but considered it a coincidence as he cautiously stepped from the relative shelter of the oak tree to the corner of the dirt crossroads.

"Hey there," JaMark said to the man as they both entered the intersection.

The man blew his harmonica once more.

JaMark called out again.

"Hey!" JaMark yelled.

"Lord have mercy, boy," the man with the white suit said, finally noticing JaMark. "You ain't gotta yell. I'm right here."

"Sorry, sir," JaMark said as he walked towards the middle of the crossroads to meet the man. "I just wanted to get your attention."

"Well, you got a funny way of asking for it," the man said. "You got my attention. Now, what can I do ya for?"

"I'm looking for a woman," JaMark said.

"Son, ain't no women out here," the man replied with a smile. "You want a woman, you need to go back into town where I'm going. That's where you find a woman."

"No, no," JaMark said, "I'm looking for a woman who can help me with a deal."

The man's posture stiffened, and his eyes grew wide.

"Inga," he said to JaMark in a serious, hushed tone. "You're looking for Inga. Inga Roosevelli."

"You know her?" JaMark asked.

"Go down the way I came about a mile. Look to the left. Your nose will tell you where to go from there," the man answered.

"Thank you," JaMark said.

"Oh, and one more thing," the man replied.

"Yes?"

"Tell her Sonny Boy sent you," the man concluded. The stranger in the white suit, white top hat, black string tie, and white shoes tipped his hat towards JaMark, turned towards Rosedale, and continued his slow walk.

From the middle of the crossroads, JaMark watched the man continue on his way, letting out another wail from his mouth harp.

JaMark turned towards the direction the man came and began his own walk. After a few steps out of the intersection, JaMark took a look back, curious to see if he could see the small man with the white suit through the prevailing mist. Although the sound of his harmonica still echoed, the man was nowhere to be seen, vanishing into the mix of fog and darkness.

CHAPTER 51

Though he could barely see through the thick midnight fog, JaMark walked the dirt highway from the crossroads away from Rosedale. Almost half an hour later, a familiar smell wafted in the air and caught his attention. He remembered the old man in the white suit said to look left after a mile, but JaMark wasn't sure how far a mile was. But JaMark also remembered the old man said to follow his nose, so JaMark thought it best to follow that part of the man's directions and head toward that familiar aroma that permeated the night air.

JaMark stepped into the cotton field on the left side of the dirt highway, where the smell was strongest. He thought if he was going in the right direction, perhaps he would find a trail to the woman's house. Unfortunately, the thick fog cloaked any semblance of a path, leaving JaMark to the fate of his other senses. He took caution and walked slowly through the bristle, vines, and other assorted vegetation. The fog became thicker as he walked, but his nose still held a recognizable smell he couldn't quite place.

Fumbling through the fog-infested cotton field for what felt like forever, JaMark finally came to a clearing, albeit one he could barely see. Through the thin spread of moonlight, the former baseball player saw a building at the far end of the clearing, closest to a gaggle of trees. JaMark walked towards the building, no longer worried about tripping over cotton plants, but worried instead about who or what was in the building.

JaMark knew the smell came from the building he was walking towards. As he stepped closer, he finally placed the smell, recognizing it from his grandmother's kitchen – soul food mixed with fresh home spices – spices and flavors unique to the Delta. Solving the mystery left JaMark curious as to who was cooking in the darkest hours of the night.

Circling the building, JaMark finally found the front of the establishment. From what JaMark could see in the thick fog, the building was a house. He wondered if it was the home of the woman Uncle Rufus mentioned. JaMark hoped it was, because if it wasn't, he knew he would be trespassing, which might not be looked upon kindly in rural Mississippi.

The house was a two-story, wooden farmhouse typical of those scattered throughout the Delta. Although most of the ones JaMark had seen were in poor shape, victims of neglect and abandonment, the house he approached was in near-perfect condition, with none of the roof slats missing – missing roof slats were a trademark sign of neglect. It was painted red, with a yellow front door and two front windows centered evenly on the center of the home. Across the front of the house, in front of the windows, was a covered porch with a wooden bench and a small wooden table on the far left and a rocking chair on the far right.

JaMark walked up the few, small steps onto the front porch and looked into the window to the right of the front door. Although he saw a light on, he was hesitant to knock. He knew it was well past midnight, although he was not certain of the exact time. Unsure what to expect, JaMark took a deep breath and knocked.

JaMark was surprised to hear footsteps quickly advancing towards the door. He took three steps from the door, so he wasn't directly in front when the mystery person answered. JaMark thought how Betsy would feel if she opened the door and saw a tall, athletic man in the wee hours of the night. He would probably advise her to only open the door after she called the police or armed herself with a knife, preferably the largest one in their kitchen.

The door opened, and a short, elderly white woman with jet-black hair appeared. While she had European features, fitting of the name Inga Roosevelli, she was dressed in an African dashiki, kept her hair up with chopsticks, and wore glasses that were far too large for her face.

"Hello?" the woman calmly said as she looked up at JaMark. Her lack of surprise made JaMark wonder if late-night visitors were a regular occurrence in her home.

JaMark looked at the small woman in her eclectic outfit and wasn't sure what to say. He wasn't sure how to approach the subject of the Devil or even if she was the woman he was looking for, although he couldn't imagine many other people were awake in the area, let alone lived in the area.

"Sonny Boy sent me," he said.

"Sonny Boy?" she repeated, stepping out of the house and partly closing the door behind her as if she didn't want JaMark to see inside.

"Yes," JaMark replied. "He wore all white and played a harmonica. I met him at the intersection down the road, and he told me you were here. He said he knew you."

"Dear," the woman said, peering over her oversized glasses and looking intensely at JaMark. "Sonny Boy has been dead for fifty years."

Fear gripped JaMark. The night was too dark, he was in too deep, and he wanted to wish everything away. And now he might have been confronted by a dead man.

"So, the man I saw was ..." JaMark said, leaving the sentence open and hoping the elderly woman with the oversized glasses and jet black hair would finish his thought.

"He was probably a ghost, dear," she said matter of factly. Then she smiled.

"Don't worry about it. It happens all the time. But if he told you to come here, it was probably for a good reason. Please, let's go inside."

The woman led JaMark into the home, which JaMark discovered also doubled as a small country restaurant. Walking through the threshold, JaMark followed the old woman past the foyer and through a room that was probably once a front living room but had been converted into a dining room. It was furnished with several tables, most having four chairs and a few having six. The walls were decorated with unique, kitschy country kitchen decorations, such as signs that said, "Don't kiss the cook if you don't like garlic!" and "You can't fatten pigs with bacon alone!" On a window sill nearest the door was an upside-down flower pot painted with rainbow stripes. When she saw JaMark staring at the flower pot, the woman told him it was good luck, as upside-down flower pots never hold dead plants. JaMark smiled, unable to argue with her logic.

JaMark followed her through the dining room, and to the far right of the house. They walked through a swinging wooden door and into a kitchen, which JaMark realized was the source of the aromas he had been following from the dirt highway. JaMark looked around the kitchen and saw Inga was cooking a feast. In one large pot was black-eyed peas, in another collard greens, in a third, vast amounts of cheese and macaroni. But JaMark was most impressed with the large amount of meat she was slow-cooking. JaMark saw ribs, pork, brisket, and many other dishes typical of the area.

"I start early," the woman said. "You never can start too early when it comes to slow cooking. Those ribs have been in that oven for a few hours and should be done by the time the dinner rush arrives. Same with those briskets."

Once settled again in her kitchen, the small woman swarmed over her food and tended to the preparations. JaMark felt guilty. He had interrupted her, and she looked like she had her hands full. He stood on the far right of the kitchen, on the house's far wall, away from the kitchen apparatuses, and watched the small woman with chopsticks in her hair bounce from one dish to another, mixing and making, testing and tasting.

After twenty minutes, JaMark noticed she slowed down. Perhaps, he thought, the food was almost completely prepared and ready for cooking.

"Do I want to ask why you were at the crossroads tonight?" she said, surprising JaMark with her forwardness.

"Well, ma'am," JaMark began.

"Please," the woman interrupted, "call me Inga. It's my name, and it's what people call me. Too many people in this region were forced to call people 'ma'am' or 'sir', whether they respected them or not. I don't like it. Please, it's Inga."

JaMark nodded.

"Inga," he started again, unsure of the first-name power he was just granted, "Sonny Boy told me where you were because I asked. I was told to see you. That you would be able to help me."

As she nodded to show she was also listening, Inga walked to one of her three ovens. She cracked the oven open, letting the smell of cornbread into the room and into JaMark's nose.

"Let me guess," she said as she looked at the cornbread. "You made a deal you shouldn't have, didn't you?"

"Yes, m..." JaMark caught himself before committing a second violation. "Yes, I did," he said.

"You a musician?" Inga asked, again peering over her over-sized glasses to get a close look at JaMark. "I don't think I've ever seen you before."

"No," JaMark answered. "I am ... I mean ... I was a baseball player."

"Baseball player, huh?" Inga said. "I never heard of a baseball player making a deal around these parts. You any good?"

"I like to think I was," JaMark said. "I like to think I was one of the best in the world."

"That sounds about right," Inga said conclusively. "Come, tell me everything."

CHAPTER 52

JaMark followed Inga out of the kitchen, down a hallway, and into the small living room. The room was furnished only with a lime green, leather recliner, a small, hot pink love seat, and a small television with metal antennas, all of which appeared to JaMark as if they were made in the 1970s. There was a small window in the middle of the far wall that JaMark assumed looked out to the side of the house. As Inga took a seat on the recliner, she indicated for JaMark to follow suit on the love seat. Although it was comfortable, JaMark noticed the cushions of the love seat were stiff, as if no one had sat on them for a long time.

For the next three hours, JaMark told his story. Inga listened intently, taking only periodic breaks to check the food in her kitchen. He told her everything, from his high school stardom to his fall to his rise in professional baseball to his meetings with the Devil to his eventual loss of talent, resulting addiction, and even the details of his trip to her restaurant.

"Very interesting," she said when JaMark finally finished. She rubbed her hands together and looked down. "There is a lot to think about."

JaMark looked past Inga for a moment and looked out the window. The sun broke the horizon and was starting to rise on a new day.

"You better go to sleep, dear," the old woman said, looking at JaMark. "I have two spare bedrooms upstairs. They're small, but I think you will fit in either. Pick whichever one you'd like. There are sheets in the closet. We'll talk more after you are rested."

At nearly ten o'clock the next morning, JaMark awoke to the smells of Inga's familiar cooking. The aroma of bacon, sausage, and waffles filled the air and lured JaMark awake, similar to the dishes of the previous night. JaMark rose from the bed, utilized the facilities, and walked downstairs towards the kitchen. He found Inga engaged in cooking a full course breakfast with all the fixings. JaMark saw the table full of food, from the bacon that caught his attention to eggs, grits, biscuits, and sausage gravy.

"Good morning," Inga said as JaMark came through the hallway and entered the kitchen. "I hope you slept well."

"I did," said JaMark. "I needed that. I haven't gotten much sleep in the last week."

"Well," Inga said, "you can have yourself some good meals while you are here. We'll talk while we work. I was thinking last night about what you told me. We need to keep talking. But for now, would you be a dear and bring me a bag of potatoes from the pantry over there? Those potatoes get heavier every year I try to carry them."

JaMark moved quickly from the threshold of the kitchen to the large pantry closet in the back of the kitchen, farthest away from the wooden door that led to the dining room. He brought Inga her potatoes, then volunteered to peel them, mash them, and add the butter, milk, and other ingredients Inga requested. After he was done with the mashed potatoes, JaMark assisted with vegetables, then checked the bread, and mixed Inga's homemade coleslaw. By the time he could catch his breath from all the cooking, it was nearly noon.

"Get yourself something to eat, dear," Inga said. "After you finish, we'll be finished. Then we open for business."

JaMark sat down to his still-warm breakfast of eggs, grits, biscuits, sausage gravy, and orange juice. Even though he had eaten the same meal dozens, if not hundreds of times, something about the way Inga cooked made this breakfast the best he ever tasted. He couldn't put his finger on it or find it with a fork, but when the food hit his tongue, it tasted different. Through the entire meal, he tried to figure out why, but the meal didn't last long enough to find any answers as he ate it so quickly.

As Inga predicted, after JaMark finished, people started arriving at Inga's house. JaMark looked out from behind the swinging wooden door and saw every table in Inga's former living room filled with patrons. He watched the old woman swarm from table to table, taking care of her guests.

JaMark was amazed at Inga's ability to wait tables, prepare meals, and serve. After watching for several minutes, JaMark realized none of the patrons used a menu. They all just told Inga what they wanted. JaMark also noticed although she carried a notepad and a pen, Inga rarely wrote down their orders. They were all very familiar with each other and the food, JaMark noticed, as if they were all long-standing regulars who always sat in the same seat and ordered the same meal.

After collecting all the orders, Inga returned to the kitchen and began preparing meals from the food they made in the morning and the meat she made the night before. JaMark volunteered to assist however he could.

"You can help put together the meals," Inga said, "but I have one rule: you always stay in the kitchen. Never go in the dining room and serve my guests. They are very picky, and some have been coming here for a very long time."

JaMark thought her request was unusual, but he accepted the conditions. If Inga was going to help him with his deal, the least he could do was to help her with her meals. Over the next two weeks, JaMark discussed his life with Inga and helped every chance he could. There was a calm about him in Inga's kitchen. He felt so safe he forgot about the outside world. In Inga's kitchen, he mixed, he mashed, he baked, he battered, and he learned to make food he never made before.

CHAPTER 53

As JaMark helped, he learned a lot about Inga. The elderly woman opened up to JaMark in ways he didn't expect. During his first week in her home, Inga told JaMark that she was a widower who lost her husband, Sir Reginald Roosevelli, to a mountain climbing accident in the Himalayas in the late 1960s. According to her story, a Sherpa accidentally zipped her husband inside his sleeping bag and left him to suffocate.

"If a man can't be free from harm on the top of a mountain," she said, "I am not sure where he can be safe."

Inga also told JaMark about the couple's trip to China for the 1967 global stamp collectors' convention. According to Inga, Reginald introduced her to Buddhism during the trip, and there he decided to be part of the first rock'n'roll band to play a song on the top of Mount Everest. Upon their return to the US, he recruited his friends, saved money, and eventually made what would be their first and final trip as a group. JaMark felt bad when Inga told him that the news of her husband's demise took away her desire to see any more of the world.

The money Reginald and his band made during their brief stint as musicians led Inga to the Mississippi Delta, where she bought her restaurant. At the time, she thought houses and businesses in the area would expand in quantity and begin to fill the land bordering her old, wooden farmhouse. Unfortunately, the economic expansion never happened, and Inga's restaurant remained on the outskirts of Rosedale and the rest of the Delta. Inga smiled as she told JaMark how, after two years of struggling and numerous thoughts of closing the restaurant, a young guitar player saved her venture.

"I will never forget him," she said. "It was the winter of

1970. His name was Johnny Allen. He quietly approached the restaurant, sat on the porch bench, and played the most beautiful set of local standards I had ever heard. As he played, dozens of people walked up to the restaurant. People I had never seen before just appeared from beyond the crossroads. Since that day, the restaurant has stayed full and I've been working in the kitchen ever since with not a single day off. I get tired, but I still love it. It keeps me busy."

JaMark also received lessons in Buddhism from Inga. Although he wasn't raised Buddhist, nor had he ever had exposure to the Buddhist religion, JaMark was impressed by Inga's belief that cooking, although work, focused the mind into something constructive. Whereas he initially thought his labor in the kitchen was work, after a month studying both cooking and culture with Inga, he began to appreciate her approach to and philosophy behind the art of cooking.

JaMark was also intrigued by the library of occult literature Inga kept in the remaining upstairs bedroom. Many nights, after he finished cleaning the last of the pots and pans, he would catch Inga studying books such as *Prayers of the Blue Midnight, Witches, Warlocks, and White Wizards, Going Green on the Left-Hand Path* or other less colorful titles. One night during the second month of his stay, JaMark asked Inga why, as a practicing Buddhist, she would read such dark and malicious texts.

"There are a few things I have to keep secret from you, dear," she said with a smile. "Perhaps one day you will find out."

JaMark's conversations with Inga and his long hours in her kitchen prevented him from calling Betsy often. On the first day of his third week at the restaurant, after lunch but before dinner, while the daily brisket was slowly cooking, JaMark asked Inga if he could take a quick break and borrow her phone. Inga pointed him in the direction of the back porch, where she had an old rotary phone. JaMark was surprised there was a dial tone on the ancient device. Before he could spin the correct numbers, he felt Inga's hand on his arm.

"Be careful what you talk to her about," she said. "Things here aren't always what they seem."

JaMark wasn't entirely sure what Inga meant, but he had seen enough during the last few years to know she was serious. He nodded and returned to the ancient contraption to make his call. For over an hour, he talked to Betsy, calming her nerves, and reassuring her that he was in good hands. He told her he found the woman Uncle Rufus described, and with her help, he was getting closer to the end of his saga, although he didn't know if that was true or not. Although Betsy asked, JaMark didn't tell her where he was, nor did he mention that Inga's collard greens were slightly better than Betsy's own recipe.

JaMark called Betsy every other night throughout the fall. With Inga's permission, he rewired the phone from the old woman's back porch to his room, giving him a place to talk in private. Although it was hard being apart, JaMark never sensed any thought of infidelity, as he was busy working in the restaurant, and Betsy was busy with her job as well as trying to keep Uncle Rufus from further legal trouble. Despite Betsy's efforts, JaMark was not surprised to hear Uncle Rufus was arrested and put in jail for ten days for wiping his nose on the sleeves of unsold merchandise at a local men's clothing store. During the trial, Rufus admitted to the crime but stated that due to the Act of God of allergy season, his actions were exempt from prosecution. His defense was blown away by the store's sale on handmade handkerchiefs.

CHAPTER 54

For the next three months, from the colorful fall of October to the brisk December winter, JaMark assisted in Inga's restaurant. All day he prepped and cleaned, and all day she cooked and served. Every other Sunday, Inga went to Rosedale to get supplies and ingredients in her faded yellow 1968 Volkswagon bus. JaMark wondered what general store Inga went to, as he thought he knew everyone who frequented Rosedale. Then again, he never knew there was a soul food restaurant tucked away off the old dirt crossroads. Nor did he know there were crossroads until he found them on the night that changed his life.

As time passed, JaMark thought about home often and started to question his stay at Inga's. Although he was still learning about Buddhism and cooking and told stories about his time in baseball, JaMark began to feel antsy and impatient. Not that he didn't believe Inga, but after a few weeks of considering the consequences, he decided to challenge Inga's first rule and leave the kitchen when customers were present.

Inga often told him she told her guests about her new cook and often pointed out the meals he made. She relayed their rave reviews to him and once even kidded with him that perhaps one day he could take over the restaurant and she could retire. JaMark wondered why he couldn't learn about the customers who were learning about him.

On a cool Wednesday afternoon during the last week of November, after working on several dishes, including a huge pot of grits he was quite proud of, JaMark approached the large wooden swinging door connecting the kitchen with the dining area. He was nervous but overwhelmed with curiosity. He opened the door cautiously, poked his head outside, and hoped

Inga wouldn't see him. He saw her on the far end of the dining room, facing and conversing with a table of customers.

JaMark looked around the dining room. The patrons were oblivious to the world around them, and their eyes were occupied only with the food they were voraciously scooping into their mouths. JaMark was amazed at their food focus and culinary concentration. He was awestruck by the fact that the whole room was only eating and chewing, eating and chewing. There was no banter, no movements to and fro, no looking around, and no conversations, except with Inga. They were transfixed by food.

The attire of the guests caught JaMark's eye. Each was dressed very formally, the men in black suits and the women in long white dresses. JaMark guessed they must have come from a local church in the area, but he could not think of one that held a Wednesday morning service.

JaMark stepped out from behind the wooden door, exited the kitchen, and walked squarely into the dining room. Unfortunately for JaMark, he released the wooden door to the kitchen too soon, and it slammed shut with a loud bang. Realizing his racket, JaMark turned his head to the dining room, worried he woke the patrons from their hypnosis. Only one woman lifted her head from her meal to see the source of the racket.

JaMark saw the old woman at the same moment she saw him. She was sitting in the middle of the dining room, eating with three other women at a table for four. While the others stayed entranced in their vittles, the woman turned to see the commotion. JaMark's eyes locked with hers for a moment, and she smiled at the former baseball player.

Her face had a familiarity JaMark could not place. As he tried to remember where he knew her familiar features from, Inga walked quickly towards him and pushed him stiffly into the kitchen.

"I told you to never walk out there," she said sternly.

"The woman in the middle table," JaMark said, "I have seen her before."

"She is new here," Inga said. "What do you mean you have seen her before?"

"Her face looked familiar," JaMark replied. "But I don't know where I've seen her before."

Inga's facial expression softened from anger to concern.

"Did she gesture that she knew you as well?" she asked.

"I think she smiled at me," JaMark answered as he walked towards the oven to check on the latest loaf of bread.

"Think long and hard, JaMark," the old woman said, walking towards JaMark. "Where do you know her from? It is important."

JaMark turned towards the oven, opened it, and examined the baking bread. He closed the oven and looked back at Inga.

"I think," JaMark said. "That was Gertie Dupree. I saw her play bingo on television years ago." His voice trailed off as he finished speaking.

"I met someone here in Rosedale a few years ago," JaMark continued as he struggled to piece together his thoughts. "A competitor of hers from years earlier. A woman who acted paranoid around me. Her grandson wore a Gertie t-shirt and told me Gertie was …"

JaMark paused, hesitant to complete his thought.

"Dead," Inga finished his sentence for him. "She died a few years ago. That's why she is new here."

"I'm not sure I understand," JaMark said.

"JaMark, this is not a normal restaurant," Inga explained as she sat at the kitchen table. "No one who eats here is from here. Yet they all have something in common. Something most people would never know anything about. Something you know."

"I don't understand," JaMark said.

"They all made a deal," Inga explained. "They come here to try and undo that deal. But for them it is too late. Yet they keep coming here. The food keeps them busy. I wish I could, but I can't help them."

"Are you saying Gertie Dupree made a deal with the

Devil?" JaMark asked.

"I'm sure she did," Inga explained. "She wouldn't be here if she didn't. They don't tell their stories, but they all have that in common."

"I heard she was the best bingo player in the world," JaMark said.

"They all become the best," Inga said. "That's the part of the deal they can't refuse. You should know that."

JaMark looked at Inga. He knew she was right. Although he made his deal so he could play baseball again, he always wanted to be the best. He was as guilty as anyone else. Had he not cared so much about being on the pitching mound, he might never have fallen as he did, leaving him vulnerable for the Devil's opportunity.

After several moments of silence, Inga smiled at JaMark.

"You should get back to cooking," Inga said as she walked towards the large wooden swinging door and towards the dining room. "We're expecting a good crowd for dinner."

CHAPTER 55

O n the Sunday before Christmas, a year to the day the
Devil confronted JaMark and stripped him of his ability,
and six and a half months after JaMark walked away
from baseball, a rare winter thunderstorm soaked the Mississippi
Delta. Sheets of rain fell, and thunder rumbled through the
region. As the storm passed Rosedale and ventured east, a bolt
of lightning coursed through the sky and struck the center of the
old highway crossroads. The bolt lit the earth and caused a small
blaze. The soaked mud burned as if made from the pyre of Hell.
From the burning earth, a chasm opened where once mud stood
firm.

A tall, slender man wearing a black suit, tie, and matching
top hat rose from the hole, brushed crumbs of mud off his suit,
and walked towards the restaurant of Inga Roosevelli.

"Time to collect," the Devil said aloud.

Although JaMark had seen the restaurant full during
similar downpours, Inga was adamant the weather was to blame
for the lack of patrons that afternoon.

"It has to be the weather," she said. "There is no other
reason. We always have patrons here."

By JaMark's count, they hadn't served anyone since the
end of the breakfast rush. Inga paced the dining room,
rearranging silverware and napkin stands on every table. JaMark
remained in the kitchen, cleaning the breakfast pots, pans, and
plates. He propped the swinging door to the kitchen open,
allowing him to keep an eye on the dining room, and to
occasionally talk to Inga as she wandered and waited for the next
customer.

After finishing her third round of rearranging, a tall man
in a black suit, tie, and matching top hat knocked on the front

door of the restaurant.

"Hello?" the Devil said. "Are you open?"

When JaMark saw the Devil open the door to the restaurant, he immediately closed the swinging door and fled to the sanctuary of the kitchen.

Catching his breath and regaining his composure, JaMark peeked from behind the door. He saw the Devil take a seat in the middle of the dining room. Inga met the man and engaged him as if he were any other customer. Unlike her other customers, the Devil didn't give Inga his order immediately. JaMark strained to listen, but the noise of the downpour outside drowned out the conversation. JaMark watched Inga and the Devil converse. He saw the Devil raise his hand and say something to Inga before the old woman returned to the kitchen. JaMark was curious what the Devil said. He wondered if the Devil was there for his soul or a healthy serving of soul food.

A moment later, Inga walked through the swinging door and into the kitchen.

"What a curious man," she said. "Even though it is raining cats and dogs, and he said he arrived on foot, there is not a drop of water on him. How in God's name is that possible?"

JaMark looked at Inga with a look of concern.

"Because he is not God," JaMark said. "Inga, that's the Devil."

Inga stopped. In the three months JaMark worked in the kitchen, he never saw Inga come to a complete stop when there were customers waiting. He saw a look on her face that he had never seen before.

"All the years I have been here and all the people I have met who have made deals, I have never seen him," the elderly woman quietly said. "I didn't expect him to look like that. Are you sure?"

"That's definitely him," JaMark said. "Did he order anything?"

"Yes, he did," said the elderly woman as she tried to regain her composure. "Chicken wings, the hotter, the better. A side of greens. And a diet soda."

Chapter 55

JaMark watched Inga prepare the chicken wings. Although wings were a typical order, she prepared the Devil's wings slightly different than she did for her usual patrons. JaMark stood aside as she searched through several cabinets on the far side of the kitchen. She returned from her search with a small jar.

"What are those?" JaMark asked.

"Ghost peppers, dear," the old woman replied. "I got them from a Sikh who came through here once many years ago. He was not only in the wrong place but in the wrong time. But he did stay for lunch. He gave me these from his native land."

Inga pulled a ghost pepper from the jar. From several feet away, JaMark's eyes watered from the pepper's potency. Inga plunged the sizzling wings deep in frying oil, then soaked them in the typical hot sauce accompanied with the ghost pepper. JaMark watched as the pungent smell permeated the entire kitchen. The wings soaked in the blazing concoction as Inga prepared the rest of the Devil's food and poured his drink. JaMark was amazed the smell didn't bother Inga as she put the wings on the plate adjacent to the greens. She walked through the large swinging wooden door and brought the meal to her only customer.

JaMark watched Inga through an inch-wide opening in the large wooden door. He saw her walk into the dining room and approach the Devil's table. The Devil looked calm, JaMark thought. He wondered if the Devil realized he was nearby. The Devil had to know he was here, JaMark thought to himself. He quickly became tired of conversing with himself and asking himself questions he couldn't answer and continued to watch Inga.

Inga placed the plate in front of the Devil as she had before so many others in the restaurant. JaMark watched the Devil and Inga engage in a few moments of friendly banter. JaMark even saw Inga laugh. Although she smiled plenty of times for plenty of customers, JaMark rarely saw the old woman laugh. But she laughed for the Devil. JaMark gently closed the large wooden door and began quietly cleaning the pots and pans used for the sole lunch patron.

Several minutes later, Inga entered the kitchen.

"How did it go?" JaMark asked quietly.

"Not bad," Inga replied as she walked to JaMark and helped the clean-up effort. "He was interesting. Very charming. I can see why people fall for his approach."

JaMark glanced at Inga with a sullen look.

"Oh, sorry," she said. "On the positive side, he didn't say anything about you. I'm sure that was worrying you."

"It still is," JaMark said as he wiped down the final pan, placing it in the dishrack to dry.

"Don't worry," Inga said. She put a reaffirming hand on his shoulder. "You'll be fine. I promise."

After a few more moments of cleaning, Inga exited the kitchen to check on their only guest. JaMark decided not to watch, but instead finished wiping down the countertops, poured a glass of iced tea, and sat at the kitchen table. A few minutes later, he folded his arms on the table, placed his head on his arms, and dozed off.

"JaMark, wake up." JaMark felt the slight nudge of Inga's hand against his shoulder as he began to open his eyes. "Our guest is gone."

"He left?" JaMark asked.

"Yes," replied Inga. "He finished the meal, said my wings were the best he ever had, paid, and left. He said he needed to visit an old friend."

JaMark wondered why the Devil came to the restaurant but didn't bother to confront him. Maybe the Devil didn't know he was there. The situation confused JaMark.

"He did say he would be back tomorrow," Inga continued. "He didn't say why, but he smiled when he said it. He was surprisingly pleasant for a timeless demon."

Hours later, JaMark and Inga sat at the kitchen table through the empty dinner hours, saying little about the eerie happenings of the day. Afterward, JaMark retired to his room for the night. The Devil's unexpected afternoon visit made him both anxious and exhausted. Before collapsing on his bed, he reached for the phone on the nightstand and called Betsy. He told her about the Devil's visit to Inga's restaurant and the Devil's impending return.

"JaMark, I'm going to be there," Betsy said. "I need to be there."

"No," JaMark said. "If it happens, I don't want you to know. It needs to be just me and him. That's the way the deal is supposed to go down."

"But JaMark," Betsy pleaded. "What if I never see you again?"

"Betsy, you can drive to Rosedale," JaMark instructed. "I will see you there, no matter what. If anything happens, you will be with friends and family. As much as I want you near, you can't be here. This is my moment. I have to finish this. You will be with me in my heart. But I just can't have you here in person."

"JaMark, I am leaving for Rosedale right now," Betsy said. "I will be there waiting. I miss you, and I love you."

"I miss you, and I love you, too," said JaMark. "Good night, Betsy. I will see you soon."

JaMark hung up the phone, rolled over, and tried to sleep.

CHAPTER 56

JaMark awoke at six the next morning and met Inga in the kitchen. She had already begun scrambling eggs and cooking cornbread. JaMark started preparing the country gravy that he had grown quite good at making. Inga once told him the country gravy was a favorite of many of the patrons, and one even said he liked JaMark's recipe better than Inga's. JaMark didn't believe the comment at first, but it gave him the pride he needed to keep cooking the entrée, tweaking and tasting until even he thought it was as good as Inga's recipe.

As JaMark watched the slow boiling gravy, he shifted his focus to making his fruit salad. He cut apples, bananas, peaches, and pears and even added cherries for sweetness. Inga never told him if the patrons liked the fruit salad, but he thought it tasted good and he enjoyed making it.

By seven o'clock, JaMark and Inga were finished with their preparations. Inga also straightened the dining room, placing silverware and napkins at every seat at every table. They had the routine down to a science and always finished at the same time, moments before the first patron walked to the door.

That morning, however, on Monday, three days before Christmas, no one arrived. The restaurant was as empty as it was for lunch and dinner the previous day.

JaMark and Inga waited for their first guest. Eight o'clock turned into nine o'clock, and still, they waited. Ten o'clock came and went. At nearly eleven o'clock, Inga and JaMark both decided to make their own meals and began cleaning up the excess food, which had become cold and unappealing. Inga was not accustomed to throwing out food, as she always knew exactly how much food to prepare for the same regulars who frequented her restaurant every morning for over thrity years. As she poured the leftover eggs into the garbage, JaMark saw a tear roll down her face.

With the kitchen cleaned, JaMark and Inga were at a loss. Three meals passed, and no one visited the restaurant except for the tall, slender man with the black suit, tie, and matching top hat. While Inga sat in the dining room amidst the unused tables, chairs, forks, knives, and napkins, JaMark took a break from the kitchen to go upstairs and prepare himself for the rest of the day.

JaMark came down the stairs twenty minutes later and walked into the dining room. He glanced out the window overlooking the front yard. He could see the old dirt highway. He saw a familiar figure emerge from the cotton fields walking slowly towards the restaurant. JaMark knew it was the same ominous figure who had visited the day before – the same tall, slender man with the black suit, tie, and matching top hat. The same Devil.

As the Devil came closer to the restaurant, JaMark noticed he had something in his hand. At first, JaMark thought it might have been a guitar case. As he moved closer, JaMark realized it was not a guitar case, but a baseball equipment bag. The former big-league pitcher took a deep breath. The time had come. He was going to pitch for his soul.

"Inga," JaMark said as he found the old woman in her small living room looking out the window at the woods alongside the restaurant. "Inga, he's back."

Inga turned towards JaMark with a look of surprise.

"He's back?" she said.

Before JaMark could reaffirm, there was a knock on the door.

"Excuse me, are you open?" the Devil asked loudly to no one in particular.

Inga dashed down the hallway, through the kitchen, and out of the dining room to greet their patron. JaMark followed not far behind but stopped when he reached the swinging door to the dining room, opting to again stay in the kitchen and not face the Devil. Although hidden in the kitchen, JaMark could hear Inga speak to the Devil as there was no longer the disrupting sound of rain on the rooftop.

"Yes, sir," she answered as she entered the dining room. "We are open. Just a little slow at the moment."

JaMark heard Inga pull a chair out for the Devil and heard the shuffling of silverware and the jostling of other accoutrements. Inga made a place for the Devil nearer to the kitchen than his seat the day before.

"Thank you, ma'am," JaMark heard the Devil say as he took off his hat and sat down, the sound of his sports equipment bag clanging on the floor beside him. "The food was so good yesterday, I had to come back. I do hope you remember me."

JaMark noticed the Devil's tone seemed louder than it was the day before. JaMark wondered if the Devil was speaking not only to Inga, but perhaps to him as well.

"Of course, I remember you, dear," Inga replied. "You were the gentleman who ordered the hot wings. I never forget someone who braves the ghost pepper."

"Well, ma'am," the Devil said. "I have always had a way with ghosts."

JaMark saw Inga pause. Watching the interaction from the kitchen, JaMark remembered Inga had little experience with the Devil and his sarcastic quips. JaMark wondered if Inga thought as he did, that the Devil was the reason none of their regular patrons visited the restaurant recently.

"Would you like a plate of wings today as well?" Inga asked the Devil. "And can I get you something to drink?"

"Well, ma'am," the Devil answered. "Those wings were delicious. Probably the best I've ever had. And I've had my share of wings. But today, I would like something a little more living. May I have a pitcher, please?"

"I'm sorry, we don't serve pitchers," Inga answered instinctively, without realizing the Devil's obvious play on words.

"You soon will," the Devil said, his tone changing from sarcastic to serious. "When I have his soul. Why don't you call him out here?"

JaMark watched Inga take a step back. He knew she was unsure what to do next, and he couldn't keep her in that situation.

"I'm here," JaMark said as he opened the swinging door and walked into the dining room.

Inga and the Devil turned towards JaMark as he walked towards their table.

"JaMark, it is a pleasure to see you again," the Devil said as he rose from his seat. The Devil pulled a baseball out of his suit pocket and placed it on the table. "Are you ready?"

"Why don't we eat first?" JaMark countered. "This way, no matter what, we'll have the good times. Just like in Durham."

JaMark felt the Devil's eyes look him over. He knew the Devil could deny dining and insist they get to business, but he also knew the Devil enjoyed the volleys of a worthy foe.

JaMark sat in the chair across the table from the Devil while the Devil returned to his seat. The two men stared at each other in awkward silence for several moments before the Devil turned his glance to Inga, who stood tableside during the entire exchange.

"May I have a menu, please?" he asked. "And a glass of water."

"The same," JaMark said.

The awkward silence between JaMark and the Devil lasted several more moments before JaMark said the first word.

"So, you enjoyed the wings yesterday?" he asked the Devil.

"Best wings I have ever had," the Devil replied. "And as I told you in Durham, I am a bit of an expert in having wings."

"I remember," JaMark responded, ignoring the Devil's religious doublespeak. "The place with the great water."

"The water was good," the Devil said. "But the wings left a little to be desired. The wings here, though – the best ever. So good, I'd serve them in my own kitchen. Did you have anything to do with cooking them?"

"No," JaMark said. "There were all Inga."

"Inga," the Devil said slowly, letting each letter roll off his tongue. "Inga. A beautiful name. And a great cook. Interesting."

Chapter 56

A moment later, the door to the dining room opened, and Inga arrived with two menus and two glasses of water.

"Here you go, gentlemen," she said to the two men as she placed the glasses on the table. "And here are your menus."

JaMark and the Devil looked over their menus for a minute before looking up at Inga.

"I'll have the hot tamales," the Devil said. "Please make them red hot."

"Sure thing, dear," Inga said as she took the menu from the Devil.

"Can you please make my favorite: a peanut butter, banana, and bacon sandwich," JaMark said, realizing this would be the first time he ate in the dining room. "And a side of toasted white bread. Dry."

"Ok. Thank you," Inga said, taking the second menu from JaMark. "I'll get that right up."

Inga walked into the kitchen. JaMark watched the door close behind her before returning his attention to the Devil. For the next four minutes, the two men exchanged small talk and pleasantries on the weather, the ambience of the restaurant, and stock market investment strategies. JaMark discussed how he invested a portion of his baseball income in the top American companies and was surprised to learn the depth of the Devil's involvement in margin investing and optimal subprime loans.

Before JaMark could get any investment tips or learn any risks in the Devil's investment plan, Inga returned with the two meals.

"Here you are, gentlemen," she said, placing each respective dish in front of the person who ordered it. "Enjoy, and I will be right back with two more glasses of water."

JaMark and the Devil ate their lunches without saying much. JaMark looked up to see the Devil devouring his hot tamales as if he hadn't eaten in days. JaMark took a more methodical approach to his sandwich, eating it slow bite by slow bite. By the time he had finished half, the Devil was finished with his meal. But as JaMark continued, he realized how little hunger he had, as his appetite was pushed aside in favor of nervous anticipation. He knew the grand moment was coming, and felt it in his gut as well as in his arm. While he ate, he wondered how he would do and how is arm would feel, as he hadn't pitched or even thrown a ball in months.

"You are nervous, aren't you?" the Devil asked.

"Slightly," replied JaMark.

"You have nothing to fear," the Devil said. "Let me hit the first pitch, and it will be all over. Pitch one down the middle of the plate."

JaMark finished the last bite of his sandwich and washed it down with the last of his glass of water. The Devil's comment struck a nerve. JaMark wasn't about to back down. He grabbed the baseball off the table and stood up.

He rubbed the smooth baseball in his hands, letting its stitches run along his palms. His long fingers instinctively settled across the seams in a traditional fastball grip.

The Devil reached down and picked up the sports equipment bag.

"How sad would it be if you hurt your arm again trying to strike me out, JaMark?" the Devil asked. "How sad would it be if you hurt yourself only to fail? The pain in your shoulder would live forever, plaguing you and reminding you of your biggest failure."

The Devil's words grated JaMark, but he knew he couldn't reply. He grabbed the sports equipment bag from the demon and walked towards the kitchen. He heard the Devil behind him rise from his chair, push his chair back in, and follow.

"Behind the restaurant, there is an open grass field," JaMark said to the Devil as he pushed open the swinging door to the kitchen. "Satan, I believe it's time to go."

CHAPTER 57

JaMark led the Devil through the kitchen and past Inga as she finished cleaning the dishes she used to cook the two lunches. Through the corner of his eye, JaMark saw Inga smile at him. He remembered when he first arrived, she told him to trust her and that she would help. He wasn't sure how, but he hoped she was right. He needed as much help as he could get.

JaMark walked through the house's side door and exited to the right side of the house. He walked through the grass along the house for several paces before waiting for the Devil to also exit the house. Several seconds later, the tall, slender man with the black suit, tie, and matching top hat walked out, closing the door behind him.

"There is a good spot around the side here," JaMark said, pointing towards the grass field to the rear of the restaurant.

Along the backside of the old farmhouse was a wall with no doors. The only window was the living room window near the far right corner of the house. Although trees and cotton fields surrounded the area, immediately behind the house was an empty patch of grass approximately 100 meters wide and 100 meters deep. During one of his many talks with Inga, JaMark learned her original intent was to build a small cabin directly behind the house and convert the entire farmhouse to a restaurant. According to Inga, the land was cleared, but because of the restaurant's initial lack of business, the cabin was never built. All these years later, the old woman could never explain why she kept the land open. As JaMark and the Devil walked side-by-side to the rear of the house and faced the grass field, JaMark was thankful Inga never did build her separate cabin.

JaMark and the Devil stopped in the middle of the rear wall of the house. After JaMark placed the sports equipment bag on the ground at the Devil's feet, the Devil took off his black suit jacket and his top hat and laid them down a few feet from the wall for a makeshift home plate. The Devil then traced his finger along the cement wall. JaMark watched the Devil's finger burn a coal-black square resembling a strike zone on the back wall of the former-farmhouse-turned-restaurant.

JaMark stoically stared into the box the Devil drew on the wall. He took a deep breath and began to walk the approximate sixty feet and six inches required to create a makeshift pitcher's mound. After settling on a spot, he dug his sneaker into the ground to mark the spot in the grass. He looked up to see the Devil take several practice swings, each motion brimming with confidence. The Devil was right-handed, JaMark noticed.

JaMark took another deep breath and exhaled, trying to clear his mind and focus only on the task at hand. He tried to remember his glory days in the Major Leagues, but they seemed so far away. He glanced at the ball in his left hand, but that also looked unfamiliar. He rubbed his left shoulder with his right hand, hoping his arm had three more pitches in it. Three more, he thought to himself, and his soul would be free.

Before JaMark threw his first pitch to the Devil, as he stood with his hands together and faced the makeshift home plate in a routine he had done repeatedly since his days flinging strawberries on Uncle Rufus's farm, he was interrupted by a loud noise.

"Woooooooooo. Wooooooooooo."

The noise grew louder with each repeating wail. After he heard the noise for the third time, JaMark recognized the sound as the same tone he heard the night he returned to the crossroads.

While the Devil waited patiently at the makeshift home plate, JaMark stepped away from the makeshift pitcher's mound and turned towards the huge field. From the tree line surrounding the field appeared the usual patrons of Inga's restaurant. On the left side of the tree line emerged the man he knew as Sonny Boy, playing his harmonica as he did the night at the crossroads months earlier. On the right side of the tree line was Gertie Dupree, looking as she did weeks earlier at the restaurant, and still years younger than she was when JaMark saw her on television. Between Gertie and Sonny Boy were numerous other men and women. Many of the men were dressed similarly to Sonny Boy in suits, straight-laced ties, and old fashioned top hats, while the women wore white dresses, their hair in different styles.

Behind the usual patrons in their suits and dresses, a large group arrived from the tree line dressed in various types of attire from different periods of time. JaMark noticed most had something in their hands. Some carried books, some carried small pieces of art, and others carried various items such as sculptures or trinkets. JaMark also saw a young man among the group carrying a guitar and dressed in flowery attire with his hair in an afro. Among the masses emerging from the woods were also athletes who wore uniforms of different sports, from basketball to golf to both types of football. They all carried a piece of equipment from their respective sport. As JaMark looked out to most of them, he realized he was rubbing a baseball, his own personal totem.

Before JaMark had enough time to observe all the people walking out of the woods, he was brought back to the moment by the Devil's voice.

"It is great to see you all again," the Devil said, addressing the crowd. "Soon, there will be another among you. Behold, a young man who thinks he can defy me and salvage his soul. You all know how this will end."

JaMark turned to face the Devil as the dark deity was in the middle of another practice swing. JaMark took a deep breath and returned to his pitching position. He rolled the baseball in his fingers. Although it had been months since he faced a batter with anything on the line, he thought back to the lessons he learned in the Major Leagues. JaMark knew that his weak left shoulder was well-known to the Devil. He also knew the Devil would easily hit a less-than-fast fastball. As he did on rare occasions in the big leagues, he decided to throw his curveball first and pitch "backward" to the Devil. JaMark smiled at the irony of throwing the Devil a pitch the Rosedale locals once called "Legba."

Slowly, JaMark stepped back with his right leg, leaned back, pivoted his body, brought his right leg up high in front of him, and went through the same pitching motion that served him since his days in Rosedale High School. After his right leg hit the ground nearly a full meter stride from where he was standing, his arm followed through with a curveball that had as much rotation as he could muster.

Less than a second later, the ball struck the line of the black finger-drawn strike zone with a thwack, curving from the left upper corner of the strike zone to the lower right corner of the box, inches from the Devil's knees. The Devil watched the pitch strike the wall. He picked up the baseball with his right hand, and threw it back to JaMark.

"Strike one," JaMark said confidently as he caught the ball.

"That ain't my style," said the Devil with a smile.

CHAPTER 58

JaMark turned his back on the Devil and looked towards the group in the open field. As far as he could see, they were smiling and clutching tightly to their instruments and miscellaneous tokens. JaMark smiled back and nodded to them. He didn't want to show them how his shoulder seared with a pain he had long forgotten about until now. The pain pulsed and quivered with each heartbeat, ripping through his muscles. JaMark took a deep breath, tried to forget about the pain, and turned to face the Devil.

Again, JaMark stood approximately sixty feet and six inches from the Devil. Again, the Devil took a batting stance to the right of home plate. Still feeling the throbbing pain in his shoulder, JaMark peered in to the back wall and stared at the black outlined box. From the corner of his eye, he saw the Devil again take several practice swings. Keeping with his plan of pitching backward, JaMark again fingered the ball with a curveball grip.

Standing in his pitcher's position with his body facing the Devil, JaMark placed his right hand over his left. He covered the baseball with his right hand as if he were wearing a familiar baseball glove. The once-great pitcher took another step back with his right foot, rocked his body back, raised his right leg, and set into his pitching motion. His leg again landed nearly a meter from where he once stood, only a centimeter from where his foot landed on the first pitch.

When his leg hit the ground, JaMark's arm quickly followed, whipping across his body, and letting the baseball fly. As he set the ball in motion, he heard a cacophony emerge behind him, a din of harmonicas, guitars, and loud human voices.

The wall of sound struck the Devil first. The demon

froze in surprise, distracted by the noise. JaMark's pitch curved from the middle of the Devil's strike zone towards the inside, traveling just behind the wall of sound. The Prince of Darkness gave the bat an awkward stroke, and his follow-through caused him to lose his balance. His bat missed the ball as it struck two inches to the right of the strike zone with another loud thump.

"Strike two," JaMark said.

Recovering from his off-balance attempt, the Devil grabbed the baseball, and held it in his right hand. He held his bat in his left hand, its barrel top barely touching the grass.

"If you intend on trying to defeat me with tricks and outsiders," the Devil said as he glared at JaMark. "I will damn you to Hell for all eternity where your carcass will burn with the heat of a thousand fires, and your soul will scream in torment. Do not cross me, mortal."

The Devil threw the ball to JaMark and addressed the crowd in the grass field.

"Begone, all of you," the Devil yelled to the congregation. "You all had your moment, and each lost. Mettle not in business that is not yours."

JaMark turned to see the people who arrived from the woods disappear into the tree line.

Only one remained.

In the middle of the tree line, alone in the vast field, stood Dusty Polichardo. The diminutive pitching legend was dressed in his baseball uniform and clutched a baseball in his hand.

JaMark watched Dusty waddle towards JaMark's impromptu pitcher's mound much as he did every Spring Training. The old pitcher's unorthodox gait made JaMark remember better, more innocent days. Days spent throwing baseballs for fun, not to avoid eternal damnation.

"Dusty," JaMark said as Dusty neared. "It's great to see you."

"Here," Dusty said, handing him the baseball he was carrying. "Give me your ball and use this."

Without hesitation, JaMark accepted the new baseball

from his old friend and gave Dusty the ball he pitched twice to the Devil. JaMark looked at the new baseball and rubbed his hands over his friend's gift. It felt like a new ball, with seams tight and covered by the slick sheen of new horsehide.

"Thank you," JaMark said.

"JaMark," Dusty said.

"Yes?" JaMark replied.

Dusty paused for a moment.

"Do it for us," Dusty said.

At that moment, JaMark realized why Dusty was in the grass field with Inga's regular patrons. He understood who the Devil had visited the night before.

JaMark looked at Dusty and nodded his head. More than ever, he understood the weight on his shoulders.

"Do it for me," Dusty said.

Dusty turned towards the grass field from which he came and walked in his typical odd fashion, still carrying the baseball he took from JaMark. JaMark watched his old friend slowly wobble through the field and into the tree line, where he disappeared from sight.

JaMark rubbed the new baseball and turned to face the Devil. The Devil smiled at JaMark, tapped the bat on the ground near his suit jacket, and took two more practice swings.

Gripping the new baseball, JaMark's unnaturally long fingers settled into a natural fastball grip. During his brief conversation with Dusty, JaMark didn't acknowledge the searing pain in his left shoulder. Looking towards the finger-drawn box on the wall approximately sixty feet and six inches away, his eyes struggled to focus through the pain.

JaMark stood on the impromptu pitcher's mound. He knew the pain wasn't going to get any better as long as he had to throw one more pitch. While the Devil continued to stare down the former big leaguer, the pain forced JaMark to step away from the pitching spot. In an attempt to massage the pain away, JaMark roughly rubbed his new baseball into his shoulder, grinding the seams into his muscle. Although he knew it wasn't a long-term cure, it did momentarily ease his pain.

CHAPTER 59

J aMark resumed his spot on his impromptu pitching mound and took a deep breath. He focused on the finger-drawn strike zone and tried to ignore the batter at the makeshift home plate. He moved his hands in front of him and again instinctively covered the ball with his right hand as if he were wearing a baseball glove. He took a second deep breath. He wanted desperately to get in the same zone he enjoyed years ago when he controlled pitcher-batter match-ups. But the pain continued to interrupt his mental process.

JaMark glanced over to Inga. While the Devil stood at the middle of the rear of the house, the short, elderly woman stood at the far end of the back wall of the house, observing the matchup of man against immortal. She smiled at JaMark, although JaMark also sensed her concern. He wondered if the cacophony during the last pitch was orchestrated by her. If so, he would have to thank her. But he knew she could aid no more. His final pitch was his alone.

A moment before he started his windup, JaMark reflected. Thoughts of his life with baseball came to mind – how his love for the sport began years ago in Uncle Rufus's strawberry fields, how he dealt with early fame during his brief but misguided time at Rosedale High, his tragic injury, his need to play again and his deal with the Devil, his return to success, and his tragic end. It all went so fast, JaMark thought. Now his entire life with baseball, his entire life in general, was down to one pitch.

If he struck out the Devil, he was free to live, albeit with an arm no good for baseball. If he failed, and the Devil made contact, he would eventually join the Devil on a trip to Hell. Either way, he was about to deal his last pitch and say farewell to baseball forever.

After pitching two curveballs, JaMark knew he had to put everything he had into the fastest fastball he could possibly throw. He took one more deep breath, took his last step back with his right leg, and started his pitching motion.

One more high leg kick.

Another long stride.

His right leg landed at the same spot it had the previous two pitches.

His left arm rotated towards home plate.

He released the Dusty-given baseball as fast as he could.

When JaMark's arm finally stopped moving, the pain caught up with him. He fell to his knees and clutched his left shoulder, as he did nearly ten years earlier in his last game at Rosedale High School. This time, however, the baseball didn't roll meekly to the dugout. This time, it flew directly where JaMark wanted it to go.

As JaMark fell to his knees in pain, the ball ripped through the air. JaMark didn't see the Devil give a mighty swing on the chest-high fastball, nor did he see the ball sail over the Devil's uppercut swing. But JaMark heard the ball smash into the back wall of the farmhouse and embed into the concrete, a permanent marker of the Devil's strikeout.

JaMark also heard Inga's celebratory yell as she saw the Devil miss JaMark's third and final pitch. Still wincing in pain, he looked in her direction. As he struggled to his feet, he clutched his left arm, trying desperately to hold it close to his body. He saw Inga walk along the rear wall of the house towards the Devil.

JaMark watched Inga approach the Devil. He couldn't hear what she said to the Devil as the immortal demon put on his hat and jacket. But JaMark saw the Devil smile. The young pitcher then watched as Inga took a step closer, leaned in, and kissed the Devil on the cheek.

"We'll talk soon," JaMark heard Inga say to the defeated Devil after her kiss. Inga then turned towards JaMark. She smiled at the former baseball player, and walked towards the door on the side of the restaurant, leaving JaMark alone with the Devil.

JaMark stood in place as the Devil walked towards him and closed the ground between them. Within a few moments, the Devil was an arm's length away.

"You did well, Mr. Reliford," the Devil said. "Very well."

"Thank you, Mr. Devil," JaMark answered.

"For your victory, your soul is yours," the Devil said, extending his right hand to JaMark. "Do with it as you please."

JaMark shook the Devil's hand, as he did years earlier at the crossroads under the old oak tree.

After their final handshake, the Devil walked past JaMark. JaMark watched as a hole in the earth slowly opened in the middle of the field behind the farmhouse. Smoke poured from the growing chasm, and JaMark could swear he saw the brimstone of Hell.

JaMark watched the Devil walk into the hole, now wide enough to fit a man's figure. The pitcher stood amazed, but not completely surprised, when the Devil didn't fall, but rather slowly descended in the hole, tipping his hat towards JaMark and vanishing from the earthly toil. After the top of the Devil's top hat vanished, the hole from which he descended closed, leaving no evidence of its existence.

CHAPTER 60

While JaMark was occupied with the disappearance of the Devil, he failed to notice the many regulars of Inga's restaurant reemerging from the tree line. Again they were dressed in peculiar attire, from the dapper suits of yesteryear to historical dresses to professional sports uniforms. Upon their return, however, none carried any trinket, token, totem, relic, book, instrument, or piece of sporting gear.

In mass, they walked to JaMark, careful to avoid the spot in the field where the hole to hell once existed.

The harmonica-playing man from the crossroads reached JaMark first.

"Thank you," Sonny Boy said.

"You're welcome," JaMark replied as he watched a growing number of people emerge from the tree line.

"May I shake your hand?" Sonny Boy asked. "It would mean so much."

"Sure," JaMark answered as he extended his hand, unsure of what might follow.

Sonny Boy extended his arm and clasped his hand on JaMark's, shaking the hand of the man who struck out the Devil. JaMark saw Sonny Boy smile as he pulled his hand away from JaMark.

"Thank you," Sonny Boy said again as he took a step back. Sonny Boy put his hands together in front of his chest as if in prayer. A moment later, Sonny Boy's entire being dissolved into a small stream of smoke rising towards the heavens.

One by one, each of the wayward souls held hostage by the Devil walked to JaMark. One by one, they shook JaMark's hand, took a step back, smiled, put their hands together, and disappeared, their smoky trails ascending into the air.

"You must be Johnny Allen," JaMark said as a young black man with an afro approached wearing flowery attire.

"Please call me Jimi. Jimi Hendrix," the specter said before shaking JaMark's hand and disappearing.

"Thank you," said Gertie Dupree when it was finally her turn to meet JaMark.

"You are very welcome," JaMark said in return, as he smiled at the disappearing bingo legend.

"Thank you," said every soul that shook the hand of the man who struck out the Devil.

JaMark stood in the field, shaking hands and watching souls rise to the heavens for hours. After all the souls left, only one visitor remained, JaMark's former coach, Dusty Polichardo.

"Thank you, JaMark," Dusty said as he finally reached JaMark. JaMark noticed Dusty looked happier than he had ever seen him.

"No, Dusty, thank you," JaMark replied. "I had no idea."

"This is a good thing, JaMark," the legendary pitcher said. "It's over. He found me."

"I understand," JaMark answered. "At least you were able to spend your time here with us. Instead of being lost."

"Oh, I was lost," Dusty said. "I was very lost before I found you. And I would still be lost if it wasn't for you. But now I must go."

The old pitcher extended his hand to JaMark.

"Dusty," JaMark said as he took Dusty's outreached hand, "I couldn't have done it without you."

"Good luck," Dusty said. He let go of their handshake and took a step backward.

"You too," JaMark said. JaMark watched the small streak of smoke that was once Dusty Polichardo rise several feet before his friend evaporated into the clear Mississippi night.

CHAPTER 61

JaMark looked at his surroundings. He stood alone in the field. The sun was gone, and the moon and stars shined bright over the Delta sky. He walked to the wall where the Devil stood, swung his bat, and struck out. Gone was the finger-drawn coal-black outline of a strike zone. The baseball JaMark threw past the Devil for strike three was also gone. JaMark knew it embedded in the wall, and he didn't see the Devil pull the ball from the wall before he vanished. He also knew Inga didn't grab the ball from the wall. Yet it was gone, as was the hole the ball would have made in the wall. Every trace of the Devil was gone. It was as if nothing had happened at all.

Even if there was no physical evidence, JaMark knew what he accomplished. He struck out the Devil and freed not only his soul but the souls of so many before him who had been trapped in fair deals gone wrong.

JaMark turned and took a final look at the field from where he pitched and beyond that, where dozens, if not hundreds of lost souls gathered to cheer him on. He reached his right arm to his left shoulder. The pain was still there, but it subsided drastically in the hours since he struck out the Devil.

As he rubbed away the pain, JaMark walked around the restaurant to the side door, the same door he walked out of hours earlier with the Devil. He walked through the empty kitchen and through the swinging wooden door that led to the dining area. He saw Inga sitting at the same table where he and the Devil had eaten lunch. Her head was in her hands, and she was crying.

"I did it," he said as he walked up to her and placed his hand on her shoulder.

"I know," the elderly woman said, looking up and smiling at JaMark. "I am very proud of you."

Inga placed her hand on the hand JaMark placed on her shoulder.

"Thank you," JaMark replied. "I couldn't have done it without you."

Inga let out a deep sigh.

"They are never coming back," she said. "They were my best customers. Before they arrived, there was maybe one person here a day. After Johnny Allen played, they came here every day. I am happy for all of them, but now I have no one."

JaMark sat across from the old woman, holding both of her hands in his.

"You have me," he said. "Come with me back to Rosedale. There are people there who would love to have a great cook in their presence. And I am going to need someone to vouch for me when I tell them what happened here. I don't think anyone will ever believe it."

"They'll believe it," Inga said. "Trust me."

Inga smiled. Her smile caused JaMark to smile, although he had no idea how the people in Rosedale would ever understand his confrontation with the Devil.

"No reason to stay here," Inga said. "Go upstairs, get your things, and come down when you are ready."

JaMark stood up from his seat and ran up the stairs to his bedroom. He grabbed his few possessions, and ten minutes later, he was back downstairs, eager to return to Rosedale. He hoped Betsy made the drive and would be there to meet him. He knew he would miss Inga and her restaurant, but he missed the love of his life and his family more.

JaMark was waiting by the front door of the restaurant with his backpack over his shoulder when he caught a glimpse of Inga. She carried her keys, a small picture frame, and a handful of old books. After making sure they had all they needed, JaMark and Inga climbed aboard Inga's faded yellow 1968 Volkswagon bus and drove the dirt highways to Rosedale.

Moments after they left the restaurant, JaMark and Inga stopped at the intersection where JaMark first met the Devil. The large oak tree, the old stop signs, and the unpaved roadways weren't as ominous to JaMark as they were in the past.

"It doesn't look as scary anymore," JaMark said as the wheels of the Volkswagon rolled directly over the scar of burnt soil where the Devil ascended to make his first appearance to JaMark so many years before.

Twenty minutes later, with few words spoken between them, Inga and JaMark passed the "Welcome to Rosedale" street sign. They drove past the general market where Inga bought food for the restaurant, past Rosedale High School where JaMark had his first brush with fame, and past the movie theater where JaMark encountered the Devil for the first time after making his deal. They almost drove out of town before turning right at the last block before the "Thank You For Visiting Rosedale" sign. They passed five houses on the left and four on the right before turning into the driveway of JaMark's grandmother's ranch-style house.

They sat in the driveway in silence for several moments.

"This is where we part ways," Inga said.

"Are you sure?" JaMark said.

"JaMark, you don't need my help anymore," Inga said. "You did a great thing, and now your life is up to you."

"I'll never forget you," JaMark said as he exited the Volkswagen bus.

"I hope not," Inga said with a smile. "Maybe one day we will cross paths again."

"I would like that," JaMark responded before closing the passenger door of the Volkswagon bus.

JaMark walked to the front of the bus with his backpack over his right shoulder. Inga put the bus in reverse and rolled down the driveway. JaMark had no idea where the old woman was going or whether he would ever see her again. But he knew her days serving lost souls were done.

The Volkswagon bus drove down the last road before the "Thank You For Visiting Rosedale" sign. JaMark watched the bus turn right, the opposite direction Inga needed to return to the restaurant. As the taillights of the bus disappeared from his line of sight, JaMark heard a familiar voice, a voice he had only heard over the phone during the last four months.

"JaMark!"

JaMark turned to see Betsy running out the front door of his grandmother's house. The woman who was with him throughout his baseball career closed the ground between them in a fraction of a moment and threw her arms around him before he could return her hello.

"I missed you so much," Betsy said before kissing him.

They stood in the driveway with their arms around each other.

"It's over," JaMark replied, looking down into Betsy's eyes. "I did it. I struck out the Devil."

Betsy cried as she hugged JaMark tighter. He kissed her forehead as she looked up at him with a smile.

As their embrace began to ease, the couple realized they were not alone. JaMark's grandmother and Uncle Rufus joined them in the driveway.

Rufus walked up to JaMark and Betsy and put his hand on JaMark's shoulder.

"Good job, boy," Rufus said. "I don't know how you did it, but I had faith in you."

JaMark turned towards his uncle as Betsy took a step away.

"Thank you," JaMark said to Uncle Rufus, shaking the older man's hand. "Inga helped. A lot."

"You went to see Inga?" JaMark's grandmother asked. JaMark's grandmother stood between the driveway and the front door with her arms crossed.

"Yes, ma'am," JaMark replied as he walked towards the matriarch of his family.

"She helped cure you of that devil you had runnin' around in you?" JaMark's grandmother asked. "She's always been a weird one, that one. Never saw much of her, but heard she would take in any lost soul. Not too many willing to do that, I guess. Still, an odd bird, if you ask me. Now come inside, it's late, and it's gettin' cold."

JaMark, his grandmother, Uncle Rufus, and Betsy walked

inside the house. Over the next hour, JaMark told his family of his months living with Inga, how he learned to cook, how he fed the ghosts of those who made deals with the Devil, and how he struck out the Devil with two curveballs and a fastball. JaMark smiled when Uncle Rufus interrupted him to remind everyone that it was he who taught JaMark how to pitch. After Rufus's less than humble interjection, JaMark told his family that his shoulder no longer hurt.

After reuniting and catching up, JaMark and Betsy finally retired to the guest bedroom. JaMark looked at the bed and realized how long the day had been. Although it was mathematically as long as any other day, and the Earth took as long to rotate on its axis as it had for millions of years, the events of the day and their emotional toll made the day seem much longer. But at last, JaMark's soul was free and he was beside the love of his life and was finally at peace.

CHAPTER 62

The next morning, as the clock neared nine, JaMark awoke to the smell of bacon and the faint aroma of pancakes. His family was already sitting at JaMark's grandmother's kitchen table, feasting on breakfast cuisine when JaMark came down the stairs. Although Inga was a better cook than his grandmother, JaMark knew meals with the solitary old woman were missing the key ingredient of family. For the first time in months, JaMark feasted on food with people he loved.

Later that day, after lunch, but before his grandmother began to cook dinner, JaMark sat in his grandmother's living room, and turned on the television to watch the sports news of the day. He hadn't watched sports in months and was curious about how the Saints were doing without him. After a few college football scores, some professional basketball analysis, and a highlight of a monkey riding a Shetland pony attempting to lasso a chicken, the sports newscaster's announcement caught JaMark's attention.

"In baseball news, former all-star pitcher JaMark Reliford was given his unconditional release today," the newscaster said. "According to the St. Petersburg Saints, the left-handed pitcher hadn't been heard from in months. Given that he was on the last year of his contract and that he showed early signs of arm trouble in Spring Training, the team decided to part ways with the former superstar."

JaMark watched in shock as two entertainers posing as sports analysts added salt to the wound by debating for the next five minutes whether the Saints made the right move by severing ties. Neither one of them made any sense to JaMark as they were both so over-the-top and theatrical in their arguments. While one concluded JaMark walked away because he was jealous of the success of Pete LaGib, the gypsy knuckleballer JaMark dueled with in the Minor Leagues, the other was even more off-base, suggesting JaMark was leaving baseball to try his hand in basketball. JaMark shook his head as one sports analyst said unidentified eye-witnesses claimed to see JaMark play basketball in Chicago while wearing a fake mustache and an afro wig.

JaMark didn't know whether to laugh or cry. He decided to call Barry Carusowitz, his longtime baseball friend. Although JaMark knew he could never play again, he wanted to let someone in baseball know he was alive and well.

His old teammate-turned-coach updated JaMark on the happenings of the team, as well as some of the politics behind his release. Barry told JaMark that a new majority shareholder wanted to rebuild the Saints with younger, cheaper talent. Most of the players who won the World Series years earlier were traded, released, or not re-signed. According to Barry, even though JaMark was still a year away from free agency, he was already too costly for the new majority owner. With no other team willing to trade for a former all-star pitcher with an injured shoulder who disappeared from baseball for over six months, it was best for the Saints to let him go.

JaMark understood. He apologized for not staying in touch and told Barry that although he had eventually overcome his pain killer addiction, he still couldn't raise his arm above his shoulder and definitely couldn't pitch anymore.

"Are you sure you want to walk away?" Barry asked.

"Yeah," JaMark said. He knew that no matter how much he wanted to or how much he loved baseball, he was physically unable to play at a professional level ever again. "I'm sure. I'm done."

"Well," Barry concluded, "if you ever want to visit, we'd be happy to see you. You were one of the best I've ever seen. Best of luck to you."

"Thanks," JaMark said. "Best of luck to you too."

JaMark hung up the phone and took a deep breath. He saw Betsy enter the living room from his grandmother's kitchen.

"Who was that?" she asked.

"You remember Barry, my old catcher, right?" JaMark replied. "I just told him I was done."

"A few weeks ago, the sportspeople on television said the Saints were thinking about releasing you," Betsy said.

"The news today said they did," JaMark said. "But I still wanted to tell them I was alive and well. The television analysts were crazy with their ideas on where I was and what I was doing."

Betsy walked over to JaMark, squeezed his hand, kissed his cheek, and led him into the kitchen for another family dinner.

CHAPTER 63

The following day was the day before Christmas. Although JaMark, Betsy, and Uncle Rufus accepted JaMark's grandmother's offer to stay in Rosedale through the holiday, they quickly discovered the old woman's pantry had barely enough food for one, no less four. Needing to get out of the house, JaMark and Betsy volunteered to go to the Rosedale General Store and the Rosedale Farmer's Market for groceries.

The open-air Rosedale Farmer's Market sat on the southern edge of the small town. Usually only open on weekends, on this Christmas Eve Day, it was bustling with families, shoppers, and vendors plying their wares. JaMark had never seen the farmer's market so busy. There were aisles upon aisles of merchandise, from furniture to clothing to made-for-TV trinkets to barely used auto parts.

JaMark and Betsy finally found the produce section and strolled through the vegetable vendors, booths of banana bunches, distributors doling dairy, and salesmen selling steak. JaMark wondered about the quality of the steak but didn't care enough to ask.

For several minutes, the couple examined produce, discarded the bruised and overripe fare, and put aside their picks. As they picked their top tomatoes, a young man in his early twenties approached JaMark. He was not quite as tall as JaMark but similar in slenderness. He looked well-traveled with a dusty gray sweat jacket, torn jeans, and a faded West Mississippi Tech baseball cap hiding his blondish brown hair.

"You," the slender man said as he stood next to JaMark. "I know you."

JaMark looked at the young man and had no idea who he was.

"You don't know who I am, do you?" the young man said.

"No, sorry," JaMark replied. "I can't say I do. How do you know me?"

"Well, I know you used to pitch in the Major Leagues," the young man said. "And I know you gave my grandmother quite the scare a few years ago at the bingo hall."

Despite the years that passed, JaMark never shook the memory of the frantic old woman screaming and lunging at him at the bingo hall, even if he didn't completely remember the appearance of the woman's grandson.

"Oh," JaMark said. "I'm sorry, I remember you now. I remember your shirt. Weren't you traveling bingo players? Are you still in Rosedale?"

"Yes," the young man said. "My grandmother said we'd stay until we won. I hadn't won a game since the night before we met you. But I won last night. Grandmother said she knows what happened. She said you freed Gertie Dupree. She also said I would meet you here today."

"Tell your grandmother she is right," JaMark said. "Gertie is free."

The young man stuck out his hand and gave JaMark a firm handshake.

"Thank you," he said. JaMark sensed a burden lifted from the young man.

"Best of luck to you," JaMark said. The young man smiled before he walked away and disappeared into the crowd of the market.

JaMark returned to the produce to find Betsy examining some asparagus. He had learned the finer points of asparagus ripeness from Inga, and he joined Betsy in looking through the stock. A few moments later, he felt a tap on his shoulder.

"Excuse me, sir," a voice behind JaMark said. JaMark turned to see a short, middle-aged black woman. Like other shoppers in the market, she was dressed casually and pushed a shopping cart half-full of meats, vegetables, and other assorted products.

"Yes?" JaMark asked in response. He wondered why she wanted his attention as he wasn't standing in the way of any items or vendors.

"Sir, I would like to thank you," the woman said.

"May I ask why?" JaMark asked. Although she sounded sincere, JaMark couldn't imagine why she was thanking him.

"I hope I don't have the wrong person," she said. "I believe it was you who freed my grandfather, Blind Albert Jones, and let him go to Heaven. He was one of the best blues musicians in this area back in the 1940s. When he died in the '70s, people whispered that he made a deal with the Devil to be as good as he was. Last night, he came to me in a dream for the first time since I was a little girl. He told me a tall black man who played baseball finally allowed him to go to Heaven. I don't know any baseball players, and I am not really sure why, but I had a feeling just now when I saw you that it must be you. If I have the wrong person, then this must not make any sense, and I am really sorry."

JaMark looked at the short woman. "No, ma'am," he said. "It makes sense. That is me. And you are very welcome."

The woman looked at JaMark again and reached towards him to give him a hug. "Thank you," she said as she embraced him. "Thank you for giving him peace."

Following their embrace, the woman smiled, rubbed a tear from her eye, and walked away from JaMark to continue her grocery shopping.

The longer JaMark and Betsy stayed in the farmer's market, the more people approached JaMark to say thank you, shake his hand, or, like the short, middle-aged woman, give him a hug. By the time JaMark and Betsy left the market, over a dozen Rosedale residents had thanked JaMark for easing the pain of their loved ones. Even a vendor at the market showed her gratitude by not charging JaMark and Betsy for their items. As the couple approached the market exit and headed to their car, a group of men, one of whom already approached JaMark on behalf of his father, put down their purchases and applauded the man who struck out the Devil.

The next day, JaMark and Betsy spent a quiet family Christmas with JaMark's grandmother and Uncle Rufus. Using some of the culinary skills he learned at Inga's restaurant, JaMark helped his grandmother in the kitchen for the first time. Although there weren't many presents exchanged, it was the best Christmas JaMark celebrated in a long time. His soul was free, and his heart was full of love.

CHAPTER 64

Two days after Christmas, after all the Christmas dinner leftovers were eaten, JaMark, Betsy, and Uncle Rufus said their tearful goodbyes to JaMark's grandmother and began their return to the Chicago suburbs. They took their time along the eighteen-hour trip, driving casually and staying a night in a hotel in northern Tennessee. While neither Rufus nor Betsy had to be back to work before New Year's Day, JaMark had nowhere to go and no idea what was next. But instead of fearing the unknown, he felt a sense of freedom.

As the months of the new year progressed, JaMark's feelings of freedom fled fast. While he was trying to walk away from baseball, everyone in the Chicago area still knew him as the former Major League All-Star who walked away from the game. Whenever he left his house, neighbors, strangers, and passersby asked why he left the Saints. He couldn't tell them his miraculous left arm was a gift from the Devil that came with the price of his soul. He also couldn't tell them that in order to save his soul, he had to travel to Mississippi to strike out the Devil using a baseball given to him by a ghost. No one would understand. Those who would understand had risen to the heavens. JaMark knew that even the relatives of the freed souls, the people of Rosedale who thanked and cheered him and knew he had a role in their loved ones' release, even they did not fully understand what he had been through.

While fans were consistently curious, the sports media was downright damning. Writers, television analysts, and sports talk radio personalities called him a "flash-in-the-pan" and accused him of being weak, timid, and a burnout. They frequently compared him to other Major League pitchers with brief but successful careers, often including Dusty Polichardo. If only they knew how much he and Dusty really had in common, JaMark thought.

Unfortunately for JaMark, conversations about Dusty were frequent, as many in the media eulogized the late pitcher for his remarkable performance in the 1952 World Series. In an announcement by the Saints, JaMark learned the Saints players planned to wear a black stripe on the left sleeve of their uniforms to commemorate Dusty's passing.

On May 8th, JaMark's twenty-eighth birthday, he and Betsy traveled to the local stadium to watch the Saints play Chicago. Weeks prior to the game, JaMark called Barry Carusowitz and expressed interest in seeing the Saints when they came to Chicago. Before the new season, Barry was promoted to the coaching staff of the Saints, and JaMark knew his old friend could easily acquire tickets to the game. Barry provided JaMark and Betsy two tickets near the Saints dugout, as close as JaMark could get to his former teammates without being on the field.

As he looked out on the field, JaMark felt a sense of strangeness. Many of the teammates he won a championship with were gone. He remembered Carusowitz discuss the owner's intent to rebuild, but didn't realize he would only see two of his former teammates on the field, the second baseman and the left fielder, both of whom were rookies during JaMark's last full year in the Majors.

Pitching for the Saints was a rookie pitcher JaMark never heard of. After the first three innings, the Chicago team scored five runs and hammered eight hits as the young pitcher struggled to contain the Chicago lineup. Watching the kid on the mound struggle made JaMark feel guilty, both for the overwhelmed young pitcher and for his former teammates. JaMark knew it could not be easy to stay on a losing team while wearing a uniform that had symbolized winning for so long.

In the fourth inning, a fan wearing a Saints jersey with the name "Reliford" on the back recognized JaMark. The fan, who sat a row behind JaMark, stated the team would be better if JaMark was still pitching. JaMark politely thanked the man for his recognition of JaMark's contribution and abilities.

As the game progressed and alcohol became a bigger influence on the man's one-sided conversation with JaMark, the fan in the Reliford jersey became more unruly, calling JaMark a "quitter," a "bum," and a "loser," and started blaming him for the team's performance on the field that day and in the days earlier. By the sixth inning, the Saints were losing nine to nothing, and other frustrated Saints fans found JaMark and joined the heckler in expressing their frustrations and taunting the former All-Star pitcher. Their actions forced JaMark and Betsy to alert security.

In the seventh inning, security finally made their way to JaMark and Betsy and removed the unruly fan and quieted his choir. By then, the Saints were behind twelve to one, and JaMark and Betsy couldn't bear to see any more. They thanked the security guards for their efforts and asked a stadium police officer if he could provide the couple an escort to the parking lot. On their way home, JaMark called his friend Barry and left a message, thanking him for the tickets.

As the spring turned into summer, JaMark shifted his focus and his life further and further from baseball. The early season team struggles, the uniform sleeve reminder of Dusty, and the feigned enthusiasm by manager Hiroki Montana after every loss caused too many pangs of guilt. By July, he could no longer even enjoy watching the game on television. JaMark again felt trapped in his own home. His inability to shake the shadow of baseball and his former fame worried him.

In early August, curiosity about JaMark's career decision crossed the line from benign to badgering. For reasons JaMark could not imagine, a small group of obsessive fanatics discovered JaMark's relationship with Betsy. They sent several questions and accusations to her work email, insinuating that perhaps she was behind his departure from the game. Betsy explained to JaMark how she tried to block the emails, but they became more persistent.

"Maybe it's time to move," JaMark proposed. "Maybe it is time for you to get a new job and for us to get away from all this."

"Are you sure?" Betsy asked.

JaMark looked around the house. He was done living in the Chicago suburbs. Although they could still afford to live in a metro area, having built an admirable nest egg during his playing career, JaMark wanted to go somewhere more laid back, somewhere quiet, somewhere where he could disappear into anonymity among people who had achieved more.

"Are you thinking about moving back to Rosedale?" Betsy asked.

"No," JaMark said. "Things would never be normal there either. I was thinking about Florida, like those condos we stayed in during Spring Training. Small, peaceful, beachside condos where we can fit in. Where seeing athletes and former athletes is not a big deal. A place where I can make money without people pointing fingers. A place where I can see a baseball game without it turning into a circus. I don't know. That's what I was thinking."

Betsy walked to JaMark, reached up, and put her hands on his shoulders.

"Sounds good," she said, reassuring him. She stood on her toes to kiss him. "I like the idea. Let's start looking tomorrow."

CHAPTER 65

Two months later, after a Labor Day weekend visit to Clearwater to look for a new home, JaMark and Betsy settled on a small beachside condominium on the west coast of Florida. In the middle of October, the couple packed everything from their suburban Chicago house and, with the help of Uncle Rufus, who surprised everyone by staying out of trouble and finding a place of his own in Chicago, JaMark and Betsy moved their belongings to Clearwater Beach.

Mr. JaMark Reliford and Mrs. Betsy Reliford settled quickly in Clearwater Beach. The following years brought a son and daughter and forced the growing family to move from their small condominium to a mid-sized beach home. Betsy took to the laid-back Florida lifestyle and motherhood with ease. She often told JaMark her job as a case worker, guiding grown men away from a life of adventurous petty crime, was good practice for raising children.

Although the rare fan asked for an autograph on his famous picture with Pete LaGib and he answered the occasional "Where are they now?" interview, JaMark was able to make peace with himself and with baseball at last. Inspired by his children, he finally took to the game again. This time, however, his involvement was coaching his children's little league teams, all of whom were sponsored by Colonel Crispy's Frosted Sugar Bombs.

Outside of baseball, JaMark followed the path of many former athletes in the Tampa Bay area and became a part-owner of a small beach bar. While rock bands, reggae groups, and deejays provided the music on the weekends, JaMark made sure to keep one night a week open for the sweet sounds of an aging French horn player and his peace-loving female companion.

Finally comfortable in Clearwater and surrounded by the sounds of his family, friends, and a French horn, JaMark Reliford never again heard from the Devil.

CHAPTER 66

Welcome back to the Clearwater Beach Little League Age ten through twelve Baseball Championship on Tampa Bay's sports radio. Today the Colonel Crispy Frosted Sugar Bombers are taking on the Renegades of Ray's Auto Sales. If you are just joining, we have seen a great game by two of the best teams in the area. The score is three to two Renegades as we enter the bottom of the sixth inning in a six-inning contest.

Per Clearwater Beach Little League rules, games only go six innings. If the Bombers tie the game in this frame, we play a seventh inning. If neither team scores in the seventh, we call the game a tie and have co-champions for the first time since 1981.

Leading off the inning for the Bombers is Bethany Reliford, the number two hitter in their lineup, and youngest child of team manager and former Saints All-Star JaMark Reliford. The switch-hitting second baseman is one for two today with a single and a stolen base in the first inning. She has also played flawless defense at second, including turning a double play in the fourth inning.

The first pitch to Bethany by the Renegades pitcher is a ball, low and outside. Bethany has a great eye up there and doesn't show any fear, which is surprising and inspiring for a ten-year old. Very impressive considering this twelve-year old Renegades pitcher is one of the hardest throwers in the league.

He winds up and delivers. Bethany bunts down the third baseline. The third baseman charges the ball, but struggles to pick it up, and Bethany Reliford is safe at first with a single. One on and no out for the Bombers.

Now batting is the number three hitter in the Bombers lineup, Hunter Flossman, their eleven-year old catcher. Flossman is two for two today with a home run and a double. He lists Cincinnati shortstop Diego Cabrera as his favorite player, and his favorite food is chocolate ice cream.

Flossman steps to the plate. The first pitch to Flossman is a fastball *for strike one. I don't think the young man thought that was a strike. But the umpire called it a strike. Flossman can't dwell on a bad call. He has to focus on the next one.*

The Renegades pitcher winds and delivers. There goes Bethany Reliford trying to steal second. The pitch is a ball outside. The catcher throws to second and Reliford slides in with her second stolen base of the day.

Now one and one to Hunter Flossman with the tying run on second. The Renegades pitcher looks over at Bethany Reliford, looks back at his catcher, winds, and pitches.

Flossman swings and hits a fly ball to deep center field. The centerfielder makes the catch and Bethany Reliford tags and runs to third base. The tying run for the Bombers is now only sixty feet away.

Stepping to the plate is JJ Reliford, Bethany's brother, and the oldest child of JaMark Reliford. JJ has struggled today, striking out both times. But like his sister, he has played great defense, making two running catches in center field.

The left-handed-hitting Reliford looks into the dugout before stepping into the batter's box. His father, JaMark, goes through the signs. JJ tightens his batting gloves and steps to the plate.

The right-handed Renegades pitcher looks over at Bethany Reliford on third and delivers. A fastball high for ball one. This kid is still throwing hard this late in the game.

JJ Reliford steps out of the box, tightens his batting gloves again, and looks to the dugout. His father, JaMark, gives him a thumbs up. No more signs, time to swing away. He glances down to third, where his sister is yelling words of encouragement.

The Renegades pitcher steps back on the mound, winds, and here is the pitch.

JJ Reliford swings and hits a long drive to deep right field. That's back, back, back, and gone over the right field fence. A game-winning home run for JJ Reliford. He knew a fastball was coming, and he hammered it.

While the Bombers pour out of their dugout, Bethany Reliford is standing by home plate, waiting for her brother to round the bases. What a moment for young JJ Reliford.

JJ steps on home plate and his greeted with a big hug by his sister and many high-fives by his teammates. Standing outside the dugout is his very proud father with a huge smile on his face.

While you have to be very happy for JJ and Bethany Reliford and their teammates, it's great to see JaMark Reliford this happy again. For all he went through, the ups and the downs, leading this team to a championship has to feel good – as a coach, but also as a dad.

Great to see the parents and fans in the stands also recognize the moment. They are giving the Bombers a standing ovation. Of course, there is Betsy Reliford, JaMark's wife and JJ and Bethany's mother. Even fans in the opposing bleachers are applauding. Look at the gentleman in the black suit, tie, and matching top hat. He is giving the Relifords a very enthusiastic round of applause."

ABOUT THE AUTHOR

Michael Lortz has written about sports and music in the Tampa Bay area for over 12 years. He has written for the Tampa Bay Times, Fangraphs, The Hardball Times, Deadspin, The Shadow League, SplitSider, Minor League Baseball.com, and several blogs. His writing and research have been quoted in USAToday, on ESPN.com, and at local county commissioner meetings. Michael has a Bachelor's Degree in Creative Writing from Florida State University. Curveball at the Crossroads is his first novel.